The MIT MURDERS

The MIT MURDERS

STEPHEN L BRUNEAU

THE MIT MURDERS

iUniverse books may be ordered through booksellers or by contacting:

iUniverse
1663 Liberty Drive
Bloomington, IN 47403
www.iuniverse.com
1-800-Authors (1-800-288-4677)

ISBN: 978-1-5320-8737-0 (sc)
ISBN: 978-1-5320-8738-7 (hc)
ISBN: 978-1-5320-8739-4 (e)

Library of Congress Control Number: 2019917824

Print information available on the last page.

iUniverse rev. date: 10/31/2019

PROLOGUE

Cambridge, Massachusetts: Present Day

The red-and-white T bus squealed to a stop. The driver glanced in his mirror and noted a solitary passenger making her way down the aisle as fellow riders moved to let her by. With practiced disinterest, he pulled the handle of the lever next to his seat, folded in the bus doors, and deposited the young woman onto the sidewalk.

Augusta Watkins hoisted her backpack into place as the bus banged into gear and pulled away with a low growl and a trailing puff of exhaust smoke. Walking into the heat and humidity of late August in New England was like walking into a sauna. Fortunately for Gussie, as her family and friends called her, that was no problem, as she was in excellent shape. Heading east on Mount Auburn Street, she hit her stride, taking advantage of the opportunity to work a little exercise into her daily routine.

Within minutes, a thin sheen of sticky sweat enveloped her body, dampening her collared high-button blouse and releasing tiny streams of perspiration down the back of her neck. Her short-cropped brown hair matted on her forehead, and moisture collected on the inner lenses of her wire-rimmed granny glasses. Her destination was five blocks east on Mount Auburn Street and three blocks west on Brattle Street, but thankfully, as was her custom, she had exchanged her office shoes for a pair of Cole Haan Zerøgrand sneakers.

Pedestrian traffic was light as she strode past Mount Auburn Cemetery. She preferred to make the eight-block walk from the bus stop to her apartment on Brattle in the heat of summer rather than the ravages of winter. On a day like that, she visualized a cleansing, soapy shower waiting for her, followed by several minutes of pulsating cold water.

It was just past five o'clock. Wednesday nights were always fun, and she looked forward to them. Wednesday was book club night. It wasn't a huge club, just four other women and herself. The most recent addition, she had been a member of the group for just more than a year. Her friend Cicely Blackwood had introduced Gussie to replace her when she moved to Ireland. The club was a welcome reprise in her weekly routine.

Gussie was not a social extrovert. Her bent was academic, and she was selective about whom she allowed to connect with her in any way. The book club had proven to be a joyful experience. All of the women in the group were her intellectual equals. The topics were wide ranging and often stimulating. Gussie relished the camaraderie and the spirited discussion.

The group met each week at a different member's home or apartment—a five-week rotation. That night would be particularly enjoyable because it was Gussie's turn to host. Her friends would arrive at seven thirty, which gave her plenty of time to get ready. In her backpack, among other things, were two bottles of wine, one white and one red. Gussie smiled at the thought of kicking back on her couch while someone threw out a provocative comment on the club's latest read in order to get things going. Her anticipation was palpable. With a little wine and some cheese and crackers, they would be freestyling past midnight.

Gussie turned left onto Brattle Street—three blocks to go. She breathed deeply through her nose and exhaled sharply through her mouth, relishing the challenge of a brisk step in the oppressive heat. The other benefit of that particular Wednesday night was that once she cleaned up and cooled down, she would be in for the night. She enjoyed the hospitality of the other women's homes, but it was always nice as hostess not to have to commute home when the evening was done. That night, as an added benefit, she would not have to venture out into the blast furnace again. She might even get an early start on her first glass of wine while awaiting her friends' arrival.

Two blocks ahead, her six-story low-rise apartment building came into view. The apartment had been a great find. The building was eighty years old and, thanks to rent control, had been spared from condo conversion. Many of the building's original features were still in place, as the landlord had opted for basic maintenance over unaffordable remodeling. That was fine with Gussie. She appreciated the charm of the place, and the way things were in the Greater Boston real estate market, despite her not insignificant resources, she likely never would have been able to handle the rent if the place had been renovated or converted. She didn't even know who the landlord was, at least not on a personal basis. The small plastic sign on the side of the building read "Brattle Realty Trust," whoever that was. In her mind, she pictured some faceless, nameless person counting rent money, operating behind a curtain of anonymity like the wizard in Oz. Whoever Brattle Realty Trust was, to their credit, they had installed a worthy superintendent in the basement apartment, and while amenities were sparse, the old antique of a building was kept in good repair.

Technically, it wasn't even Gussie's apartment, though she had lived there for two and a half years. One of her few undergraduate friends at Harvard had grown up in Cambridge, in that very apartment. The daughter of a single mom, Cicely had qualified for a full academic scholarship out of high school. When her mom had died unexpectedly during her junior year at Harvard, Cicely had found herself the sole occupant of the rent-controlled unit, where she'd remained for several years.

Cicely was brilliant. Gussie missed her friendship. After Cicely had completed her PhD in English literature, she'd been offered a two-year assistant professorship at Trinity College in Dublin. Not wanting to lose rights to the $600-per-month apartment, Cicely had struck an arrangement with Gussie. The apartment had stayed in Cicely's name. Gussie had moved in. On the first of every month, Brattle Realty Trust received a personal check from Cicely Blackwood. On the first of every month, Cicely Blackwood received a check for $600 from Gussie Watkins. No one knew the difference, or if they did, they apparently didn't care.

Gussie reached her apartment building, bounded up the front stairs, and paused on the landing as she punched in the security code on the keypad next to the door. The door opened, and she stepped into the deep foyer with raised fifteen-foot ceilings. Old-fashioned wainscoting circled the lower perimeter on most of three walls, with painted-over wallpaper above. The woodwork was ivy in color, and the upper walls were shaded in a pale light green. The original granite floor tiles were well polished, but stains and scratches from eighty years of foot traffic were evident. There were no windows save for the side panels to the oversized glassed entryway. The rear wall consisted of an aging elevator centered between a narrow banister staircase on the left and an array of wood shelving and oversized built-in metal mailboxes on the right.

Most days, Gussie would finish her mini-aerobic workout by high-stepping up the stairs to her fifth-floor apartment. Surprisingly, that day, there were two orange cones on the bottom step, with a crude handwritten sign taped to one of them: "Wet paint. Please use elevator today."

Gussie stood at the bottom step and peered up the stairwell, looking for some sign of work in progress. Seeing none, she sniffed the air, but she could detect no odor of paint. Joe, the super, must have had a good reason for blocking the stairs. Perhaps the painted area was a level or two up, beyond her view. Gussie shrugged, though no one was there to share her puzzlement. She crossed the small lobby and pushed the call button for the elevator. Immediately, the doors opened, as if they had been anticipating her arrival.

Gussie stepped across the threshold and into the confines of the elevator. The space was cramped, no more than four feet deep and five feet across. With her index finger, she jabbed the white inset button for the fifth floor, and then she settled into a rear corner for what she knew would be a painfully slow crawl to level five. The public areas of the building, including the elevator, were not air-conditioned. Gussie was already sweating profusely, but psychologically, the claustrophobic space was even more stifling. The car groaned reluctantly and set into motion for the slow climb. After several seconds, the floor indicator light above the doorframe changed from one to two. Gussie folded her arms across her body and waited. The indicator light passed from two to three. Gussie's chest swelled gently up and down as her breath slowly recovered, and her heart rate returned to normal.

Suddenly, there was a loud thump, and the elevator lurched to a stop, throwing Gussie slightly off balance. She used her hand to steady herself and immediately looked at the floor indicator light. She appeared to be stuck between levels three and four. *What the hell?* She didn't need this right now. Gussie's first reaction was to push the button for level five. She stabbed at the button again and again, but the button was ambivalent. The elevator, which a moment ago had seemed to be waiting in place for her, now had no reaction whatsoever to her efforts. Gussie started banging on the wall with the palm of her hand. For a full minute, she shouted for help and pounded her fist and palm on the elevator door.

Nothing.

Gussie became concerned. She didn't panic yet, but she feared she might be stuck there for a long time, maybe even hours. Perhaps she could summon help on her cell phone. A sharp click and a scraping sound from the top of the elevator interrupted her thoughts. Before she could understand what was happening, a hatch on the roof, something she had never noticed before, popped open, and she could see the outline of what appeared to be the lower body of a person standing astride the narrow opening. What the hell was this?

"Can you help me?" she cried out.

There was no response.

"What's happening? Who are you? Can you help me? What do you want?"

Still, she received no response.

Gussie shrank into the corner of the now alarmingly small elevator car. She could not see a face, and the silence was unnerving, but clearly, there was a person up there. Panic welled up within her.

"Why won't you answer me? What are you doing? Please help me!" she pleaded.

The ambient light from the open hatch door shifted, indicating movement above. Gussie recoiled farther into the corner, if that were even possible. An arm protruded through the opening. In the unknown person's hand was a small pistol-like object. It was not exactly like a firearm. The device looked vaguely familiar, and Gussie tried to place where she might have seen it in the past.

It all happened in a millisecond. Before she could process anything, two wires shot out from the barrel. One attached to her at the lower part of her neck, and the other, through her blouse, attached just above her right breast. Fifty-five thousand volts of electricity coursed through her body. Immediately, she lost all muscle control, her body went rigid, and she toppled forward onto her face. An agonizing scream rose in her head but never made it past her throat. She felt as if a thousand bees swarmed over her, impossibly stinging her everywhere at once. She tried to push up off the floor, but her limbs would not respond.

Despite her pain and terror, she was fully conscious and aware. Above and slightly behind, she sensed motion as her assailant dropped fully through the hatch and onto the floor behind her. Why was this happening? Who would have wanted to do this to her? Tears formed in her eyes, but she could not blink them away. In the background, she heard a constant clicking noise as the current continued to surge through her body. Her heart rate rocketed far in excess of any workout she had ever experienced. She wished she could pass out, but she was trapped, suspended in burning, biting hell.

Then there was a new sensation. She felt it before she saw it: a knife had come from behind and was now pressed to her throat. A sharper, more specific, more intense burn became superimposed on top of all the buzzing bees that continued devouring her body. A white-hot blade of fire, held in a gloved hand, was slicing through her throat!

The angry bees began to subside. Gussie could not breathe. She felt as if she were drowning, drifting away, but thankfully, her eyes began to close. *A glove. A rubber glove,* Gussie thought. Her last thought was of a rubber glove, and then her world went dark.

◆ ◆ ◆

Joe Bucci was pissed off. It was not in his nature to be so. Pissed off for Joe was probably the equivalent of mild irritation for most people. Joe was an affable fellow, a go-along-to-get-along type of guy. Nonetheless, with mounting annoyance, he glanced at his watch for the fiftieth or sixtieth time in the past hour.

The message, a text, was from Gussie Watkins and had been unexpected. It was technically business in nature, but it wasn't business as usual. Normally, tenants dropped him a note in his mailbox or left a voice mail on the business line when they had a request for repairs. The recorded answer on the business phone provided his cell number for emergencies, which obviously was how Gussie had obtained it; however, calls to his mobile were rare and usually after-hours. It was the first time he had ever received a text from a tenant and certainly the first time anyone had requested a meeting in a coffeehouse—or anywhere else off property, for that matter.

Joe did not have much of a social life. Truth be told, he had no social life, yet he suspected that most everyone he came in contact with thought of him as the stereotypical nice guy, unfailingly friendly and anxious to please. Inside, he often felt like the invisible man, a cutout that other people either looked right through or looked right past. On some level, he recognized that all his relationships were superficial, yet it was important to him to be liked.

At age thirty-eight, Joe felt his most recent gig as a live-in residential maintenance and building supervisor was a good fit. Prior to that opportunity, he had lived at home in his parents' basement and bounced around in a variety of odd jobs. Now, as of three years ago, he had his own basement, a unit in the bottom of a six-story low-rise apartment building in Cambridge. Gussie Watkins was one of the twenty-four tenants he now considered friends. Joe looked at his watch again. "Where are you?" he whispered, his annoyance increasing.

The other customers in the coffee shop were busy talking, eating, and sipping their coffee. His had gone cold, and he didn't want a refill. If she didn't show up soon, he'd be out of there.

In the text he'd received from Gussie, she'd asked him to meet her at five o'clock, ostensibly to go over a list of tenant requests. But why ask to see him off-site at a coffeehouse? That never had happened before, not with Gussie or any other tenant. There must have been some additional reason—some possibility. Maybe on the inside, she was as lonely as he was. Maybe there had been some unspoken interest the day he'd fixed her shower.

It was now six o'clock. He knew she was not coming, but he did not want to give up. Joe realized it was not a real date exactly, but it was as close as he was likely to come. Why would she do this to him? He had spent the afternoon thinking about what to say. This time, he would be prepared. He would ask her where she was from, where she worked, and maybe if she'd had any pets when she was a little girl. Reluctantly, Joe downed the last of his cold coffee in one gulp, crushed the large paper cup in his oversized hands, and headed out the door to catch the next bus home.

Joe walked the short distance to the bus stop. The bus

arrived a few minutes later, and it was packed. Joe's mood did not improve as he noticed it was standing room only. The ride back to the building was mercifully short. He got off the bus. As he approached his building, he slipped down the narrow alleyway between properties to the small rear courtyard, where four steps led down to his basement unit.

The apartment was tiny, barely nine hundred square feet, but it was more than enough for Joe, and it was free, part of the package in his job as property manager. There was no closet, but Joe used an exposed ceiling pipe to hang a small assortment of shirts, pants, and two coats, one light and one heavier. That day he had worn his best plaid shirt, corduroy pants, and clean sneakers. He carefully removed his shirt and pants, hung them on the pipe, and opted for a pair of dungaree shorts and a worn "Boston Strong" T-shirt he removed from an old used bureau tucked into one corner of the space.

Joe paced back and forth, not sure what to do with himself. He clicked on the TV and flopped onto his bed. He couldn't get his mind off Gussie and why she hadn't shown up for their meeting. After all, she was the one who'd texted him. Five minutes passed, and Joe realized he hadn't heard a single word spoken by the newscaster on the screen. He clicked off the TV and headed for the door. In addition to Joe's modest unit, the rest of the basement level consisted of the boiler room and a storage space. The elevator did not extend to the basement.

A thought occurred to him. What if Gussie had left him a note in his lobby mailbox? Maybe her phone had run out of battery, and she couldn't call or text him. It was possible she might even have lost her phone. That would have been a good reason not to show up. Joe decided to take a look. If there were no note, he might even take the elevator up to the fifth floor and pretend to do some work in the hallway. Maybe he'd run into her, and she'd apologize, explain about her phone, and invite him in for a cup of coffee. *All's well that ends well.* Joe smiled and trudged up the stairs, buoyed by his new line of thinking.

The lobby was deserted. Joe started to cross to his mailbox, when he noticed a small handwritten note taped to the frame of the elevator, just above the call button. What the hell was this?

"Out of order. Please take stairs."

Joe didn't know anything about this. The elevator had been working fine when he'd left three hours ago to meet Gussie at the coffeehouse. Puzzled, he pushed the call button.

There was no response.

Joe had a key ring hanging on a peg by the door back in his apartment. Among those keys was an override tool that would enable him to open the elevator doors. He hustled back down the stairs and retrieved the ring. He also grabbed a small folding ladder and pocket flashlight out of the storage area before returning to the lobby. Joe had only done this a couple of times before. He hoped it would work. The override key was a six-inch-long piece of narrow, angled aluminum that fit into a corresponding slot centered at the top of the elevator doorframe. The insert pushed a small lever that released the tension on a spring that kept the door cables taut and held the doors in place. Once he released the spring, he could pry the doors open with a screwdriver and pull them apart by hand.

Joe climbed atop the ladder and after several attempts felt the catch release. He stepped back down and with some effort managed to muscle the doors open and take a look. The elevator was not there. He looked up into the darkness of the shaft and could see the outline of the bottom of the car about thirty feet above. It appeared to be stuck between levels three and four. *Shit!* There was no way to climb past the elevator car from down there. He would have to go up to level four and repeat the procedure of opening the doors once again. From there, he could climb down to the top of the car and access the interior through the roof hatch. There didn't appear to be anything mechanically wrong beneath the car. Perhaps from level four, he could determine what the problem was.

"Hello?" he called. "Anyone in there?"

He received no response.

He tried once more. "Hello? Is anyone there?"

Still, there was no response.

Joe folded up the ladder and started up the stairs to level four. Moments later, he was inside the shaft, looking down at the stuck elevator. The roof of the car was about five feet below the fourth-floor corridor opening to the shaft. The shaft's temperature made him feel as if he were entering a baking oven. At six feet and 275 pounds, Joe was not built for that type of work. He was sweating profusely, and his T-shirt was plastered to his body. His hands felt slippery on the rungs built into the shaft wall as he maneuvered himself down to the roof of the car. The ceiling hatch door was closed. Joe stood on top of the car and paused as his eyes adjusted to the dim light, and his breathing slowed slightly, recovering from the physical exertion of getting into position.

Gathering himself, he glanced about, looking for whatever had caused the elevator to get stuck. Joe played the flashlight beam up and down the shaft. At first, he couldn't find anything out of order, but then he saw something high above his head, at the top of the shaft. The ancient elevator was operated by a cable system running through a series of pulleys and driven by an assemblage of electrically powered gears. Wedged into the exposed gears he saw a small, triangular wooden shunt. What the hell was this? Who could possibly have done that—and why? No one would ever have climbed around inside the elevator shaft without his knowing it, not a tenant and certainly not the landlord. Yet someone had apparently deliberately jammed the gears, not only stopping the elevator in its tracks but also causing the small electric motor to burn out, killing the power to the elevator. Who? Why? It did not make any sense.

Joe reached down, grabbed the handle of the hatch door on the elevator roof, and yanked it open in one quick motion. He shone the light through the opening and fell to his knees when he saw what was inside.

CHAPTER 1

Police Headquarters, Cambridge, Massachusetts

Chief Homicide Investigator Dimase Augustin let out a long sigh and tossed the crime scene folder back onto his desk. In his fifteen years in the department, including the last eight heading up homicide, he had never seen anything like this. Cambridge was not Boston. The Boston side of the Charles River averaged ten times more murders than the half dozen or so each year in Cambridge. Most homicides in Cambridge were drug related or maybe a mugging or robbery gone bad. There were occasional crimes of passion; he'd seen perhaps two or three in his years as chief investigator. This was different.

Dimase reached into the inner pocket of his navy-blue sports coat and fished out a half-full pack of Marlboros. He tapped out a cigarette and rotated it between his index and middle fingers. He knew he couldn't smoke inside police headquarters, but he found some comfort in the familiarity of the unlit cigarette in his hand. Real or imagined, the routine seemed to help him think and had a calming effect when he started to feel stress. He was feeling stressed now.

Dimase got up from his desk; stretched his legs, coming to his full height of five feet eight inches; and began to pace. The stress ebbed slightly. He knew stress was bad—it could kill. But his biomass was fine for his weight of 175 pounds, which he carried on a thin, solid frame. On the outside, he looked to be the picture of health. So far, good genes had apparently outweighed the impact of a caffeine- and nicotine-fueled diet augmented by fast food and TV dinners. The first-generation son of Haitian immigrants, Dimase had a quick mind, but as much as anything, his willingness to put in long hours and outwork the competition had driven his rise to chief investigator—and he knew it. There was no time for a wife or family. He was married to the job.

Dimase sat down again, feeling a little better. He put the unlit cigarette in his mouth, picked up the crime scene folder once again, stared at it for a few seconds, and without opening the file, tossed it back onto the desk in disgust. This murder was different. It had the feel of a ritualistic killing, carefully planned and meticulously executed. Yet the man waiting for him in the interview room, despite his newly declared willingness to confess, seemed incapable of such sophistication. Three hours earlier, the man had been apprehended at the crime scene, in the elevator shaft. Now he sat down the hall, and he had just informed the attending officer he was ready to make a full confession. It was going to be a long night.

For the third time, he picked up the folder. This time, he opened it to reread the summary and re-create the scene in his mind. Dimase often found it helpful to bring a written report to life by allowing a narrative to play out like a video, filling in gaps with imagined conversation or action. It was too soon to know what really had happened, but he closed his eyes and tried to put himself in the place of the responding officers and rescue personnel.

The first call to 911 came in at 7:15 p.m., followed in quick succession by additional calls at 7:16 and 7:19. The initial call, from a tenant, reported an open elevator shaft on the fourth floor of a residential apartment building at 645 Brattle Street. When the caller looked down the shaft, he could see a man lying on top of what appeared to be the roof of the elevator car. The man was sobbing and talking to himself but unresponsive to the tenant's inquiries. Lighting was so poor in the shaft that it was difficult to tell whether or not the man was hurt or simply delusional.

The succeeding calls came from visitors to the building who entered the lobby through the front entrance and also encountered open elevator doors with no elevator present. They too could hear muffled sobbing. The first responder was a foot officer on patrol in the general area. By the time she arrived at 7:29 p.m., a small crowd of tenants and visitors had gathered in the lobby. The officer used her flashlight and determined that the elevator was suspended some thirty feet above her head. She also could hear subdued whimpering but elicited no response when she called out.

A tenant informed the patrolwoman that the fourth-floor elevator doors were also ajar, exposing the open shaft, and that a man appeared to be lying atop the stranded elevator. At 7:38 p.m., an ambulance, along with two EMTs, immediately followed by two patrol cars, pulled curbside in front of the building. Leaving one officer in the lobby to secure the area, they proceeded as a group up the stairs to the fourth floor. The senior officer on site, Sergeant Robinson, took charge and, after a brief assessment, radioed for tactical backup, including temporary lighting and rappelling equipment. The man on top of the elevator could be seen more clearly now in the crossbeams of three different flashlights. He was conscious but apparently incoherent and continued to be unresponsive.

At 8:31 p.m., a tactical support van arrived, and temporary lighting was rigged up to illuminate the shaft from both the lobby level and the fourth floor. One of the EMTs was hooked into a safety harness, but he used the ladder built into the shaft to get down to the elevator. As his feet touched the elevator car, the man lying on the roof rolled into a sitting position and held his hands out with palms up in a position of submission. The EMT handed the man a bottle of water, which he accepted and gulped greedily.

"Are you all right?"

The man shook his head and directed his gaze to the open hatch door beneath their feet. The EMT looked through the two-by-two-foot opening and immediately pulled back. "What happened to her?" he asked.

The man just continued to shake his head.

"Did you do this?" the EMT asked.

Again, the man just shook his head. It was clear the woman was beyond any chance of help.

"Are you armed?"

The man again shook his head.

"Are you hurt? Are you going to hurt me? Do you have any weapons?" the EMT asked.

The man remained silent, his face contorted, with tears forming in his eyes.

"Stand up. I'm going to have to frisk you, and then we have to get you out of here. You got anything sharp in your pockets, like a needle or something?"

The man shook his head. The EMT quickly determined that he was unarmed. He also noted that the man was quite overweight. It was not going to be easy to get him up the shaft if he did not cooperate. The EMT stepped out of the harness and hooked it up to the man. With three responders pulling from above and the EMT in the shaft pushing from below, they managed to haul the dazed man up to the open fourth-floor doors and out into the corridor. In the full light of the hall, he appeared to be in a catatonic state. They quickly checked again for injuries or weapons and, finding none, placed a pair of flex cuffs over his wrists. Sergeant Robinson asked him several questions about what had happened there, but the man just hung his head, mumbling incoherently to himself.

In the shaft, the EMT turned his attention to the interior of the car. The arc of his flashlight beam played across the inside of the car. He could see the twisted body of what appeared to be a young woman. Her body was wedged unnaturally into a corner of the car, with her head tilted at an impossible angle. There was blood everywhere. Something was off about her face. It was difficult to tell exactly what from the perspective of the EMT, who remained outside the car for fear of contaminating the scene. The woman was not fully facing him; her head leaned back and to one side, bathed in the surreal lighting of the flashlight. There was something ghoulish about her appearance. The EMT extended his torso partially through the roof opening in order to get a better look. She was clearly dead.

The EMT did not want to enter the elevator and risk disturbing evidence in any way. Bracing himself with his feet and one arm, he maneuvered his head and shoulders as far as he could through the opening. The coppery smell of fresh blood assaulted his nostrils. He craned his neck to get a better view and pointed the beam of light directly at her partially turned face. What he saw shocked him. Despite many years of experience in responding to every manner of disaster and carnage, the EMT recoiled, almost dropping the flashlight from his hand. Her face was reminiscent of a wax figure in a haunted house of horrors. Someone had fully excised the woman's eyes from her head, leaving only dark, shadowy sockets where her eyes should have been.

Dimase Augustin turned off the video replay running through his head and returned to the moment. Based on the report and on what he'd seen earlier in person, he figured he'd reconstructed the scene accurately enough. The narrative ended with the macabre discovery by the EMT that the case was far from a routine robbery or impulsive act. There was something more going on, but Dimase was damned if he could figure it out. Yet thirty feet down the hall, the man they had pulled from the elevator shaft was now willing to talk. He supposedly wanted to confess, as Dimase had already been told, but something seemed off.

It would be hours before Dimase received the follow-up report after the crime scene was cleared. There would also be an autopsy and preliminary cause-of-death finding within twenty-four to forty-eight hours. Without those pieces, it was impossible to understand exactly what had happened. Dimase was still trying to get his head around the end result, let alone what could possibly have led up to such a bizarre outcome. One thing was sure: the vic's name was Augusta Watkins. They'd found the lady's wallet in her purse. She'd been a tenant in the building, which meant the suspect had known her.

◆ ◆ ◆

Joe Bucci sat passively at the small conference table, jiggling his legs and fidgeting compulsively with his thumbs. He'd seen enough TV to assume they were watching him from the other side of the mirror on the wall in front of him. The initial shock and confusion from his grisly discovery in the elevator had somewhat abated. His first reaction had been total paralysis, with all of his senses overwhelmed at once by the sudden jolt to his system. The heat, blood, smell, sweat, lighting, and twisted body highlighted by the beam of his pocket light had short-circuited his brain and sucked what little air there was from his lungs.

The situation was incomprehensible. Who could possibly have gained access to the elevator shaft—and how? Who was the poor woman in the elevator? He had a sick feeling about that. The sneakers and backpack looked familiar, and the general frame of the woman made him think it might have been Gussie. After his first crippling glance into the car, he hadn't looked again. He'd been unable to look again. The horrible image would be with him for the rest of his life. He hadn't needed to look twice.

If it was Gussie lying in the elevator, that would explain why she had not shown up for their meeting at Simon's Coffee Shop. Why would anyone have wanted to hurt Gussie? She seemed harmless and innocent. Had she simply been in the wrong place at the wrong time? Somebody had gone to a lot of trouble to stall the elevator. Joe had seen the wooden shunt jammed into the gears. That was how the perpetrator had done it. What had happened after that was hard to say. Why there, and why like that? If it was Gussie, did her killing have anything to do with the unusual meeting she had scheduled with him at Simon's?

None of it made sense to Joe, but as he calmed down and his panic receded, he realized something. The officers at the scene who'd pulled him from the shaft had treated him with a great deal of respect. True, they had handcuffed him, but they had not been rough. They'd asked him questions politely and called him "sir." Joe still had been reeling at that point, unable to respond and still trying to process what he had just seen. Nonetheless, his rescuers had been considerate and deferential. When they eventually had escorted him down the stairs, through the lobby, and into the backseat of a patrol car, Joe had noticed that bystanders and law enforcement personnel alike paused briefly to look at him.

He was important. For the first time in his life, he was the center of attention. Maybe he'd grab the limelight just for a little while.

The doorknob turned, and a wiry black cop entered the interview room and took a seat opposite Joe on the other side of the conference table, giving Joe his name as he did so: Dimase Augustin. Joe made brief eye contact and then stared at the table, waiting for the cop to make the first move. The cop took a digital voice recorder from his jacket pocket and placed it on the table between them.

"Mr. Bucci, you haven't been arrested yet. You're here to answer questions. Is that understood?"

Joe nodded.

"I am going to record our conversation. Okay with you?"

Joe raised his eyes and nodded his assent.

"I understand from the other officer that you wish to make a confession. Is that also correct?"

"Yes," Joe replied.

"All right then. Please tell me slowly and calmly in your own words what happened here."

Joe had already decided to operate on the premise that it was Gussie Watkins in the elevator. Sooner or later, his story would not tie together anyway. His goal was to gain some notoriety, garner some attention, and eventually be cleared. On the off chance Gussie was not the victim, he would simply be exonerated sooner than he would have liked. Either way, reporters would be waiting for him upon his release.

"I think I did it," Joe whispered.

"You think?" Dimase said. "Either you did or you didn't. Why do you *think*?"

"I went into a rage. A quiet rage—no one else could see it. I kept it inside of me. When that happens, sometimes it's hard to remember. Things become a blur. I don't think. I just act."

"Okay," Dimase said. "What triggered this rage? Where were you? How did it start?"

"It's Gussie—Gussie Watkins. She's the girl in the elevator. I killed her, I think."

Dimase raised his eyebrows and, despite the recorder on the table, pulled a small notebook from his breast pocket and started to jot down a few notes. "Tell me what you remember. Start at the beginning."

Joe let out a long breath, squirmed in his chair, and for the first time looked Dimase straight in the eye. "Gussie is a tenant in the building. Lives on the fifth floor, number 503. She's been there about two and a half years. She seemed like a nice girl. I knew her a little bit, just like I know all the tenants. I'm the building supervisor. I'm good at it. They call me, and I fix it. I keep the building clean. I do repairs—whatever it takes to keep the building in good shape."

"So you were saying, Mr. Bucci, you went into a rage, you don't remember everything, and you believe you are the person who killed Ms. Watkins. Why?"

"I was angry. I thought we had a date. I was waiting for her, and she stood me up."

"Where was the date?" Dimase asked.

"At Simon's Coffee House, near Harvard Square."

"What time were you supposed to meet her?"

"Five o'clock."

The cop shuffled some papers and took a sip of coffee. "Did

you often date tenants in the building? Had you ever dated this woman, Gussie Watkins, before?"

"No. Not her and not anyone else. I don't really date."

"So how did this date come about? Did you ask her?"

"No, she sent me a text. It was kind of a work date. She wanted to go over a punch list of repairs, but she suggested we do it away from the property, at a coffeehouse—you know, like a date."

"Would that text still be on your phone?" Dimase asked.

"I suppose so," Joe replied. "I didn't erase it."

"So what happened? She didn't show up for the date?"

"No, I waited over an hour. I grew angrier and angrier. Finally, something just snapped. Like I said, it was all a blur. I got back on a bus, went back to the building, and killed her."

"Where did you kill her?" Dimase asked.

Joe was puzzled by the question. "Well, in the elevator, I guess."

"Were you initially in the elevator with her, or did you climb in through the roof hatch?"

"No, no," Joe stammered. "Not the roof hatch. I got on the elevator with her."

"Then how did you wind up on the roof?"

Joe was confused. "Well, I got in the elevator with her, then I did it, and then I panicked. I didn't want anyone to find her, at least not right away. I figured I could disable the elevator, and that would buy me some time. I didn't know what to do. I couldn't believe I might have killed her, so I got out of the elevator real quick. I rigged the scene to look as it did."

"If you did that to buy time to get away, then why didn't you just make a run for it?"

Joe was starting not to like this cop, and he was starting to think he'd made a big mistake. Maybe the limelight, at least under those circumstances, wasn't so cool after all. "I dunno. As I said, Detective Augustin, I was in a frenzy. I wasn't thinking straight."

"But why go to the top of the elevator?" the cop said. "I'm confused."

Joe took a deep breath and buried his face in his hands. "I'm confused too. I don't remember what happened exactly. I told you I—"

"Yeah, yeah. You don't remember. But surely you remember how you killed her."

"What do you mean?" Joe asked, feeling an increasing amount of fear and confusion.

"Did you strangle her? Beat her? Stab her? How did you do it?"

"I stabbed her," Joe said flatly.

"Where is the knife?"

"I got rid of it when I left the elevator. I'm not sure. I don't remember. I dumped it somewhere in the building. I'm sure it will turn up. I'll try to remember."

"Okay, Mr. Bucci," Dimase said, leaning back in his chair. "There's only one problem with your story."

"What's that?" Joe asked.

"It's total bullshit!" the cop screamed, banging his fist on the table. "You didn't kill that girl!"

"Why not?" asked Bucci, deflating somewhat.

"For one thing, there's not a drop of blood on you. I was there two hours ago. I have rarely seen so much blood in such a confined space. You were never in that elevator, Joe. I don't know what your game is, but you didn't kill Augusta Watkins! That's why we haven't charged you, and we most likely will not, at least not for murder. Now, as for obstructing justice …"

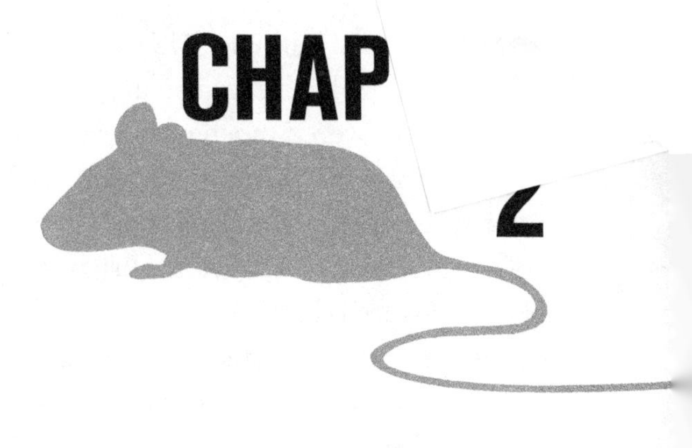

CHAP 2

The next morning at nine o'clock, operating on short sleep and several cups of coffee, Dimase Augustin was back on the scene at 645 Brattle Street. He was accompanied by a team of three detectives who also looked somewhat the worse for wear. Dimase had already reviewed the updated files and photos, and he wanted to return to Brattle Street a second time to compare what was in the file to the reality of the scene, so it would all be properly calibrated in his mind.

Yellow police tape still surrounded much of the lobby, and a young patrolman stood guard, forcing tenants to use the stairs. Dimase knew what to expect from having been there the previous evening and also from having seen the photos, but he wanted to see again for himself. He nodded to the officer on duty, opened the elevator doors, and peered inside. His colleagues leaned in behind him, straining to get a look over his shoulder. With the body gone and the elevator functional once again, the only indication of the violence that had occurred there was the blood. There was no weapon, nor had any been found elsewhere in the building. There was no damage to the interior of the car or evidence of a struggle. There was just the blood. Dark stains covered much of the carpeted floor, particularly in the corner where the body had been. Brighter red splatter marks were spread across the lower portion of two walls in the same corner. Scrawled on the wall in bright red blood was the cryptic phrase "Justice is blind."

Forensics had concluded, based on the nature of the throat wound and the pattern of blood spray, that Gussie Watkins's murderer had cut her throat with a knife. Dimase tried to imagine how the assailant had come at her. The report said the angle of the cut indicated the assailant was most likely right handed and had attacked the victim from behind. The autopsy would have to confirm that preliminary conclusion. How had the attack begun? Had the attacker entered the elevator with Gussie and surprised her? If that were the case, how would it have been possible to jam the elevator by wedging the wooden shunt into the gears at the top of the shaft? Gussie would not have entered an elevator that was already disabled. She clearly could not have entered after the elevator was stuck between floors. She certainly hadn't stepped into an exposed shaft and climbed up to the elevator.

Dimase pondered the dilemma and turned to the other detectives. "So I'll ask the obvious: Was she attacked by one person or two?"

One of his subordinates ventured an answer. "It had to be two, Chief. She gets in the elevator in the lobby. Someone else gets on with her. Everything is normal. The guy who gets on with her somehow signals a second guy, who disables the gears, stopping the elevator between floors. Maybe they don't even need a signal. What if the second guy is just supposed to jam the elevator if it rises above a certain floor? The guy on the elevator could push the button for floor two if he's not in there with the intended victim. If it's a false alarm, he just gets off the elevator and walks back downstairs. If he is on with the intended victim, the second guy, up in the shaft, knows to shove the shunt in the gears once the car passes beyond the third floor. When the elevator stops, the guy on board does the dirty deed and takes off with the weapon."

Dimase stepped away from the elevator and clasped his hands behind his back. He paused, thinking that his next stop would be the fifth floor to survey the vic's apartment.

"Makes sense," Dimase replied. "If that scenario is true, it brings our building supervisor back into play. I initially ruled him out because he didn't have a speck of blood on him. I suppose he could have been the second man, waiting in the shaft. Something about his story still doesn't smell right, though. I don't think he did it."

"Why not, Chief?" asked a female detective in her early thirties, a pretty Latina by the name of Juanita Gonzales.

"Call it a hunch. Bucci's alibi stick?"

"Yeah, we got witnesses who saw him at the coffee shop between five and six o'clock, just like he said."

A couple of people Dimase figured were tenants approached the elevator, saw the sign saying to take the stairs, and turned away.

"The second-man theory can work, but it's a bit out there."

"But—"

Dimase raised an index finger. "Does our supervisor man appear to be capable of organizing something like this? If his motive was actually based on anger at being stood up, is it logical that he would be able to recruit a second person—a second person who would commit the actual murder? Do we have any witnesses who saw anyone lurking around the lobby, waiting for Ms. Watkins? How did they even know when she might be returning to the building?"

The third detective, a short, stocky Irishman closing in on retirement, said, "The second-man theory is just that, boss. A theory."

Dimase smiled and shook his head. "We all must keep open minds. Come on. Let's go see the vic's apartment to see what we find."

As Dimase led the way up the stairs, the conversation between the detectives continued. He was pleased that his colleagues were thoroughly engaged with the investigation. They might have all been tired, but they were doing their jobs—and doing them right, as always.

"What do you think about that weird message?" Gonzalez asked no one in particular.

"And what's with the missing eyeballs?" the Irish cop asked.

"Guys who are in a frenzy of anger don't write messages like that in their vic's blood," Dimase said. "They beat the hell out of them, cut them, and shoot them. But do they stop to write a message? I think not."

"Sounds like a serial to me," Gonzalez said. "Serials would do something like that."

"You're right, Detective," Dimase said, shooting her a grim smile over his shoulder.

◆ ◆ ◆

Joe Bucci lay on a cot in his holding cell at Cambridge Police headquarters. The physical and emotional strain of the past twenty-four hours was catching up to him, and he drifted in and out of fitful sleep. He was having the kind of partially remembered dreams that occupied the space between the conscious and the subconscious. For a moment, he was back in the elevator shaft, trying to climb out. He climbed toward the top—only there was no top. The shaft was the height of a skyscraper, and every time he made progress, a few more stories appeared. The more he climbed, the farther he had to go.

They would clear him—of that Bucci was certain. Perhaps a psychiatrist would say the shock and gruesome nature of the murder had triggered temporary amnesia. Joe had said he couldn't remember doing the actual murder, nor could he recall how he'd disposed of the murder weapon. He would say he'd just assumed he had done it because he'd woken up on top of the elevator. Like the cops, he'd thought, *Who else could it have been?* When the police came to the inevitable conclusion of his innocence, he would become a famous person without actually being guilty of the crime.

A voice called to him. "Joe, wake up! Joe, we need to talk."

Suddenly, Dimase Augustin was there in the holding cell, standing over him, gently shaking him awake. Joe's eyes opened with a start. At first, he was disoriented. Slowly, he realized where he was and who Dimase was.

"Joe, you awake?" Dimase said.

Joe took a few minutes and sat up on the edge of the cot. He made eye contact with Dimase, remained silent, and waited for Dimase to make the first move.

"Joe, I have reconsidered your position," Dimase said bluntly.

"What do you mean?" Joe blinked rapidly.

"You claim you don't remember killing this poor girl. I believe you. I believe you because the best liars always incorporate a little bit of truth."

Joe just stared at Dimase, not yet comprehending what he was trying to say.

"It is true. You did not directly kill the girl. That I believe. It is clear you were never in the elevator with her—but you did have an accomplice who killed her. Didn't you, Joe?"

Joe gulped for air. "Why do you think that?"

"It took two people working together to make this happen: one in the elevator with Ms. Watkins and the other up in the shaft—where you were, Joe—to disable the elevator. You were that second person. You were in the shaft. You disabled the elevator."

Joe hadn't expected this. Was he for real? He seemed to be. Joe was unsure how to respond. "I don't know," he stammered.

Dimase banged his fist sharply on the table, sending a jolt through Joe that reflexively knocked him back. "You don't know?" he shouted. "How else did you come to be in the shaft? Do you often go climbing about in such a place? For what other purpose might you have been there?" Dimase's manner and speech reflected a blend of exaggerated politeness with a sudden strong hint of island accent.

"I told you. I don't remember," Joe said.

Dimase continued in a calm, measured tone. "We have the text Ms. Watkins sent. You were at the coffee shop when you said you were. So you're not a complete liar."

Joe began to panic. "I didn't kill her," he said, leaning forward toward the cop.

"Now you're changing your tune?"

"Yeah, I am. I got it all wrong, except the stuff about the text and being in the coffeehouse and finding her in the elevator when I looked in from the fifth floor." Joe could tell the cop was pissed off. Now Joe was scared. "I was lying about going into a rage and not knowing anything."

The cop leaned forward, bringing his face closer to Joe's. The man was formidable looking, with flashing brown eyes, close-cropped black hair, and the deep dark-chocolate skin tone of his West African ancestors. "And why did you lie to us, Mr. Bucci?"

Joe shook his head. "I dunno. Just did, I guess."

"So why did you confess?" the cop asked. "Enlighten me."

"It was stupid," Joe said, shaking his head. "I liked the attention. It was an impulse. I knew I didn't do it. I knew you'd figure that out sooner or later. I thought I could milk it—become a celebrity and maybe make some money. I don't know. It seemed like a good idea at the time. I wasn't thinking straight. I'm sorry."

"I'm sorry too, Joe," Dimase said, folding his hands on the table in front of him. "This is a very serious matter. It seems odd that you have such different stories. Perhaps that is part of your plan to throw us off."

"What do you mean?" Joe was alarmed.

"I mean that we believe there is a very real possibility that two people worked together to commit this murder. We think it is likely one person was in the elevator and did the actual killing, and the other was in the shaft, positioned to disable the elevator at just the right time. If that is true, you would be the person in the shaft. You would be the accomplice, Joe. Do you expect us to believe that someone else was crawling around in the shaft, and you just missed them? Possible, but not likely. Who are you protecting, Joe? What are you hiding from us?"

"Nothing," Joe said. "I'm not hiding nothin'. It was a bad idea. That's all. I see that now. I didn't do anything."

"Okay, okay, Joe. We will see. Perhaps you will have more to tell us in the days ahead."

"Days ahead? What do you mean? I told you I didn't do anything. You yourself said I didn't do it. I was never in the elevator. I couldn't have done it."

"Yes and no, Joe. You are correct in that you were never in the elevator, but here is da ting. I think you know who was."

CHAPTER 3

Somerville, Massachusetts: Present Day

Hans Berger sat alone in his second-floor apartment near Davis Square in Somerville. Proximate to Tufts University, Somerville was a curious mix of college town and blue-collar working neighborhoods. Berger was a relatively new arrival, having moved in within the past few months, but he had spent the past seventeen years living in and around the Greater Boston area.

The apartment was Spartan, reflective of a man living alone who was focused on things other than housekeeping and cleanliness. He had no roommates, a condition that further reduced the need to keep up appearances. Strewn about the cramped studio apartment were a wide assortment of scientific journals, newspapers, and contemporary magazines. A dozen cardboard boxes, some torn open and others still sealed, were stacked against one wall. They were labeled in thick black magic marker that identified the remnants of Berger's former life. He'd obtained what little furniture there was at a used furniture exchange on Harvard Avenue in Allston. For an extra fifty dollars, a guy with a pickup truck would toss the stuff into the back and help wrestle it up or down stairs and in or out of various locations around the city. The amenity had proven useful to Berger because he'd had no other method to transport his newly purchased third- and fourth-hand items. He also appreciated that both the purchases and the delivery had been anonymous cash transactions.

A mattress on the floor with a few tangled blankets served as his bed in the open-area apartment. The kitchenette had a small wooden table and two mismatched chairs. Berger was not expecting to entertain. An old couch and battered wooden coffee table completed the arrangement.

There was an internet and cable hookup. After all, it was the twenty-first century, and this was a college town. Berger was extremely competent and intelligent. It had been nothing for him to obtain a black box on the secondary market and clandestinely connect his laptop and a flat-screen TV. Sometimes, other than his predawn runs, he didn't leave the apartment for days on end. It was both through his nature and by design that he kept a low profile, shunning contact with neighbors and the public in general. As far as the world was concerned, Berger was off the grid. It had not always been that way, but that was his reality now.

A small pot of water began to boil on the electric stove, and Berger stirred in some ramen noodles, his midday meal. Whether or not one was hungry, one had to maintain nutrition. The Davis Square section was heavily populated with students and recent graduates who stayed in the area. Youthful in appearance and only eighteen years removed from his own MIT graduation, Berger was invisible when he ventured out to the street, a perfect accessory to the ubiquitous ebb and flow of student bodies.

Grasping the steaming cup of noodles, Berger settled into the sagging couch and grabbed the TV clicker with his free hand. He liked to keep up on the news, relying on both his laptop and the various cable news channels. He found it interesting to compare the different spins and biases of the talking heads from one network to the next. Most of them were contemptible, seemingly incapable of independent thought beyond the groupthink of whatever preconceived agenda was evident at their own particular outlet. It was an entertaining, intellectual exercise for him to break down specious arguments, revealing false premises, incomplete facts, and straw dogs purposefully propped up to make a misleading point. He recognized the propaganda for what it was, reaffirming the clarity of his own logical positions.

Berger skipped through several channels before a byline on Fox News caught his attention: "Feminist Discounts Due Process." Berger turned up the volume just as the host asked his guest, "What do you say to the innocent men who may have been caught up in this movement and been falsely accused?"

Berger leaned forward on the couch, interested in her response, even though he was certain of the direction it would take.

"I can't be concerned about that," the young woman replied. "This movement is far too important to let it get derailed by a little collateral damage. It's unfortunate, but the greater good must be served. It is far, far beyond the time for women to be treated equitably in every level of society. Sometimes you have to break a few eggs to make an omelet."

◆ ◆ ◆

Boston, Massachusetts: Present Day

Angela Mancini rose early, as was her habit. No alarm was necessary; her body clock was dependable and accurate to within seconds each day. Angela was not one to stir slowly awake—quite the opposite. Each morning, at precisely five o'clock, her eyes popped open, and she was instantly awake. At age thirty, her daily predawn routine was deeply engrained from years of repetition.

Angela stood and languidly stretched her arms above her head, feline in her mannerisms. Living alone, she was comfortable in sleeping in her own skin. She crossed the bedroom naked and drew back the window shade. Downtown Boston had not yet begun to come to life. Below her, the streetlights cast dim illumination over conical slices of sidewalk, and the few spots available for on-street parking were still occupied by dormant vehicles. A lone *Boston Globe* delivery truck moved slowly down the street and passed out of sight around the corner.

Angela regarded her image in the bathroom mirror.

Not bad, she thought. *Not bad at all.*

Folded on the counter were gym shorts, panties, and a sports bra, which she'd laid out the night before. She dressed quickly and, still barefoot, went to the kitchen and popped a Green Mountain Keurig cup into the machine. After cutting the coffee with a splash of organic whole milk, she sat on a stool at the kitchen counter and checked the weather on her laptop. For more than a week, Boston had been in the grip of a stifling heat wave. According to Weather.com, that day would be no different. No need for rain gear—that morning would be a dry run. Angela didn't mind running in the rain. There was something both vaguely romantic and, at the same time, enjoyably melancholy about running in weather.

That day, however, would be a more exhilarating run down Commonwealth Avenue, across the Boston Common, over Storrow Drive, and along the bank of the Charles River—light gear and a fast pace. By the time she returned, the sun would just be coming up.

Angela was an attractive woman, half Italian and half West Indian. The only other person she knew who shared the same ethnic blend was her younger brother. Her natural skin tone was a light bronze that darkened considerably in the sun. She'd inherited her high cheekbones and brooding brown eyes from her Trinidadian father and her shoulder-length raven hair from her Italian mother. Both parents had bestowed her with an innate intelligence that belied her stunning looks.

Math was her thing. Numbers always had made sense ever since she was a young girl. As an adult, she'd gravitated to computer science, specifically code writing. After graduation from MIT, she'd worked for a couple of start-ups that eventually had gone bust. By the time she was twenty-five, she'd settled into a comfortable niche, freelancing for two or three small companies at a time. The money was good, not spectacular, but the freedom and control of being her own boss more than offset any perceived benefit of being someone else's employee. She often wondered if she was still capable of ever working for any boss other than herself.

Angela loved her morning run. She usually cranked out five to seven miles seven days a week. The runner's high was an addiction to her. The euphoric surge of invincibility, even superiority, made her feel in command of her world. It was almost a sense of immortality. If each day began with an all-out run, why wouldn't she be able to do it the next day and the next and each day after that? Why would it ever end? What could ever change so dramatically that she wouldn't be able to repeat only one day later what she had just done yesterday?

Of course, intellectually, Angela realized she was mortal just like everyone else. Nonetheless, it was a comforting illusion. She did some of her best thinking as she ran, gliding effortlessly as the miles rolled away beneath her feet. Most of the city was still asleep, and her own mind was transported to another place, not even aware of her body's physical effort, as she pondered some piece of code or elusive equation.

Angela's mother had chosen to maintain her maiden name, Mancini, and so too had Angela carried on her mother's line. She loved her father well enough, but it was empowering that both her parents had honored her mother—and all women, in a way—by choosing the Mancini surname at her birth.

Angela pulled on a pair of Peds, slipped her feet into a set of Nike running shoes, and laced them up tightly. She unbolted the deadlock on the door; placed the key to her apartment beneath a potted plant in the hallway; and, eschewing the elevator, took the stairs two at a time down to the street. On the sidewalk, she began to stretch, separately propping each leg up against the side of the building. Despite the early hour, it was already 75 degrees out, probably on the way to 90 by noontime. *Perfect running weather,* Angela thought to herself as she went through a dynamic five-minute warm-up in place.

At length, she was ready to go and set out at a slow jog to the intersection three blocks away where she would pick up Comm Avenue down to the Public Garden. Comm Avenue was starting to see some light early morning traffic, but the cars were few and far between, and she was able to run in the street, lengthening her stride as she approached the Public Garden. By the time she hit the Frog Pond, she would be at full speed, her torso and head balanced with hardly a bounce, her legs pumping rhythmically beneath her at a seven-minute pace.

Angela crossed Arlington Street, picking up speed, and

followed the paved path into the Public Garden. The dark of night was reluctantly yielding to the steel gray that briefly preceded dawn and the sun's first breach of the horizon. The path was lined with plantings and flowers in full bloom, though their brilliance was not yet on display. On some subconscious level, she was aware of the flowers' outline—like a charcoal sketch on an artist's palette, waiting to be brought to life with color. The multitude of species and genera enveloped her in a pungent fragrance that only enhanced her high. The endorphins released in her brain, the peak performance of her body, and the herbal aroma of the fauna sent her to a place she had never experienced in any other part of her life. She felt like a beautiful machine. Her lungs and legs were working at full capacity, but there was no pain. *Let the rest of the city sleep.* This was her daily ecstasy—sheer, raw, pure joy. It had been hers every day for as far back as she could remember, and it would be hers for each day going forward, with each day linked together in an unbroken chain. Immortality.

Angela crossed the divider road and started across the Common. She passed a sleeping homeless person awkwardly stretched out on a park bench. Angela started to work an equation in her mind. *Of course.* Why hadn't she seen it yesterday? The solution seemed simple.

Angela swept past the Frog Pond at full speed. She wound around the Parkman Bandstand, her body mindlessly leaning into the curves like a racehorse at full gallop.

Sheer exhilaration! The rim of the sun barely crested the Boston skyline to the east, highlighting the building tops. The only sound in Angela's head was her own breathing. Her eyes focused robotically on the path ahead, her mind totally separated from the automaton that was her physical self. It was an out-of-body experience, better than an orgasm.

Suddenly, something was wrong. Her body continued on automatic pilot, running fifteen more strides at full speed before a plume of blood spewed from her mouth. Her brain refocused on her body, which was now stumbling forward. Her momentum carried her another ten yards before her lungs exploded, and she collapsed face-first to the ground.

Angela realized she was dying, but she didn't know why. Was that what a heart attack felt like? Out of the corner of her eye, she saw a fading image of the Boston Massacre Monument. The sun edged slightly higher in the early morning sky, and as Angela's world faded to black, she thought, *Immortality.* She had known it had to end someday. She hadn't thought it would be that day.

CHAPTER 4

Police Headquarters, Cambridge, Massachusetts

Dimase Augustin pulled one last drag on his cigarette and squished the remains underfoot on the cement floor in the same manner one might have killed an ant. He had a prime reserved spot near the elevator on the third underground floor of the subterranean police parking garage. His last hit of nicotine would have to last at least two or three hours. He stole a glance at the security camera and gave his digital watchers a cooperative smile. Dimase couldn't bring himself to chew nicotine gum or use a patch. That meant the stimulant of choice for most of the morning would now default to caffeine.

He leaned in through the driver's-side door of his department-issued Ford Police Interceptor Utility vehicle and grabbed the full cup of steaming black Dunkin' Donuts coffee from the cupholder. An empty twin Styrofoam cup remained in the adjacent cupholder—one for the road and one for the office. The autolock beeped as he clicked the lock button on his key fob, not that he should have had to worry about getting ripped off in the police garage.

Dimase entered the elevator and punched the button for the seventh floor, where he would preside over the morning briefing for the Watkins task force. As chief homicide investigator, he had two full-time detectives assigned to him, but the department gave him great latitude in accessing other resources, particularly if his workload was backed up or they had a brand-new case. Everyone recognized that the odds of solving a case went down dramatically if they didn't come up with something quickly.

Just two days had passed since Gussie Watkins's murder in the elevator on Brattle Street. When Dimase got on the parking garage elevator, he couldn't help but think about what the poor woman's last moments must have been like. The first morning after the murder, he involuntarily had cast a glance at the elevator roof, checking for a hatch door. Of course, he knew modern elevators didn't have visible hatches. There was a false ceiling in the parking garage elevator, and there was no obvious method to gain entrance other than through the passenger doors. In his normal course of business, Dimase had been on several elevators, and not one of them had had an obvious roof hatch of any type. He wondered if there were any statistics available on how many elevators in the Greater Boston area were old enough to have old-fashioned hatches. That line of thinking always led him back to Joe Bucci.

Dimase had charged Bucci with suspicion of murder just to keep the suspect on ice while the investigation played out a little more. The prosecutor argued for $50,000 in bail, which was no small amount for most people but for Bucci was totally unattainable. It might as well have been a million dollars. Dimase knew the judge was not predisposed to keeping a person in jail unless he or she posed a serious flight risk or the crime was so heinous that a premature release might boomerang back at the judge after the fact if the suspect did anything inappropriate postrelease. As crimes went, the murder of Gussie Watkins was pretty heinous.

Bucci was appointed a public defender, who argued for house arrest and pointed out that Bucci had recanted his original confession. The DA successfully argued that Bucci could be a threat to himself or others, he had confessed with no coercion or undue influence, and circumstantial evidence strongly supported his likely involvement. In the end, the judge was persuaded, perhaps by fear of tarnishing his own reputation as much as anything else.

The public defender was only twenty-five years old and fresh out of Suffolk Law School. He was clearly out of his element and in over his head. Dimase imagined that if Bucci ever actually went to trial, he would probably wind up with a high-profile defense attorney on a pro bono basis. After all, the case was about as sensational as it got, probably one of the most notorious in the city's long history. The Cambridge City Police Department, at Dimase's direction, had kept two key details from the public. It was news enough that a vibrant young woman had been brutally murdered in an elevator right in the heart of one of the most liberal, academic, and sophisticated cities in the world. If the media got wind of the fact that Gussie Watkins's eyes had been cut out of her head or that the cryptic message "Justice is blind" had been scrawled on the wall in the victim's blood, the headlines would scream from every tabloid in the country. Small wonder the judge was hesitant to release Joe Bucci.

The elevator stopped on the fourth floor, and two detectives from robbery stepped on, nodding in acknowledgment toward Dimase. Every time Dimase had gotten on an elevator over the past few days, he'd asked himself the same questions: How many elevators were still around that had trapdoors, and who knew where they were? That was why he always thought of Bucci.

It seemed clear there likely had been two perpetrators. The crime had to have been painstakingly planned to the last detail in advance and timed perfectly. Had the assailants specifically targeted Gussie Watkins for some unknown reason and then later devised the methodology of the elevator attack, or had it been the other way around? Had the assailants been aware of the antique elevator and the unusual hatch door first, with poor Ms. Watkins simply a random victim?

The doors opened at floor seven, and Dimase, as well as both detectives, disembarked. They proceeded as a group down the hall to conference room B, where the rest of Dimase's hastily assembled task force were waiting. Dimase took his place at the head of the oversized conference table, and all eyes turned toward him. In light of the seriousness of the situation and as a sign of respect for Dimase, they dispensed with the usual banter.

Dimase took a small sip from his coffee and glanced around the room as he gathered his thoughts. "Does anyone have any new developments to report?" he asked.

Chen Li from forensics raised his hand halfway, indicating a desire to speak. "We've completed our analysis of both the victim's phone and Mr. Bucci's. The results are quite interesting."

Dimase nodded for Li to continue.

"Well, as you know, we ran the phone records on the vic and the suspect right away to confirm the guy's alibi. He did get a text asking him to meet Ms. Watkins at the coffee shop."

One of the detectives from robbery spoke up. "That would seem to indicate support for Bucci's story, correct?"

"Yes and no," Li replied. "The problem is, we also completed analysis of Ms. Watkins's phone, and the text did not come from her, nor did she receive the confirmation text back from Mr. Bucci."

Dimase clasped his hands and leaned forward. "That's something new."

"Anyone could have sent that text to Bucci, including Bucci himself," said Jorgé Rodriguez, one of the two detectives permanently assigned to Dimase in homicide. The other was Bob Coyne.

"Do we know from what phone the text did originate?" asked Dimase.

"Yes," Li replied. "We were able to identify the number. It was from a burner. Working backward from where the number falls in the sequence of that lot of manufactured phones, we've narrowed it down to the CVS off Mass. Ave. in Cambridge. We believe it was purchased there about three weeks or so before the murder."

"All right," Dimase said. "I want four weeks of security tapes run through facial-recognition software. We don't know who we're looking for, but I want to identify every possible phone transaction we can from those tapes. Isolate every single image where we suspect a phone purchase, and let's see if we can get as many names as we can through the recognition software."

"You got it, Chief," Li and Rodriguez answered nearly in unison.

"There's something else," Dimase said. "When you're doing the recognition software, I also want you to scan all transactions to see if we can get a hit on either Bucci or Ms. Watkins. I want to know if either of them was ever in that store for any purpose."

Again, both men nodded in understanding.

Dimase leaned back in his chair and folded his arms across his chest. "I keep coming back to our Mr. Bucci. Perhaps he is smarter than he would like us to believe—a clever mind in an odd package."

The group was silent, waiting to see where Dimase was going with that thought.

"So we know now that Ms. Watkins never texted Mr. Bucci. In all likelihood, she never knew anything of this alleged meeting at Simon's Coffee House, supposedly to discuss building repairs. What if Mr. Bucci sent that text to himself?" Dimase paused for dramatic effect. "What if he sent the text to himself, and it was all part of an elaborate attempt to create an alibi? The text places him at Simon's for a five o'clock meeting. And so do the witnesses. He was there. No question. Yet it's possible the murder took place before or after that time. The coroner puts time of death in a four-hour window from when the body was discovered. Bucci could still have had plenty of time before or after the supposed date with Ms. Watkins to kill her or help someone else do it."

Li raised his hand again. "One other thing. Bucci was there—at the coffee shop, I mean—about ten minutes earlier. At ten to five, not five o'clock. Don't see it as all that important, but I thought you should know we have security footage of him at the counter buying a large cup of coffee at about four fifty."

"Do we have anything after that?"

"No, he may have gone off in a corner, or he may have left. The surveillance video is not panoramic, so there are large segments of the seating areas not visible."

Dimase raised his hands in feigned incredulity. "So our Mr. Bucci's alibi is really not an alibi at all."

"But, Chief," Rodriguez said, "what would be his motive? And what about the eyes and the message on the elevator wall? What's up with all that? There's nothing in Bucci's background to indicate any interest in the occult or horror movies or anything of that sort. There's no connection between him and Ms. Watkins other than their superficial contact in the building as tenant and maintenance man. Why would he do it? Why would he do it like that?"

"I agree it doesn't add up," Dimase replied. "I also know that Bucci is all we've got at the moment, and his actions and alibi don't add up either. My conclusion is that he must have been recruited. He must have been approached by someone who did have a motive to go after Gussie Watkins."

"And he set the alibi up at the coffee shop to throw us off?" Li asked.

"Yeah, but why confess to the crime if he was trying to get out of it?" Rodriguez asked.

"All good questions," Dimase said. "We have to find the motive. It has to be something in Ms. Watkins's background. Find that motive, and maybe we find the actual perpetrator, the brains behind the operation. Maybe Bucci knows this person, or maybe he doesn't, but somehow, he or she got Bucci to play his role as an accomplice, either knowingly or unknowingly. When we find the motive, it will become clearer."

"What about the eyes?" Rodriguez asked again. "Do you think the motive could have something to do with the eyes being removed and the message 'Justice is blind'? That has to be tied in, but if we can't find anything in Ms. Watkins's background related to that, it brings me back to the idea of a random crime. I really think it's a carefully preplanned crime with a random victim who happened to be in the wrong place at the wrong time."

"Very possible," Dimase said. "Our perp may have some general message he wants to deliver for whatever reason. He dreams up a crazy, dramatic scheme of an elevator killing; locates an appropriate elevator; and somehow tricks or induces Bucci into being his accomplice. Under that theory, the motive is not connected to either Ms. Watkins or Mr. Bucci. The motive is unknown, but the perpetrator is aware well in advance of the old-style elevator on Brattle Street. Let's run with that approach at the same time. I want all the tenants interviewed again. Look at all of them closely, but also develop a list for all of them of every visitor they've ever had to the building. We also need to identify past tenants. Talk to the landlord again. Go back five or even ten years if possible. We need to track down as many people as possible and develop a master list of everyone they can think of who may have ever visited the building. It won't be perfect, but it will give us a universe of people to work with. The person we're looking for had to have known about the elevator. Good old-fashioned police work, ladies and gentlemen. Anything else?"

"I might have something. I'm not sure," said Burke, the department's external liaison. "Remember that jogger who was murdered on Boston Common yesterday?"

"It was in all the papers," Rodriguez said to no one in particular. "You could hardly have missed it. How is that related to us?"

Burke continued. "We withheld the details on our case about the eyes and the message, so there's no way anyone in the general public would know about those things. I just got an updated summary of open cases from BPD this morning. It turns out there was a message in the jogger case too. Nothing to do with eyes, but it did mention justice. I thought that was a pretty strange coincidence."

"What did it say?" Dimase asked impatiently. "Give us the specifics."

"No one saw anything. It was still pretty dark. Happened around five twenty in the morning or so. They found her around six o'clock with an eight-inch hunting knife plunged up to the hilt right between her shoulder blades. The interesting part is, there was a laminated handwritten note carefully taped in place at the base of the blade, just above the handle. Whoever did it went to great pains to place the blade through a slit in the plastic laminate so the message would be pinned to the victim's back, like a kids' game."

"What did the message say?" Dimase asked.

"It said, 'Justice is swift.'"

CHAPTER 5

Dimase Augustin drove his departmental vehicle down Memorial Drive and over the Massachusetts Avenue Bridge on his way to a demonstration soon to begin on Boston Common. The events of the past several days, starting with the gruesome murder of Augusta Watkins, disturbed him. His drive alone in the SUV gave him time to think.

He knew something the media did not. Neither the Cambridge Police nor the BPD had released any information relative to the murders' one common denominator: the presence of a written message citing the word *justice*. Also, the circumstance of Gussie Watkins's eyes being excised had not been allowed to become public knowledge. The connection certainly would have thrust Gussie Watkins back into the spotlight, but for the time being, Dimase felt there was an advantage to holding the information back.

Dimase wasn't buying the media narrative that Angela Mancini had been hunted down like a wild animal by some crazed Nazi or white nationalist of some type. In his mind, the justice message left at each crime scene was an irrefutable connection. Throughout his entire career, Dimase had not seen or even been aware of a single case in which the murderer had left a written message relating to the concept of justice. Now two cases within one week and within seven miles of each other shared that distinction. Dimase was convinced the murders of Gussie Watkins and Angela Mancini had to be related. Not only was there commonality between the cases through the use of the word *justice*, but it was also clear to Dimase that the modus operandi in each case, while different, reflected consistent allegories that possibly had originated from the same mind, possibly the mind of a serial killer.

The perpetrator was obviously preoccupied with the concept of justice and wanted to deliver a message about how justice should be administered in his or her world order. In the case of Gussie Watkins, the assailant not only had made a point about justice being blind but also had gone to great lengths to leave a graphic illustration by removing Ms. Watkins's eyes. In the case of Angela Mancini, the murderer had educated his audience on the concept of swift justice, not only through the note but also by swiftly overtaking a running woman from behind and likely delivering the fatal blow before she even knew what hit her.

The murderer was angry about something, Dimase postulated—perhaps something the two women had in common. He did not know. Contrary to the media narrative, he did not think the Mancini murder was racially motivated. After all, if the two cases were connected in the way he thought, one victim had been white, and one had been brown, so while one could never rule anything out completely, it seemed unlikely that race was the motivating factor. They were both women. Perhaps the person they were looking for had a problem with women, not race. It was possible they were both random victims, even though each killing clearly had involved advanced planning.

Alternatively, there could have been some unknown connection between the two women that had triggered the murderer to carefully track and sensationally kill each of them while simultaneously delivering the dramatic messages about justice. None of Dimase's theories changed the fact that the genie was out of the bottle. There was a political and media maelstrom surrounding the Mancini murder. Multiple groups on both the left and the right were using the woman's death to project and spin their own message. The media was only too happy to fan the flames, consequences be damned.

The local TV news, national broadcast networks, and, of course, the cable news channels were all having a field day with the Mancini murder. Provocateurs, protagonists, and antagonists from across the nation were descending on Boston to congregate on the Common in what was being billed as the largest Rally against Hate protest the country had yet seen. News outlets across the spectrum speculated about the event nonstop. If expectations were accurate, there would be fascists from the right and fascists from the left, all trying to drown out or shut down the others' message. Antifa would be there, as would Black Lives Matter, various Nazi groups, and a handful of white nationalists and white supremacists. Both sides would be armed with batons and clubs at a minimum, with knives and even firearms a possibility. Many, particularly from Antifa, would wear masks to shield their identities and body armor to give themselves courage as they searched for any opportunity to violently express their views, especially in front of TV cameras. Of course, if history was any indication, all sides would direct vitriol at the police. It was going to be a volatile and dangerous situation.

Dimase wondered what purpose would be served other than

to harden preexisting positions. The majority of people on the Common would be curiosity seekers, not hard-core agitators. Some idealists would even be there in the earnest hope of genuinely supporting peace and love. The news media would not focus on them. The true believers on both sides would be seeking confrontation in a misguided effort to make their point on the nightly news, not realizing that a majority of Americans felt the violence and willingness to shut down free speech undermined the very positions they were trying to promote.

Dimase was waved through a police barricade on Arlington Street and parked his SUV in a temporary law enforcement staging area adjacent to the Public Garden. The mayor had declared a state of emergency, and the BPD was out in force, trying to maintain separation between opposing factions. Dimase was not in uniform. He was not there to support the policing effort. His purpose was entirely different.

Dimase was convinced there was a high probability the murderer of Gussie Watkins and the murderer of Angela Mancini were one and the same. If not the same person, they were at least operating in coordination with each other. Dimase had a hypothesis. It was vague and sketchy but nonetheless an angle he felt compelled to pursue. He was still in the dark with regard to any common motive the perpetrator might have had to murder both women. Still, experience had shown him that certain personality types often were drawn back to the scene of their crime, particularly if they could return anonymously. What better setting to remain invisible than in the midst of a mass demonstration among thousands of people? It might have been the longest of long shots, but Dimase's intention was to work his way across the Common to the spot near the Boston Massacre Monument where Angela Mancini had fallen. In plainclothes, a middle-aged black man, he would linger inconspicuously in the area. He had no idea whom or what he was looking for, but he hoped someone might set off his internal sensor. He would also take multiple crowd shots on his cell phone for later analysis. One never knew what was possible. If the murderer was excited by the national furor he had touched off, he might well have been lurking in the area, deriving some sort of perverse enjoyment from the chaos he'd set in motion.

Dimase walked through the Public Garden and followed the path toward the Parkman Bandstand. There must have been at least twenty-five thousand people on the Common, maybe double that. To his left, two separate columns of marchers converged toward the bandstand as onlookers parted to let them through. Each column consisted of around one hundred protestors chanting slogans as they drew closer to the object of their wrath: the police barricade and the ragged group of rightists on the bandstand. At the head of one column, supporters carried a large banner proclaiming, "Black Lives Matter." Clad in black T-shirts, they chanted, "What do we want? Dead cops! When do we want them? Now!"

The other column looked as if they were prepared for combat. Most wore masks, and many brandished clubs, shields, or batons. In the midst of their ranks, an individual wearing a bicycle helmet and covering her face with a handkerchief carried a large black flag with the word *Antifa* emboldened in large white letters. Antifa chanted, "Death to fascists."

On the Parkman Bandstand, a small circle of supporters surrounded a man speaking through a megaphone. The competing chants completely drowned out his message. Over one side of the bandstand hung a banner that read, "White Rights." Dimase could not help but be struck by the insanity of it all. He wondered if most Americans felt as he did and lived their daily lives in general harmony with neighbors, friends, and coworkers of all races and backgrounds. Of course there were problems, but surely those groups were an aberration. He certainly hoped so.

As the two columns approached the bandstand, Dimase saw a loose circle of police officers wearing full riot gear and holding shields close ranks in order to keep the groups apart. Without warning, a rock cracked off the helmet of one of the officers, and both columns of antihate protestors broke into a full all-out charge in an attempt to break the police line and engage the group on the bandstand. Hand-to-hand fighting with clubs and batons ensued between the police and the protest combatants.

The police were losing ground, and gaps appeared in their defensive perimeter. In response, the commander in charge ordered tear gas to be dispersed and called on his radio for reinforcements. Dimase's instinct was to help his colleagues, but that was not why he was there. The commander then ordered an elite reserve team stationed within the semicircle of police to use rubber bullets on anyone who broke through the first line of defense.

The bullets turned the tide of the battle quickly. The loud report of gunfire and the crowd's perception that real bullets were being fired led to a full-scale retreat by the rioters. The scene resembled a Civil War battlefield. Large clouds of tear gas floated over ground zero. A few injured bodies lay on the ground, struck by rubber bullets, felled by clubs, or trampled in the panic. Pockets of fighting continued as the fleeing protestors took down anyone in their path they perceived not to be one of them.

Dimase slowly worked his way around the bandstand in the direction of his original objective: the Boston Massacre Monument. Suddenly, he came across an officer lying on the ground in the mist, separated from his unit. The man was surrounded by several enraged demonstrators who were beating him with sawed-off baseball bats and kicking him. Another protestor had his arms around the fallen policeman's neck, trying to wrestle off his protective helmet.

Fearing for his fellow officer's life, Dimase launched himself at the thug trying to remove the cop's helmet. They both toppled to the ground, which only served to turn the rage of the attackers toward Dimase. He took three or four blows to his legs and torso before he was able to roll away and draw his service revolver. At the sight of Dimase's gun, the attackers scattered and ran. The wounded officer slowly got to his knees. He was shaken, but apparently, his armor and helmet had protected him from the worst.

"Thanks, brother," the officer said between deep breaths. "For a minute, I thought I was done for. My kids' faces were flashing through my mind."

Dimase slid the pistol back into his shoulder holster. He noticed for the first time that his fellow officer was a black man perhaps ten years younger than he. "You okay?" Dimase asked.

"Yeah, I'm fine," he said, giving a thumbs-up, as several members from his team ran to join him.

The tear gas started to dissipate. Dimase could see a large group of reserve law enforcement personnel, supplemented by state police, sweeping across the Common, forcing any remaining protestors back. Occasional arrests were made as the protestors, followed by a phalanx of police, fell back in the general direction of the State House.

Across the lower Common and toward the Granary Burial Grounds, thousands of noncombatants still milled about. Dimase reached the Boston Massacre Monument. He knew from the police report exactly where Angela's body had come to rest. He circled about inconspicuously, casually taking crowd shots on his cell phone without calling attention to himself. After an hour or so, the crowd began to thin. Dimase took a seat on a nearby bench and continued to surreptitiously photograph passersby. Another hour passed, and the last protestors wandered off. The only people coming down the path past the old monument at that point were typical tourists: families, young couples, and an occasional senior citizen. None were dressed for war. None were chanting slogans. None looked like a killer.

◆ ◆ ◆

Police Headquarters, Cambridge, Massachusetts

The following Monday, Dimase was back into his office at Cambridge Police Headquarters, once again manipulating an unlit cigarette between his fingers and absently sipping a large cup of DD coffee. Deep in thought, he scrolled slowly through the pictures he'd taken on his cell phone two days earlier at the so-called antihate rally on the Boston Common. From time to time, he used his thumb and forefinger to enlarge a face or profile in order to scrutinize the image more closely.

Dimase still had no idea specifically what he was looking for. Every now and then, he would enlarge and trim a photo and email it to himself so he could print a large color copy. His selection process was far from scientific, relying on gut instinct. With a few exceptions, he ruled out most women, overweight people, and older people, assuming the person he sought must have been athletic to be able to overtake Angela Mancini running at full speed. Mancini had been an elite runner, and the police were surprised anyone had been able to catch up to her.

Over the course of an hour or so, he built a portfolio of approximately fifty head and profile shots. Dimase realized the entire process was most likely an exercise in futility; nonetheless, the two murder investigations were moving forward on several fronts at once, and his photo library was simply one more avenue. Per his earlier instruction, detectives were continuing to interview past and present tenants of the Brattle Street apartment and compiling a list and background summary on anyone who might have visited the building and been aware of the old elevator. He would have Li and his team in forensics cross-reference photos from Boston Common with those of anyone they were able to identify from the Brattle Street list. They would also compare both those groups to the list being developed from the CVS security cameras and run headshots from all three sources through facial-recognition software and general databases. Each of the lists was far from perfect, but if they lucked out and found a match between anyone on the Common or CVS and a visitor to Brattle Street, that individual would jump to the head of the class as a person of interest.

Dimase sighed as he clicked off his phone and gathered the fifty or so headshots from the printer. Modern technology provided tools for law enforcement that would have been unimaginable a generation or two ago, but as he reminded his team, most cases were solved by old-fashioned, painstaking analysis and cross-referencing of facts.

They'd made progress since the Watkins murder. The possible connection between the Watkins and Mancini murders gave his people a lot more to work with. At the same time they were looking at different groups, his team was also starting to delve deeper into the histories of Gussie Watkins and Angela Mancini, looking for any possible motive and any commonality. Bucci was still on ice, and he most likely would remain so, unless he made bail or they cleared him once and for all.

If they couldn't come up with a suspect by working the

various lists, there was a chance they could work backward and come up with a theoretical motive that would lead them back to a candidate. As with any investigation, they would follow multiple tracks at the same time, waiting for the next break, the one piece of the puzzle that would allow all the others to fall into place. It was a slow and difficult process of trial and error and elimination.

Dimase glanced at his watch. He had asked to have Joe Bucci brought to the interview room. The compilation of photos and write-ups on visitors to Brattle Street and phone purchasers from CVS was far from complete. It might never be fully finished and totally accurate. Interviews and follow-up would likely continue for weeks or even months into the future. Dimase had on his desk two folders with the information and photographs compiled to date. He picked up the portfolios and headed to the conference room where Bucci was waiting for him. If Bucci was involved, someone must have approached him at some point. With luck, maybe he would recognize one of the photos from the Common, Brattle Street, or CVS.

Dimase entered the interview room and took a seat opposite Bucci. He spread out about twenty photos from the Brattle Street visitor file and pushed them across the table. "Good morning, Joe. How are you doing today? Do you recognize any of these people?"

Bucci looked at him sullenly and shuffled through the prints. He shook his head. "No, none of them look familiar. I don't know any of them."

"Okay, how about these people?" Dimase asked, gathering up the first batch and fanning out ten close-ups from the CVS security cameras.

"No," Bucci replied irritably. "Why would I? Listen, when

do I get out of here? I've told you everything I know. I didn't do anything, and you know it."

Dimase smiled engagingly. "You will get out when I say you can get out. You have had your hearing with the judge. This is a very serious matter. These are very serious charges. At the very least, you are a material witness, Joe. At worst, you may be an accomplice. When you tell me who was in that elevator with Ms. Watkins, perhaps then I will let you go. Who approached you? Who sent you the text? We know it was not Ms. Watkins. There was nothing on her phone. Did you send the text to yourself, Joe?"

"No. Are you crazy?" Joe asked. "Why would I do that?"

"Why have you done many things, Joe? That is what I would like to know. You are not telling me something. I want to know what it is."

"I've told you everything. I've told you the truth."

"Which time, Joe? Which time did you tell me the truth? You see, the problem when you make things up is that no one knows when to believe and when not to. Who else knew about that elevator hatch?" Dimase set out the largest group of pictures, the fifty shots from Boston Common. "Look through these please. Recognize anyone here?"

Bucci took some time to sort through the pile. After several minutes, he raised his hands in exasperation and simply shook his head.

"Okay, Joe. Thank you," Dimase said. "We will talk again." Dimase rose and turned to leave, deaf to Bucci's pleas to be released. In the hallway, he almost bumped into an excited Jorgé Rodriguez, who was rushing from the elevator.

"Chief!" Rodriguez exclaimed. "I was looking for you. I called your office, but you didn't pick up."

"What's up?" Dimase asked.

"You're not going to believe this. A walk-in. She's downstairs right now. She wants to talk to the person in charge. Says it's about Gussie Watkins. She won't talk to anyone but the boss. What should I do?"

"Bring her up," Dimase replied. "I'll meet her in my office. Did she mention her name?"

"No, she won't say anything, just that it's important. She looks scared."

"All right, let's see what she has to say."

Five minutes later, Rodriguez ushered the young woman into Dimase's office and left the two of them alone.

"Please take a seat." Dimase gestured toward the empty chair next to his desk. "What is your name, may I ask?"

"Yes, of course," the woman replied. "My name is Elizabeth McFarland. I was a friend of Gussie's." The woman looked to be in her early thirties and had shoulder-length scarlet hair. She had a thick frame, not overweight but not athletic looking. She wore minimal makeup and had on dungaree shorts, sandals, and a light pink "Carpe Diem" T-shirt. Her face was flush with emotion. She sat tentatively in the chair and appeared to be struggling with what to say.

Dimase tried to put her at ease. "Please try to relax. Take a deep breath. It will be all right. Take your time. My name is Augustin—Dimase Augustin. I am the chief homicide investigator."

Elizabeth did as he suggested. After a lengthy pause, she started to cry. "Poor Gussie. She was the sweetest person in the whole world. Mr. Augustin, I'm scared. I was supposed to meet Gussie the night she was killed. We all were."

"I don't understand," Dimase replied. "Who is *we*?"

"The book club—there were five of us. We were supposed to meet at her apartment. Now there's only three. I'm afraid I might be next. I'm afraid someone is trying to kill us."

"Why would you think that?" Dimase asked, feeling he was missing something.

"Angela. Angela Mancini. She was a member of the book club too."

CHAPTER 6

Eastman Laboratory, MIT Campus: Ten Years Earlier

Susan Pearce observed as the white lab mouse came to a T intersection and paused. His head nodded slightly back and forth, and his nose crinkled as if perhaps some familiar smell would provide a clue. The researchers had deprived the mouse of water for twenty-four hours to build thirst to an intolerable level. For the experiment, they used treated, odorless water. If the mouse was able to choose direction based on smell, the result of the experiment would be invalidated. The controlling factor had to be memory, not smell or any other extraneous factor.

Like many of his brethren before him, the mouse had been carefully and selectively bred to have higher levels of protein in his brain, specifically amyloid beta, a naturally occurring substance. There were different types of proteins manufactured in the brains of mice, as in the brains of humans. The purpose of that particular study was to develop two separate categories of mice, one with excess deposits of amyloid beta and the other with an excess of tau, another naturally occurring brain protein. The goal was to determine a baseline of memory ability for each group and then, in phase two, identify whether a reduction in the level of one protein or the other could possibly increase memory function.

The results were clear and consistent with earlier research. The control group with normal protein levels quickly learned which way to turn and within days exhibited a virtual 100 percent track record of choosing the correct path. Although there were three mazes for the purpose of efficiently building more data in a shorter period of time, each was identical. For any particular group of mice, the water was always placed on the same side, either right or left. The logical conclusion to explain the near-perfect accuracy of the normal control group was that the mice quickly memorized which way to turn in order to quench their thirst.

Interestingly, both groups with excess protein deposits in their brain fared far worse than the normal control group, but there was a significant and possibly important difference. The amyloid beta group was trending toward a 74 percent hit rate, while the tau group was lagging closer to 58 percent, which supported a general theory developed from earlier work that excess protein in the brain might have been responsible for memory loss. New was the possible revelation that tau protein might have a more deleterious effect on memory recall than amyloid beta.

Previous studies had not made as much of a distinction between protein types. If the results of that latest MIT study held up, it could have enormous medical, commercial, ethical, and political implications. Researchers could target future research toward developing a tau protein inhibitor, which could lead to a whole new class of compounds to be explored, developed, and commercialized.

The mouse sat on his haunches, rubbed his paws against his face, and darted to the right. Although there were two more turns, there were no more decisions to make. After a short straightaway, there was a ninety-degree left turn, followed shortly by a ninety-degree right turn to a dead end. No water. Wrong choice.

Susan Pearce reached into the maze, scooped up the mouse, and returned him to a holding cage where he would continue to have water withheld for another six hours. Thereafter, the mouse would be rehydrated, and approximately twenty-four hours later, he would find himself back in the maze, repeating the process yet again. The average life span of laboratory mice was between two and three years. The plan was to run each mouse through one hundred maze cycles over about a two-hundred-day period. At that point, the mouse would be given an indeterminate period of vacation, during which time various compounds designed to reduce or inhibit brain protein would be introduced.

Earlier studies had experienced some limited success with antibodies lessening synapse inflammation and enzymes decreasing the size of amyloid beta clumps. So far, researchers had found nothing to reduce or remove tau. If the current program could both establish that tau deposits were more causative than amyloid beta and develop a molecular modification to reduce or remove tau, it could be worth billions. That was the golden goose, the ultimate goal of the current program. The hypothesis was that slight modification in small gradations of the protein kinase C compound might eventually hit on a combination that would impact tau. Past studies had shown that protein kinase C influenced protein secretion. Would working through dozens of modifications prove one to be the holy grail of tau research?

Susan made a few entries on her iPad and then readied the next mouse. She reflected self-consciously on the irony of the mice repeating the same routine day after day just like many of their human counterparts. The mice and their masters all were caught up in the rat race. At least compared to the mice, for Susan, the somewhat boring routine of being an undergraduate lab assistant had some deep, meaningful purpose. Susan knew the ravages of Alzheimer's, having seen it erode her beloved grandmother's faculties day by day until she ultimately became a walking, talking shell of the human being she had once been. Her grandmother had been the most dominant influence in Susan's young life. When her mother had died in childbirth and her father had failed to stay in the picture on a consistent basis, Susan had been shipped off at six months of age to be raised by her grandmother.

Susan's grandmother was a strong, intelligent, independent, forward-thinking woman. Through inheritance and structured environment, all those traits had been passed down to Susan. When her grandmother had begun to fade over the past few years, Susan had resolved to do something about it. In her fantasies, researchers rushing toward a cure came up with some miracle drug in time to restore her grandmother to her old self. In her head, she realized that was highly unlikely. At the very least, making some progress in fighting that horrible disease and helping others would honor her grandmother and her gallant struggle as her mind and dignity were slowly stripped away. Either way, Susan wanted to be a part of it.

An excellent student, Susan had determined her direction by the middle of her junior year in high school. She'd focused everything she did toward getting accepted to MIT. Exceptionally bright, she'd studied relentlessly to reinforce and expand her natural abilities. She'd maintained perfect grades and cultivated references from all the right teachers by volunteering at every opportunity for special projects or extra credit. Essentially, she had become obsessed with MIT, and she'd taken the fast track to get there. Her efforts had paid off, and for that she was grateful. She was doing her work in the lab, and at the university in general, for her grandmother and for millions of others like her around the world.

That summer of 2009, a rising junior at MIT and a molecular biology major, she was finally involved in her first real research project, and it was exactly in line with her dream of studying and eventually conquering Alzheimer's.

At the moment, Susan was alone in the lab, although there were two other lab assistants assigned to the project who often were there as well. Susan was the only undergraduate, which was quite a feather in her cap, even though she was the low woman on the totem pole. Each of the three assistants had a quota of mice to run through the maze on a weekly basis. They were allowed to do so on their own schedule as long as they reached the assigned numbers and maintained the rigid protocols of preparation and documentation.

The flexibility of schedule was necessary to allow the lab assistants to meet their other obligations as students. Often, they were in the lab at the same time, running simultaneous trials on the different mazes. Not infrequently, they were in the lab on their own at odd hours, making sure they ran the requisite number of trials. A digital camera mounted over each maze recorded each and every run through the maze, providing documentation for the research. The cameras were synchronized with the researchers' iPads, so a few clicks identified a mouse by serial number, date, time, mouse group, and result.

Despite the monotony, Susan was excited to be part of the project, even if she was the junior member of the team. She glanced at her watch and noted it was almost four o'clock in the afternoon. She had promised to meet her roommate in a conference room at Hayden Library at five for a Sunday night cram session. One more mouse to go, and she could wrap things up and call it quits in time to make it to Hayden.

Just then, a key turned audibly in the lab door. Susan held a mouse cupped in her hands, ready to start the last run of the day. She looked over her shoulder while placing the mouse at the starting point of the maze and made a couple of quick entries on the iPad. The familiar figure, clad in a similar white lab coat, approached from behind and gently put his hand on her upper arm. Susan lifted the starting gate, and the mouse was off, quick-stepping down the first straightaway. She turned and smiled at her mentor. His lips pressed together in what passed as a toothless return smile.

"It seems like every time I randomly stop by, you are always here," he said, rubbing her arm encouragingly. "This project means a lot to you, doesn't it?"

Susan beamed back at him, flattered by the compliment. She hadn't thought he noticed. "You know it means everything to me, Professor. That's why you selected me, isn't it? I mean, of course, along with my qualifications."

"Yes, yes, it is," he replied sincerely. "There are many bright students here at MIT, Susan. None brighter than you, but that was just a baseline requirement. The reason I chose you above others is because I know what this work means to you. I know you have the passion. I know you will work harder than anyone else I may have picked."

Susan smiled gratefully as she gathered her things. "I won't let you down," she called out, heading for the door. "I'm running late for a study session at the library with my friend. Later, Dr. Berger."

Susan dashed across campus and flew into the Hayden Library like a small microburst, blowing through the doors and across the main room—not that she was loud. Rather, she was like a silent, powerful breeze creating a ring of atmospheric disturbance that encircled her and spun across the room. As she was late, she walked quickly, half running, past the book stacks and formal reading tables toward the string of conference rooms situated along the back wall. Like the wave rippling through the crowd at a football game, heads bobbed up to note the commotion and down again to resume reading in a domino effect across the great room.

Elizabeth McFarland looked up from her textbook as Susan slid out of her backpack and dropped the tote bag onto the floor.

"Sorry I'm late." Susan gasped in short breaths, trying to keep her voice to a whisper. "I got tied up with Dr. Berger just as I was finishing the last mouse run of the day."

"No worries," Liz replied. "Are we still on for Cicely at nine?"

"Sure, we just need to cram a few more chapters for the damn chem test first."

"Okay, good. Spending time with the old professor, huh? I've seen him a couple of times around campus. He's not bad looking—kind of serious, though. Does he always go to the lab with you on a Sunday afternoon?" Liz teased, her voice louder than a whisper.

"No, he just stopped by. I wasn't expecting him. He just likes to keep tabs on what's going on. It's his baby, you know. I'm just the help. This project is his life."

"I suppose," Liz said. "Are you sure he's not also interested in his beautiful young undergraduate lab assistant? You are the only woman on the team, right?"

Susan blushed. "Don't be stupid. He just came by. He does it all the time. It probably makes him feel good, just like it makes me feel good when it seems we are making progress doing something important. It's boring, but at the same time, it's exciting and fulfilling when you put it in the context of the bigger picture." Susan could tell by Liz's facial expression and body language that she wasn't convinced.

"I bet the mice aren't the only thing he finds exciting and potentially fulfilling. Did he know you would be there?"

"Well, yeah. We all log on to a live website that documents everything about the project. We can link to the digital cameras or pull up all the data. It also has an attendance record and schedule. We sign in and sign out. It becomes part of the permanent record to document man hours put in, who did which trials and with which group of mice, the results—you know, all that stuff."

"So you could log on right now and see if anyone was there and who it was?"

"Yes, actually, but what does it matter? What difference does it make?"

Liz tapped the table with her pen. She seemed to be lost in thought. "Susan, you are one of the smartest people I know—maybe the smartest—so how can you be so dense?"

Susan was starting to feel a little irritation at Liz's continued probing. "What are you saying—that he logged on, saw I was there, and only came by because he wanted to see me?"

Liz made a comical expression and hit herself over the head with her pen. "Duh."

"Give me a break!" Susan exclaimed. "You are letting your imagination run away with you. It's nothing like that. He's ten years older than me, for crying out loud. He's just interested in the work. It's his grant, his project. The work could help millions of people. He's always coming and going. His interest in me is purely collegial and academic. Besides, he's just like you and me. He has no time for anything else, and neither do I. Do you?"

Liz produced her best impish redheaded grin. "Okay, but me thinketh thou doth protest too much."

"You're impossible," Susan said.

"What does Berger say about the research? Does he think you have a chance for a breakthrough?"

"Yes, he says drug companies will compete against each other and pay a small fortune for the licensing rights to the compound even way before it gets to the FDA. They'll be willing to pay just for the potential. It may never get to humans and still be worth tens of millions."

"Holy shit, Susan. You are sitting on a gold mine."

"It's not my gold mine. I'm just an undergraduate lab assistant tracking data and watching mice. It's Dr. Berger's project—his theories, his grant money."

"Yes, but you can go along for the ride. Don't you see that?"

"Of course I see it, but I don't think I'm going to become a billionaire or anything. I'm the most junior member of the team."

"True, but I've read about how these things work. If you guys actually hit on something, Berger will leave the faculty and start a private company. It's happened hundreds of times before. He'll own the rights to his own research. MIT will be happy with the bragging rights. If Berger makes a lot of money, he'll take care of MIT through charitable contributions and foundations or whatever. Even if the rights belong to Berger, you're in on the ground floor. If you play your cards right, you could be set for life."

◆ ◆ ◆

Cambridge Police Headquarters: Present Day

Dimase was stunned; he steepled his fingers on the desk, repressing the urge to pull out an unlit cigarette for digital manipulation. "Are you telling me that Gussie Watkins and Angela Mancini knew each other?"

"Yes, very well—for at least a couple of years. They met through Cicely Blackwood. We were all in the book club together."

"Cicely Blackwood," Dimase said. "Is that not the young woman in whose name the Brattle Street apartment is held? She's a professor or something over in Europe, right?"

"Yes, Ireland, actually. Trinity College. She inherited the apartment from her mother. It's rent controlled, so kind of hard to come by. Cicely and Gussie were friends from Harvard. When Cicely went to Trinity, Gussie moved in. They had some kind of arrangement. I don't know if Cicely was ever going to move back in, but the arrangement suited both of them—killed two birds with one stone." Elizabeth blanched when she realized what she had just said.

"How so?" Dimase asked, wanting to keep her narrative flowing.

"I think the objective was to keep the unit under rent control. If Cicely ever did return, she could keep her current status. In the meantime, Gussie got a great place at a bargain rate."

"I see." Dimase nodded in understanding. "So Gussie Watkins and Angela Mancini knew each other, you say. Incredible. Two of the most sensational murders in years, and now we know they cannot be a coincidence. How well? How well did they know each other?"

"They were friends. We are—or we were—a tight circle. It

revolved around the book club. Gussie was the newest member. She replaced Cicely when Cicely moved to Ireland."

"So you say this book club was to meet in Gussie's apartment the night she was killed. Why have I not heard this before?"

"I don't know. By the time we started to arrive, there was police tape up, and they weren't letting anyone into the building. We gathered on the sidewalk along with the rest of the crowd. At that point, we weren't even sure what was happening. A rumor spread on the street that a woman had been killed—a young woman."

"How long did you stay?"

"Well over an hour, maybe an hour and a half. Eventually, they brought some guy out in cuffs. He was acting like a celebrity. They put him in a car and drove him away. A couple of officers told the crowd to move on, and we decided we might as well go home. We agreed to keep in touch by text and to let each other know if anyone heard anything or was able to reach Gussie."

"When did you find out that your fears were true—that it was your friend Gussie?"

Elizabeth started to cry once again. "The next afternoon, when your department put out the announcement and it hit the news."

"Still, you didn't think to call anyone here at the department to inform them of your connection?"

"Why? We all saw the police take that guy out in cuffs. We assumed he must have done it. What were we supposed to say? 'Hi. We're all friends of Gussie. Thanks for doing a good job'?"

"No, I suppose not," Dimase said, trying to avoid conflict and keep Elizabeth at ease.

"I mean, at that point, we focused on her parents. She was an only child, as you probably know. We were heartbroken for them. Susan even offered to fly out to California to be with them, but they said to wait until the funeral."

Dimase held up his hands. "One moment. Who is Susan?"

"Susan Pearce," Elizabeth sobbed. "She's a member of the book club too—the founder, really. Detective Augustin, these murders are not a coincidence, are they?"

"No, that would seem quite unlikely."

"That's why I'm so afraid. The main connection for Gussie and Angela was the book club meetings; that means the reason for targeting them must have something to do with the club. I can't imagine what that might be, but that has to be it. That means I might be a target. Do you see? I'm frightened, Mr. Augustin."

"I totally see your point. Help me with my math, Ms. McFarland. You say there are five members of the club. So far, I only count four: you, Susan, Gussie, and Angela. Who am I missing?"

"Ellen. Ellen Klein."

"So why are you here alone?" Dimase asked. "Where are Ms. Klein and Ms. Pearce? They must be frightened as well. Why are they not here with you? Why did you not come together?"

"That's just it!" Elizabeth cried. "I can't get in touch with either one of them. It's as if they've vanished off the face of the earth."

CHAPTER 7

MIT Campus: Spring 2009

Dr. Hans Berger slid the mouse across the dashboard on his laptop screen, saved his latest edits, and sent the draft to a printer. He permitted himself a smug grin as he removed five sorted copies, one for each member of his team. This was what they had all been working for—all the time, all the effort, all the frustration, and now, at last, something to show for it. The medical world would be stunned.

There was a brief knock on the door, and Susan Pearce entered the office without waiting for his response.

"Ah, Susan, just the woman I want to see." He had become fond of his attractive young lab assistant. She was a smart cookie and not bad to look at either.

"And why is that, Herr Professor?" she replied. No one else called him Herr Professor, but he didn't mind. They already had spent many tedious hours in the lab together when she'd tried it out for the first time, teasing him after an almost comical outburst directed at a hapless mouse. Since that time, it had been their own private acknowledgment that they were colleagues, not merely student and professor.

"Because we are this close to publication," he said, indicating a small gap between his thumb and index finger. "I've had extensive correspondence with the editors at the *Oxford Journal of Neuroscience*. They are anxious for our final draft to put through peer review and publish. You know what that means?"

Susan beamed at him and offered up a high five, which he awkwardly reciprocated. Secretly, he had been hoping for a hug, but high five it was. "It means we are on our way to some type of cure. Do you think it could ever work on humans?"

"Who knows?" he replied, regaining his composure. "That's still a long way off, but it does mean that everything we could have hoped for with this experiment has come true. We've proven that tau is an even bigger culprit than amyloid beta, and even more importantly, we've come up with an inhibitor compound that reduces its presence. The data bears it out. We could not ask for anything more."

Susan knew all about the data. Berger had molded many pages of summaries, charts, and data compilations into the current narrative. They had tried dozens of modifications to protein kinase C one molecule at a time. Some versions had had no apparent effect, while others had produced a whole spectrum of varying results in memory improvement, from slight to significant.

"I'm so proud of you, Professor," Susan said with genuine sincerity, her admiration obvious. "You have done a great thing here. Thank you for believing in me and letting me be a part of it."

"Susan, it is I who is proud of you—you and the rest of the team. You have worked hard and sacrificed much. Now we will all be rewarded. Take these." He handed her four copies of the draft, keeping one for himself. "I want you and your colleagues to each proofread and edit for my final approval. The article will be authored under my name, but you will all be listed as contributors and rightly so. It will be quite a unique achievement for everyone, but for you, my dear, being involved in a breakthrough of this magnitude as an undergraduate will be the foundation of a wonderful career—whatever direction you decide to take it. This publication will really distinguish you from the competition. You are young; beautiful, if I might add; and brilliant, and the world—the future—is yours. I'm very excited for you."

Susan was overwhelmed with emotion. Berger's kind words and unfiltered admiration for her abilities opened the floodgates, and he watched as months of stress and tension melted away. Tears of joy streamed down her cheeks. "Oh, Professor, I owe it all to you," she said, providing a heartfelt hug. She buried her head in his chest and continued to cry with deep, quiet sobs.

"What happened to Herr Professor?" he said, gently stroking her shoulder-length blonde hair. "You're not sad, are you?"

"No, no, Herr Professor," she said flirtatiously. "I've never been so happy in my life." She pulled back slightly from his embrace so she could see his face. Their arms lingered on each other.

Berger put his fingers to her face and gently brushed away a tear. She smiled back at him and nestled her head back into his chest. He stroked the side of her neck with the back of his hand and kissed the top of her head. Susan tilted her head back, and her lips parted and brushed against his. He rubbed his lips against hers and softly pulled at her lower lip. Susan's hands slipped to his butt; rubbed his cheeks in a slow, circular motion; and pulled him toward her. Without breaking the embrace, Berger led them in a twirling slow-motion dance toward the office door, where he set the lock and continued on to the couch.

◆ ◆ ◆

Susan kicked off her shoes and lay on the couch. She had never been with a man but felt no apprehension. Her senses were tingling with anticipation, and each sensation was something she had never experienced before. She had developed a strong affection for Herr Professor but never had thought of it in sexual terms. Now that it was happening, she could see it as the natural outcome. She didn't want to be a virgin her entire life, did she? Always she was dominated by rules, discipline, and singular focus. She had never known decadent pleasure until that moment. She was glad her first time would be with someone like Berger and not some teenager in the back of a car. He was strong, wise, intelligent, and gentle. If not a man like him, then who?

Susan understood the professor was forbidden fruit, and he must have been aware the same applied to her. She realized he was taking a huge risk, more so than she was. It only added to her exhilaration that he could not help himself. They were both intoxicated by the passion of the moment, taboos be damned. Enhancing the sheer, raw physical desire was an unspoken bond of trust, for in an odd way, each now had a form of power over the other that had not previously existed.

At that moment, the release of months of stress, the joy of success, and the spontaneous combustion of physical lust washed over them. The unspoken pact of crossing the line together drew them close. Susan allowed Berger to take control, and he slowed everything down. Carefully and tenderly, he undid the buttons on her blouse one by one, working his way down to her belly but leaving the garment in place on her shoulders. Continuing in the same direction, he pulled off her skirt and panties as she made it easier for him by lifting her butt slightly off the couch. He paused to fold the items and place them neatly on the end table next to the couch, prolonging the moment. Naked from the waist down, Susan smiled at him demurely, reveling in his ritualistic affection, surrendering herself completely, waiting to see what would come next.

She lay back, her mind blank, totally in the moment, as Berger started with her toes, gently kissing the tops of her feet and caressing her ankles with his mouth. Susan stretched her arms above her head, luxuriating in his every touch. Just as he had taken his time on the way down, he did the same on the way up. Catlike, she raised one leg and then the other, pointing her toes as he kissed her well-muscled calves, made his way over each knee, and settled in to concentrate on the soft skin of her inner thighs.

It was nirvana. The fact that it was four o'clock on a Thursday afternoon and that only an opaque glass door separated them from the empty laboratory augmented the carnal thrill. Someone could have walked into the lab at any moment. It was more reason to silently cherish each other—no need or inclination for a rowdy hump.

Berger kissed small circles around her belly button and eventually directed his attention to the back strap of her bra. After he made several failed attempts at the hook, Susan guided his fingers to the front clasp between the cups, and her breasts fell free as he tossed the bra away. The moment was magical for her, and she knew it was for him too.

Afterward, they lay together with Susan's head resting on Berger's shoulder. She didn't want to move or do anything to break the spell. After several more moments, they heard the muted sound of the lab door opening and closing.

"Susan? Susan, are you here?" a voice called.

Berger put his finger to his lips. Susan let out an inaudible giggle, and they held each other tighter as if that would make them invisible.

"I don't think anyone's here," a male voice said. Susan recognized the speaker as one of the graduate lab assistants.

"That's funny," a female voice replied. It was her roommate, Liz McFarland. "She was supposed to meet me a half hour ago. She said she was just stopping by here to pick something up."

Susan and the professor heard soft footsteps cross the room, followed by a sharp knock on the door. They held their breath and pressed their foreheads tightly together.

"Professor, you in there?" the male voice called. After a few seconds without any response, the footsteps receded back across the room. "Well, no one here now," the male voice said. "You probably crossed paths. I'll bet she's at the library, waiting for you now. She probably made another stop somewhere on the way."

"Probably," Elizabeth replied. "Anyway, after a while, I thought I'd walk over this way to see if she was still here."

"I'm sure you guys will catch up with each other."

"Yeah, well, I'm glad you were here to let me in. Thanks."

"No worries. I was just coming by because the professor wanted me to pick up something, but I don't see it around. I'll get it later."

Once again, footsteps echoed softly from the lab, the outer door opened and closed, and the lock clicked into place.

◆ ◆ ◆

Zurich, Switzerland: Present Day

The first rays of sunlight sliced through the narrow crack where the curtains were not completely drawn together. Like a laser, twin beams cut across the corner of the room in two bright lines across the floor, over the top of the desk, and up the wall.

Susan Pearce was oblivious to the change in lighting. She was stretched on her back in the king-size bed. A sleeping mask covered her eyes, and noise-canceling headphones adorned her head.

The Baur au Lac Hotel in Zurich was known for over-the-top pampering of guests; their five stars were well earned. Right now, the only service Susan desired was to be left alone and allowed to sleep. The conference on biochemical alternatives of molecular compounds had long been on her schedule. After the horrible murder of Gussie, she briefly had considered canceling the trip to Switzerland and instead going to California to spend time with Gussie's parents. When they'd declined, she'd decided to attend the conference after all. She desperately needed to get away. She had to regroup and clear her head.

Back home in Cambridge, there was no escaping the horrific images she conjured up in her mind. In the days since Gussie's murder, it was all she could think about. Every time she walked across campus, hopped on a bus, or entered an elevator, Gussie popped into her mind.

The meeting in Zurich was a welcome opportunity to change scenery and occupy her mind. The plane tickets and hotel reservations had been in place for weeks. Why not go? Once she'd made the decision, she'd decided to unplug from everything and get the hell out of Dodge. There was nothing more she could do for Gussie. Right now, Susan had to focus on her own mental health.

It had been almost a week since she'd flown out of Boston's Logan Airport. She intentionally had told no one of her plans, shutting off her cell phone and burying herself in a combination of technical and pleasure reading. After a full day of travel, she'd checked into the hotel and slept for eighteen hours. Although she was still young, healthy, and relatively vigorous, it seemed every time she flew on a plane, she caught some kind of bug. It might have been the altitude, the time difference, the confined space, the air circulation, or some other factor she hadn't even considered. Whatever the cause, she had been knocked on her ass the first few days in Zurich.

Susan varied her routine, sleeping at all hours of the day, relying on room service, and immersing herself in reading material. Fortunately, when she'd scheduled the trip, she'd allowed for a few days on her own before the conference began. Her original intent had been to do some sightseeing and maybe even hire a guide for some low-elevation hiking, but the energy just wasn't there. She surrendered body and mind to rest.

That day was day two of the conference and day six in Zurich for Susan. There was a presentation on molecular modifications in protein kinase C that she had marked on her calendar weeks earlier; the topic was right up her alley.

The phone on the nightstand next to the bed rang. Susan stirred, rolled onto her side, and pulled the comforter over her head, willing the incessant ringing to stop. The phone finally went silent but only for a brief interlude before the annoying ring resumed once again. Susan pushed the sleep mask onto her forehead and groped for the phone.

"Professor Pearce, this is your wake-up call," an accented male voice announced. At first, Susan thought it was a recording, but then the caller continued. "You asked me to make sure you got up by eight o'clock today. Are you all set? Is everything all right?"

Susan quickly realized where she was and what day it was. "Yes, yes, thank you very much. I appreciate it. I'm all set now."

"Very well, Professor. Let us know if you need anything at all."

Susan thanked him and hung up. For the first time since her arrival, she felt good. She stretched and opened the shades, flooding the room with sunlight. Finally, the days of R&R had overcome her physical and mental fatigue. She felt invigorated and ready to go. *Thank God*, she thought, because that day's presentation was what had motivated her to book the trip in the first place. There were a handful of groups around the world working on protein kinase C compounds, and she was anxious to stay current on the latest findings.

It had been several years since the tau research project at MIT and, later, the PKC Group. Upon graduation from MIT, she had been accepted into the doctoral program in molecular biology at the same institution, which had enabled her to continue research on the side. Throughout the years, in her pursuit of her PhD, her appointment as an assistant professor, and, ultimately, her elevation to full professorship, her quest had continued to be the eradication of Alzheimer's.

The original program she'd participated in years ago with Dr. Berger had indeed shown that tau was most likely a more significant factor in memory loss than previously thought. Unfortunately, the hope for a protein kinase C–based compound to reduce tau in the brain had proven to be elusive. In fact, to date, no one had been able to come up with an effective methodology to reduce tau deposits. Efforts were ongoing.

Susan, for her part, had expanded her focus to include bone

marrow function in the lining of the skull. There appeared to be significant differences in the operation of skull marrow compared to marrow in other bones in the body. It was not that she'd ruled out any possibility for some variation of protein kinase C or other compounds. There were teams at the finest medical and academic institutions in the world working on multiple avenues of brain disease research. That was her reason for being in Zurich: to be updated on the latest thinking from the greatest minds in the field.

Susan glanced at her cell phone to check the time and realized she had shut it off shortly after her arrival. She powered it up and quickly noted a number of missed texts and calls, most of them from Elizabeth McFarland. She scanned through the texts and read the screen printout of the voice mails. There was no specific information, but each message from Liz implored her to call as soon as possible.

Susan shivered slightly at the thought of having to reconnect so soon with her Cambridge-based world, but she felt she had little choice. Liz was her oldest friend, had been her roommate at MIT, and was of course grieving over their Gussie. It had been selfish to leave town without saying goodbye to Liz, but it wasn't as if they had contact on a daily basis. At the time, just days removed from Gussie's murder, Susan had just wanted to go. The world could catch up with her later. It looked as if later would be now or at least some time that day.

The time difference between Zurich and Cambridge was six hours. She realized it was two o'clock in the morning back home. Despite the seemingly urgent, almost desperate tone of the messages, Susan didn't feel right about calling Liz in the middle of the night and decided it would be prudent to call back later in the day. She loved Liz. She would have done anything for her. If Liz needed her, she would do whatever it took. On the other hand, whatever it was would probably not change between then and the time Liz would be awake. The sensible thing would be to go to the lectures and workshops and try to reach Liz in the afternoon, when it was morning in Cambridge.

CHAPTER 8

Cambridge Police Headquarters: Present Day

Things were moving fast now. Dimase spent the next forty-five minutes grilling Elizabeth McFarland as gently as possible. He moved her into the conference room, where they were joined by Jorgé Rodriguez and Bob Coyne, the two detectives permanently assigned to work under him in Cambridge homicide. Both had been instrumental in developing case material on the Watkins murder, and he wanted to keep them in the proverbial loop.

After everyone was seated, Dimase pulled out all three portfolios of photos from the Brattle Street visitor file, CVS security cameras, and Boston Common.

"Here," Dimase said. "Take a look at these." He pushed the folders toward her across the table. "Take your time." He watched her face carefully as she went through the prints. If she recognized anyone, she did a great job in hiding it. "When was the last time you heard from Susan Pearce?" he asked.

"About six days ago."

"Did Susan say anything about having plans to leave town?"

"No, she didn't mention anything. She was texting with all of us, and then there was nothing—no response. We had a couple of group texts going with all four of us. She dropped out of those. I just figured she was busy and would jump back in soon. Then Angela was killed, and I freaked out. I couldn't believe it. I couldn't get my head around what was happening. I still can't. One day I'm texting with all four of them, and a couple of days later, I'm all alone."

"What about Ellen Klein?" Dimase asked. "When was the last time you communicated with her?"

"Three days ago." Elizabeth started to cry again. "We talked about going to the police to tell you about the connection between Gussie and Angela. We speculated as to whether there was any possible way it could be a coincidence, and if not, was it related to the book club? We talked about going over to Susan's apartment or by her office to check on her and see if anyone knew anything."

"And did you go to Susan's apartment or office? Where does she live? What does she do?"

"No. We were going to. We were texting two nights ago. We agreed to meet in the morning and go to Susan's office. If no one there knew where she was, we were going to go to her apartment. She lives near Kendall Square. Her office is at MIT. She's a professor there."

"I see," Dimase said. "And why did you not go to her office as planned?"

"We were going to, and then Ellen disappeared. That's when I realized I was the only one left, the only one out of five. Of course, there's Cicely, but she's in Ireland. She wasn't—uh, isn't—really part of the club anymore. So two dead and two missing without a trace. Looks like I'm the last one standing, and I don't like it. Why me? Oh my God! I can't believe this is happening!"

"It will be okay, Ms. McFarland," Dimase said. "I am going to recommend that we take you into protective custody, at least for a couple of days, until we sort some of this out. After that, we can discuss what arrangements would be most appropriate for your security. Do you agree?"

"Yes, thank you," Elizabeth said. "Where will I stay?"

"You can stay right here, at least for a day or two. We actually have a couple of very comfortable suites up on the tenth floor. They are designed for situations just like this. Temporary protective custody, visiting witnesses—that type of thing. You will be quite safe there."

Elizabeth looked relieved. "Thank you again. I'm so frightened. I'm so confused. Thank you for protecting me. I'm glad I came. I wouldn't know where else to turn."

"You did the right thing," Dimase said. "What can you tell me about Ellen Klein? Where does she work? Where does she live?"

"She's a teacher," Elizabeth said. "She lives in Somerville, near Davis Square. She teaches high school biology in Dorchester. I don't really know her all that well outside of book club. You know how it is. You have work friends. College friends. Family friends. Shit like that, you know?"

"Okay," Dimase said. "We have a lot to do. I will have a matron take you up to the suite and help you get settled. We can send for your things later. Try to get some rest. We will have a lot of follow-up questions later."

Dimase looked at Coyne. "You and I are going to check out Ellen Klein. Rodriguez and Grafton can take Susan Pearce. We have to figure out what's going on with this book club. Let's pray to God they are both sitting on a beach somewhere, sipping margaritas."

◆ ◆ ◆

Dimase and his men broke into two-man teams and separately went to the living quarters of each of the missing women. The men were instructed to examine the contents of each apartment, looking for anything out of order or any clue to where the women might be. They inspected closets, mail, and toiletries, looking for any evidence of a planned trip. Nothing jumped out at them. They took pictures and talked to what neighbors they could find, briefing each other in real time over their cell phones as they worked their way through each apartment. There was no indication in either place of a struggle or sudden exit. No meals were half eaten on the table; no coffee was brewing in the pot. All the lights were off, and the doors were locked. No one saw anything. It was as if each woman had simply left for work on a normal day.

The separate teams proceeded to each woman's workplace. At Ellen Klein's school, Dimase and Coyne had a bit more luck. They learned it was the second day in a row that Ellen Klein had not shown up for work. The previous morning, the attendance office had received an early morning call that Ellen had a family emergency and would not be in for a couple of days. The school had arranged for a substitute and heard nothing further.

Dimase asked if they could listen to the recorded message, so the principal escorted them to the attendance office, where an administrative assistant was able to locate and play the message for them. At Dimase's request, she played it back several times while he recorded the audio on his cell phone. Surprisingly, it was a male voice: "Good morning. I'm calling on behalf of Ellen Klein, one of your biology teachers. This is her brother, Derek. Unfortunately, we expect a death in the family very soon, pretty much imminently, so she won't be in this week. She's indisposed at the moment and asked me to call for her. Sorry for any inconvenience."

Dimase and Coyne exchanged concerned looks but didn't want to say anything further in front of the school personnel. Under the circumstances, it struck them as unusual and not a good sign that Ellen had not called in herself. They asked a few more questions to get a little more background and learned that Ellen rarely, if ever, called in sick and was considered an excellent young teacher who loved her students and her work. Clearly, all held her in high regard.

"Is there something wrong?" the principal asked. "Why are you really here anyway?"

Dimase tried to be straightforward without giving away too much. "We have reason to believe she may be missing, but we don't know for sure. There could be any number of explanations at this point. We are just trying to find out where she is and make sure she's all right."

"Oh dear." The principal rubbed his hands together nervously. "I do hope she's okay. Everyone here just loves her."

"We hope so too," Dimase replied. "Nine out of ten times, the person turns up fine, and there's a logical explanation for their absence." He was anxious to get back to headquarters and work on the latest lead. "Have you ever met Ms. Klein's brother, the one who called in?" he asked.

"No, I've never met any of her family." The principal picked up Ellen's personnel file from the desk and flipped through a few pages. "I don't see any family listed as emergency contacts. That's the only place they might show up. We don't ask about family members in the hiring process. It says here her emergency contacts are Liz McFarland and Angela Mancini. I don't know who they are, unless they could possibly be sisters or something."

"Would you mind if we made a copy of this file to take with us?" Dimase asked.

"Well, it is confidential, but yes, you can take a copy. I just hope you find Ellen."

"Thank you. If you hear anything, please contact me right away," Dimase said, handing the man a business card.

The other two-man detective team had left Susan Pearce's apartment and headed to her office at MIT. Elizabeth McFarland had told them Susan's office was in the Eastman Laboratory building, on the second floor. As a courtesy, they called MIT campus police and arranged to be escorted.

At MIT, Grafton and Rodriguez accompanied a campus cop to Susan Pearce's office. Rodriguez wasn't confident that a looksee would make any difference, but he played along with his partner, who insisted they take a peek. *No sense in arguing about stupid shit,* he thought. *A guy's gotta pick his battles.*

The campus officer produced a key and unlocked Susan's office. Nothing appeared out of the ordinary. The computer on her desk was shut down, inaccessible without a password. There was no desk calendar, appointment book, or schedule they could locate. After ten minutes of searching through drawers, filing cabinets, and shelves, all to no avail, they were ready to wrap it up and return to headquarters for the joint task force meeting.

Just then, a young student stuck his head in the door and asked if he could be of any help. Rodriguez told him to come in and take a seat. Both detectives showed ID and explained to the young man that they were doing a wellness check on Professor Pearce because she had not been seen in several days.

"Oh, I can explain that," the student said. "I'm one of her grad assistants. We work together all the time. She's great, but anyway, she's in Switzerland right now."

"Switzerland?" Rodriguez asked incredulously. "What's she doing in Switzerland?"

"She's at a conference. It's been booked for months. She

almost canceled. She told me about her friend who was murdered over on Brattle Street. Unbelievable, huh? Say, does this have anything to do with that?"

"Not directly," Rodriguez replied. "Some of her other friends haven't been able to get in touch with her, and they were just a little concerned. Do you know when she left for this conference or where in Switzerland it is being held?"

The student looked thoughtful for a moment. "I'd say she's been gone almost a week. I don't know exactly where, but I think it's in Zurich somewhere."

◆ ◆ ◆

Two hours later, the joint task force members were assembled around the conference table in the large seventh-floor conference room at Cambridge Police headquarters. Dimase Augustin spoke. "The good news is we've located Susan Pearce, and she is safe. She called Liz McFarland on her cell phone an hour ago and explained she is at a conference in Zurich, Switzerland, confirming what Detective Rodriguez found from his inquiry at MIT. I interviewed her briefly and made arrangements to speak with her again later this evening. She was totally unaware of the murder of Angela Mancini. Needless to say, it was quite a shock. Hopefully she is safe over in Switzerland, but I advised her to exercise extreme caution. We also told her Ellen Klein is missing. She was shocked to hear that as well and didn't have any idea where Ellen might be."

"Did she have any insight on the book club connection? Any inkling of why the members might be a target?" Coyne asked.

"No, we didn't get into that yet. I think she's numb right now. I asked her to stay put and promised to talk more extensively in a couple of hours. I don't know if we should ask her to return here or stay in Zurich. She might be safer over there for the time being, but let's reserve judgment until after I get a chance to talk to her further. Bob," he said, addressing Coyne, "can you update the group on what we found regarding Ellen Klein?"

"Right, Chief. Here's everything we know. Her apartment in Somerville is untouched. It looks like you would expect it to look if she just went to work on any given day. There's a suitcase in the closet and plenty of clothes too. No obvious indication she was planning a trip or had recent visitors or anything out of place that we could see."

Coyne looked around the room, paused briefly, and continued. "She lives alone. Most people in the building were at work. I'll go back this evening and interview some more neighbors to see if anyone saw anything."

Dimase took up the narrative. "We learned a little more at Ms. Klein's workplace. She's a biology teacher at Dorchester High School. Apparently, she's very well thought of there. Rarely, if ever, absent. Well liked by both kids and colleagues. We met with the principal. It turns out Ms. Klein didn't show up for work yesterday or today. The principal took us down to the attendance office. They got a call before school yesterday saying there was a family emergency, someone in the family was going to die, and she wouldn't be in for the rest of the week. I recorded the call on my cell. I'll play it for all of you."

Dimase pulled out his phone and played the recorded phone message so all could hear. The group sat quietly, absorbing what they heard. Dimase broke the silence.

"This does not look good. The obvious question is, why have her brother call? It would only take a few moments for her to call herself, particularly an employee as reliable and conscientious as Ms. Klein. It seems out of character."

"It's worse than that, Chief," Coyne said. "We did some quick checking a few minutes ago, right before coming in here, but the way it looks right now, we don't think she has a brother."

CHAPTER 9

Interstate 95 North, Massachusetts: Present Day

Hans Berger exited Route 93 North out of Boston and merged the old Volvo 540 onto Interstate 95 toward New Hampshire and Maine. The car had belonged to Berger for many years, but he had taken it off the road a while back when the shit began to hit the fan. The idea had been for the car to drop out of sight in much the same manner as Berger himself. It had not been difficult to locate a private garage in Somerville, near his present living quarters. The elderly homeowner had asked no questions and been only too happy to collect fifty dollars each month for allowing the vehicle to be kept in his previously empty space.

Ever the frugal professor, Berger had originally purchased the car with thirty thousand miles on it back in 2007. When he first had decided to go underground, he'd taken the car off the road, canceled the insurance, and notified the registry that the car had gone to salvage. For good measure, he even had filed down the VIN number and had a cheap paint job done at Maaco, changing the color to a bland gray. Berger had become adept at lifting a license plate from a parked car whenever one was needed. The car, like Berger, was totally anonymous.

Berger was surprised at how easy it was for him to slip off the grid and become more or less invisible. Innately intelligent, he knew his way around all levels of the internet and had a natural talent for research. He'd been able to acquire a half dozen fake driver's licenses under different names and Social Security numbers. From there, he'd developed background and supporting documentation for each identity. His walk-up apartment in Davis Square was in the name of Joel Vandameer, the name of a California tech worker killed in an auto crash several years ago who would have been around Berger's age. Berger's internet and cable accounts were anonymous black-box accounts. He avoided the use of credit cards but had several bank accounts under false names. He lived off the remnants of his savings, having cashed in his 401(k), investments, and old bank accounts.

For all intents and purposes, Hans Berger had gradually gone missing piece by piece, until one day he had been gone completely. He'd taken great pains to make his few personal and distant family relationships estranged in the run-up to his disappearance. When he finally had pulled the plug, there had been no one to immediately notice. Hans Berger had certainly existed. He knew if anyone googled him, his entire history would come up, including his rise through academia, his professorship at MIT, and plenty of sordid details on the scandal that had brought him down, but that was where any inquiry would end. Hans Berger was no more, and no one could say what had become of him. His apartment, car, cash, and multiple identities were all anonymous. He was free to move about society as he pleased and do whatever he pleased to whomever he pleased.

The Volvo crossed over the Piscataqua River Bridge into Maine. It was midmorning, and Berger kept his speed at sixty-five miles per hour, blending in seamlessly with the other vehicles on the road. Traffic those days on any major highway was always at least moderately heavy. Staying in the middle lane, Berger was confident his odds of getting pulled over were miniscule. He was not afraid of being apprehended; he just didn't want it to happen before his task was complete. His plan was to disappear forever once he was done, but if not, so be it. Sooner or later, the authorities and his remaining victims would figure out what was going on. He always had anticipated that outcome. Berger was prepared to pay the consequences for his actions but only if he had no other choice. The important part was that he made a statement for all to see and hear.

On the other hand, they would have to catch him first. By the time they eventually started to fit together the pieces, it would be too late for his victims. Justice would be served. Vengeance might have been the Lord's, but Berger was more than happy to do God's work in that case. He knew what it was like to be consumed by a quest. He'd spent most of his adult life in pursuit of one truth or another through scientific methodology. That had been taken away from him.

At first, he'd been unable to believe it. Like a patient being given a terminal diagnosis, his first reaction had been denial. When it had become evident he'd lost control and events had overwhelmed him, his denial had turned to acceptance, but he'd hoped his fall from grace was temporary. When the finality of his banishment and humiliation had been irrefutable, his emotion had turned to blame and then justice. Some might have called it vengeance or revenge. It made no difference to Berger what other people might have called it; to him, it was justice.

Berger turned off the Maine Turnpike at the Portland exit

and picked up Route 302 toward Bridgeton. He was enjoying the execution of his meticulously prepared plan. There were always adjustments to make on the fly and unforeseen variables to address, but thus far, the overall framework of his scheme was intact.

There was a specific order he'd had in mind from the beginning, from the least guilty to the guiltiest of his offenders. They were all complicit, but this arrangement would disguise his true intentions a bit longer, and when recognized, it would be even more horrific for the worst of them. Each had played a role in casually tossing away Berger's life as if it were nothing. Those on the margin of events might not have even realized what they had done or the impact of their actions. That did not excuse them. It was the result that mattered, and the result was that Berger's life had been destroyed, his reputation had been ruined, and his life's work had been rendered meaningless. Even if some were too unaware and callous to comprehend the ramifications of their acts, they ultimately still were responsible. There had to be accountability. They might not have directly initiated his destruction, but their selfish, self-centered, blissful ignorance condemned them nonetheless. They not only deserved their fate but also had to play their part in the final takedown.

Berger's vision was that his end target should know and understand everything before she died. He wanted to start slowly, without the victims comprehending what was happening to them until the sequence was well underway. Like frogs in a pot of water about to boil, they would realize their predicament only when it was too late. He wanted Susan to at first think the least responsible of her friends was merely a random, tragically unlucky victim. He wished he could see her face when the next victim fell and the nexus of a connection became possible. He wanted all the others to die before her, each with a message—a message for her that he was coming. He wondered at what point she would understand, just as it had taken him time to realize what was happening to him. Yes, they were both frogs in a pot, but now it was her turn.

Berger found the dirt road he was looking for about halfway between Bridgeton and Denmark on Route 302. He noted two cars behind him in the rearview mirror and drove past the road by a mile or so before he was able to turn discreetly at an intersection and make the return trip. He was in luck the second time around, with no other vehicles in sight, and quickly swerved down the road across fifty yards of open field and plunged into the tree line. The drive was visible but overgrown with grass from lack of use. Four hundred feet farther in, up a slight elevation, the woods parted into a small clearing, and a permanently mounted trailer home came into view. The place was deserted, just as Berger had known it would be. He was becoming skilled at hiding in plain sight, but the irony of that location was particularly delicious.

Until recently, Berger had never been there before, but years ago, he'd heard Susan speak of it often. It was her grandmother's home, the place where she'd grown up. As always, Berger had done his research. The place was now in Susan Pearce's name. For whatever reason, it had not been sold after her grandmother's death. It couldn't have been worth much. Perhaps Susan kept it for nostalgic reasons. He didn't know, and he didn't care. What he did know was that she rarely, if ever, came there. Of course, she was busy with her own projects at MIT now that she was a full professor.

Berger had done a couple of recon runs in recent weeks, scouting the location to make sure it suited his purposes. The place was run-down; clearly no effort was being made at maintenance or upkeep. He had easily gained access to the inside on his first trip by forcing the door with a crowbar. It was obvious neither Susan nor anyone else had been there in some time. The door was off the refrigerator, and the electricity was turned off. Mold was starting to appear in spots on the ceiling, and cobwebs shrouded the corners. Debris was everywhere; the place was filthy. Susan would not be stopping by anytime soon for a weekend escape.

Berger had cleaned up the place a little but only enough to make it habitable for a night or two. On his second recon trip, he had confirmed that nothing had changed, and his odds of staying there undetected remained high.

The trailer home was set back from the highway. Berger parked the Volvo near the front entrance, got out, and stretched. He took his time looking around and then popped the trunk.

"Get up, Ellen. Are you still alive in there? I hope so. Come on. It's not time yet. Wake up."

◆ ◆ ◆

Denmark, Maine: Present Day

Night had fallen, and the only light in the small trailer home emanated from the glow of a Coleman lantern in the center of the old kitchen table. Berger located a hotspot that enabled him to log on to the internet on his laptop. The trailer home was not visible from the street, but as a precaution, he'd taped sheets over the windows.

Ellen Klein lay in a heap on the twin-sized bed against the far wall. She was heavily sedated and completely covered by a blanket; her hands and feet were bound by duct tape. He'd removed the gag in her mouth. Berger did not want her to suffocate during the night, and in her present condition, it was unlikely she would call out. Even if she did, there wasn't a soul within miles to hear her.

Berger set the alarm on his cell for 3:00 a.m. It would be a lot better if Ellen could make the climb under her own power, at least as much as possible. If he had to carry her as a dead weight, it would be one hell of a tough job. Either way, they would both get a few hours' sleep and be out of there in the middle of the night.

Berger, who had long since hacked the computers of his past, present, and future victims, logged on to Susan Pearce's email account and quickly scanned her mail to see if there was anything interesting. He smiled as he thought about how clever he was and how he'd been able to tap into Susan's cell to track her every physical move and use her to track down the other members of the book club. In the digital age, anything was possible if one knew how to game the system, and he did.

After Berger had gained complete access to Susan's life, it had been relatively easy to penetrate the security of the other women to one degree or another. None of them was as exposed as Susan, but he was able to track their movements, monitor their emails, and at least read text exchanges with Susan or group texts in which Susan was included.

In the end, he'd blanketed all five women in the book club with a network of hidden button cameras. None were inside their apartments, but everything in close proximity to the outside of their homes and workplaces was well covered. Cameras stuck on bushes, light poles, doorframes, potted plants, and the like were unlikely to be discovered unless someone was specifically looking for them. By the time Berger had been ready to move forward with his plan, he'd been able to run the equivalent of a sophisticated espionage operation through his phone and laptop.

The digital camera software Berger had installed on his

computer was similar to that used in his lab at MIT. The camera could be either manually activated or automatically started by sensors detecting motion. That feature enabled Berger to store, review, and fast-forward through time-stamped activity without having to deal with endless hours from multiple locations with nothing happening.

Berger found it satisfying to be able to monitor his intended victims so thoroughly. They had no idea what they were up against, but they would find out soon enough. He had a big advantage. He knew everything about them—their past, present, communication, and location. Through their texts and emails, he even knew what they might have been thinking. He knew the plan. They knew nothing. He knew in which order they would die and how. They were blind to their fate and would only understand when it was too late.

Gussie Watkins had been first because she was least likely to set off alarm bells. She had been a minor offender, but she'd signed the letter that had ultimately ruined him, and she'd made a corroborating statement. She'd had no basis in fact for her actions—no firsthand knowledge. She simply had done it to support her friend, with no consideration for the truth or the devastating impact of what she was attesting to. She had been an otherwise normal, kind woman apparently corrupted by passion for a cause or perhaps blind loyalty to a friend, or both, and oblivious to the consequences.

Throughout history, humankind had found it easy to destroy those they did not know. Bombs dropped on faceless targets; policies allowed entire populations to starve, suffer, or be purged through genocide; and internet scams robbed elders of their life savings. The list went on and on. There was no shortage of examples of what damage human beings could do to one another, particularly if they didn't have to witness the carnage.

That was what Gussie Watkins and the other members of the book club had done. They'd acted not in the name of truth but in ignorance. They'd launched missiles from miles away, oblivious to the destruction that was invisible to them. Each was guilty as charged. They'd acted with narcissistic certainty that the end justified the means and with self-righteous disregard for the life they helped destroy, and they'd moved on as if it never had happened. They were cowards—guilty, selfish, dishonest cowards.

Berger knew he was many things, but he was not a coward. He would make them understand the consequences of their actions. He would not destroy them from afar. He would not be like the bombardier from thirty thousand feet. Quite the opposite, his vengeance would be in close proximity, intimate and personal, with a specific message. Each would die directly by his hand.

Gussie Watkins had been up first. He'd followed her patterns for weeks in advance. Through group emails and texts, he had known the exact time and date of the book club meeting in her apartment. He'd placed discreet button cameras in the lobby, elevator, and hallway of her building. He'd pretended to be interested in renting a unit and had the dim-witted building supervisor show him around. Bucci was his name. Berger had seen on the news that the police were still holding him in connection with the murder. What a laugh. The guy had worked out better than Berger could ever have imagined.

At first, Bucci had mildly protested Berger's request for a tour, saying the landlord usually used a Realtor to show prospective tenants a unit, but Berger had explained he was only in town for the day, and his cousin had told him the building might have a unit about to turn over. Bucci hadn't known anything about that, but ever the affable fellow, he quickly had acquiesced and given Berger the grand tour. Bucci was easily distracted. At one point, he'd left Berger alone for several minutes while Berger faked a coughing fit, going in search of a bottle of water. By the time Berger had left the building, all of the button cameras had been in place.

Back then, all the specifics of Berger's plan had not yet been finalized. His only goal at that point had been to complete the blanket of surveillance on all five members of the book club. Over time, Berger had devised the method and specific message for each woman's demise. He'd wanted to start with something spectacular. After he'd determined Gussie would be first, the elevator idea had just come to him one day. He hadn't wanted to trigger the plan until he'd carefully scripted out all five murders, each with an appropriate message.

"Justice is blind" had been the perfect message to kick things off. What better way to drive that message home than to remove the victim's eyes? What could have been more spectacular than that? The last part might have been a little gruesome, but Berger had done many dissections in the lab, so it hadn't been his first time cutting through flesh. He'd just thought of her as a big mouse.

Bucci had been a willing foil. Berger had had to get rid of him for a couple of hours to gain access and move about the elevator shaft. The fake text message from Gussie to set up a meeting at Simon's Coffee House had done the trick. That diversion had given Berger plenty of time to put the cones in place, blocking the stairs and directing his victim to the elevator. Berger had been in the shaft, waiting for her. When she'd entered the building, he had tracked her movements on his cell phone. In his fanny pack, Berger had had the murder weapon: an eight-inch hunting knife. It was the same knife he later had used on Angela Mancini. He'd also had a Taser and worn rubber gloves. He'd watched as Gussie paused at the stairwell and changed direction to the elevator. Once she'd entered, he'd known she was his. Months of planning soon had become real.

After the murder, he'd climbed back up through the hatch, up the shaft, and out the fourth-floor elevator doors, taking the murder weapon with him. He had taken the staircase down, knowing the cones and note he'd put in place at the foot of the stairs made it unlikely he would meet someone on the way up. He'd checked the lobby camera on his cell, confirmed the coast was clear, discreetly exited the building, and disappeared down the street. Along the way, he'd removed all the button cameras and put them in his pocket, leaving no trace of his elaborate surveillance system. When he later had learned Bucci was found lying on top of the elevator and arrested, he'd been amazed. What a stroke of luck. The police would be on a wild goose chase, providing Berger a clear field for at least another murder or two.

Ellen Klein moaned, and the lump under the blanket changed shape. He hoped he hadn't given her too much sedative. He needed her up and walking in about six hours. Berger returned his attention to the laptop. There were no new emails, either incoming or outgoing, from Susan Pearce. He noted a number of texts from Liz McFarland imploring Susan to get in touch, but they said nothing specific beyond that. He also checked the digital camera storage data. The last records were of Liz leaving her apartment yesterday morning and of Susan leaving hers almost a week ago. That seemed odd. Berger hadn't paid much attention to Liz and Susan over the past few days, as he'd been preoccupied with the abduction of Ellen Klein. He was surprised to see the lack of email and text activity, and Susan had not been around her apartment or office at MIT for several days.

Switching gears, he logged on to location services for Susan's cell phone. At first, he was confused, but after he rechecked, it became apparent she was in Zurich, Switzerland. That might change things somewhat, he thought, but then again, there was plenty of time to get to Susan—a lifetime, really. Hopefully she would return sometime soon. If not, he would go to her. In the meantime, he still had Ellen to deal with and then Liz. He looked at Susan's Snapchat to see if he could get a location on Liz but came up empty.

Liz had been missing for about thirty-six hours, and Susan had been in Switzerland for about a week. He wondered if they knew yet. Regardless, he had to focus on the matter at hand. Once that was disposed of, he could direct his full attention to Liz McFarland, saving Susan for last.

CHAPTER 10

North End, Boston: Spring 2013

Professor Hans Berger stood to address his colleagues gathered around a large corner table at Davio's in the North End of Boston. He raised a glass of Taylor port and proposed a toast. The members of his original research team and the two angel investors raised their glasses in salute.

"To my wonderful team and to our new friends, thank you. We have come a long way, and it's been a long time coming. Tonight we pause to acknowledge that. We pause, and we savor the moment, but we must never stop. Our journey has only just begun. There is so much more to learn and so much work to do. There are so many lives to save."

He looked around the table for affirmation and, encouraged by the faces smiling back at him, continued. "Now that we have emerged from the laboratory of academia to enter the corporate world, may our success continue. Through your dedication and with the backing of our new partners, I know there are great things in our future. Here's to all of us, the founders of PKC Group. A cure awaits. May we find that cure."

Berger raised his glass high. His five companions responded with an enthusiastic "Hear! Hear!" and clinked glasses. Berger took a seat, and several waiters descended upon the table, clearing away dishes and presenting the main course. Conversational banter broke out while Berger basked in the glow of the moment. It was a new experience and a huge step. He was confident in his own abilities, but the business world was foreign to him. When he first had embarked upon the current project, he had known that day would have to come if they were to succeed.

It was no small thing to leave the security blanket of MIT and join the ranks of corporate America. In many ways, he was ill prepared, but he believed in the strength of the concept, and the allure of venture funding was irresistible. The promise of the early findings had been his ticket. Of course, the work was still in its infancy, but he was certain they were on the right track, and there was still plenty of time to work out any kinks. The first round of $5 million in seed funding was only meant to position them for what would likely be several additional rounds of capitalization. Inevitably, the founders' share of the pie would be diluted multiple times, but that was irrelevant if the pie was big enough.

The angel investors represented a broad group of wealthy individuals. Collectively, they had made more money than they knew what to do with. They hadn't gotten to where they were by aimlessly throwing money around. Their game was to spread relatively small amounts of start-up money across dozens of promising young companies. The earliest investors in a venture ultimately wound up with the largest percentage of ownership when it was successful and usually exercised the greatest control. Often, the companies they chose to support fizzled and burned out despite the promise of an initial idea with great potential. The angels anticipated that. It only took one home run over ten or twenty attempts to turn more profit than the average stock market investor could ever have dreamed of.

Berger had known the odds when he made the decision to go corporate, but he was also confident the newly formed PKC Group would be one of the companies to beat the odds. True to his word, when the opportunity had developed, he'd offered all three of his research assistants a piece of the action. Initially, Berger had been able to preserve a 50 percent ownership stake for himself. The angel investors had taken 30 percent and insisted on reserving another 8 percent to attract future talent. That had left 4 percent each for Susan Pearce and the other lab assistants.

Now their little team was expanding. The business plan called for lab and office space in Kendall Square. They would recruit more scientists and researchers. More business types would drive much of the decision-making. Berger was fine with that. He was more into the science than the money anyway.

Susan did not withdraw from the PhD program, but she lightened her load considerably, delaying her degree indefinitely into the future so she could devote most of her time to PKC Group. They had to get out of the college lab at some point if they wanted to develop and refine their work and eventually have it benefit the public. After the initial success with the original mouse experiment, most of their collective effort had gone into editing and publishing the work in a number of different scientific journals. In circumstances such as those, it was not unusual to have a lull in actual scientific activity while waiting for the next grant or source of funding. Berger traveled and lectured on a constant basis, authored several related papers, and generally tried to promote their findings.

As work inside the lab had slowed, he'd sensed Susan was

chomping at the bit to keep going, but with the original grant money dried up, all had agreed the best use of Berger's time was continued outreach to the greater academic and scientific community. His efforts in that regard would be the surest method to secure funding for their continued work.

The strategy had worked. In recent months, Berger had entertained a number of funding offers. Ultimately, he'd rejected the idea of additional grant money and decided the time was right to commercialize the process. That had opened the door for the angel investors, who in turn had introduced Berger to any number of attorneys, CPAs, and business consultants. There would certainly be adjustments to make, but now the corporate structure was in place, and $5 million resided in the corporate coffers. Berger and the team were relieved the decks had finally been cleared, and they all could get back to research.

With money in hand, the charge now was to duplicate and fine-tune the original results and then clear the way for human trials. It would be a long haul and many years in the making. The odds were still long. Probably one out of ten drugs that entered human trials ever made it to market. Getting to human trials in the first place was a tall order.

◆ ◆ ◆

Susan nibbled at her eggplant rigatoni and listened politely as one of the angels recited a lengthy history of how he first had made his fortune as an early developer of broadband. She stole a glance out of the corner of her eye at Berger, who was animatedly having a conversation of his own with the other financier. Her relationship with Berger had definitely changed. It was still positive, but there seemed to be an invisible barrier, an artificial formality of sorts that had taken hold.

Their passionate encounter four years prior had been a

one-off event. It was as if neither of them had known how to process it in the aftermath. Susan was not looking to be involved in an ongoing romantic relationship. She liked and respected Berger, but for her, what had happened between them had been the result of a combination of joy, relief, camaraderie, lust, celebration, and curiosity. As a virgin, she had viewed it as a rite of passage as a woman. Losing her virginity had not been something that preoccupied her either before or after the fact. She'd reserved her obsession for academics, research, and the pursuit of knowledge in search of a cure. She'd assumed losing her virginity was something that would happen someday in the normal course of events, and when the time was right, she would know. The time had been right with Dr. Berger. Their tryst had not been born out of romance. Neither had it been an ongoing friends-with-benefits arrangement. More than anything, it had been a product of biology, circumstance, and timing. She didn't regret it, but she had no desire for the complications of an ongoing affair, particularly one that was taboo.

Berger, for his part, was hard to read. She assumed he shared some of the same reservations, but they never really spoke of it. At the time, she had known they'd crossed a line. It had been a transgression that, if exposed, might knock one or both of them off the project and possibly even jeopardize their ability to stay at MIT. That was not a risk either of them was willing to take—of that she was certain.

There was no conflict between them. Berger was often on the road or immersed in his technical writing. Susan spent far less time in the lab with the temporary slowdown in research. When they were together, each was unfailingly polite and respectful to the other. If anything, they were perhaps a shade stilted and stiff in each other's presence. They no longer engaged in the light exchanges of their earlier flirtations. She no longer called him Herr Professor. If any other team members noticed a shift in their behavior, none mentioned it.

Whatever had happened between them was in the past. Susan had no regrets. She doubted Berger did either. The only mutual passion they shared now was the quest for a cure and whatever the next stage of development would bring for the newly formed PKC Group.

One of the angel investors raised his wine glass in a follow-up toast. "To the future," he proclaimed.

"To the future," all replied as they clinked glasses once again.

◆ ◆ ◆

Denmark, Maine: Present Day

The cell phone alarm went off at precisely 3:00 a.m. Berger was already awake with eyes wide open, lying on the second twin bed, fully clothed. He'd pulled an open sleeping bag across his shoulders as a blanket. Sleep largely had eluded him, as the anticipation of what was to come had run through his mind most of the night.

He threw the sleeping bag aside and sat up on the edge of the bed. A few feet away, Ellen Klein remained completely covered by the blanket he'd wrapped her in the night before. She snored gently, and he saw the blanket rise and fall slightly with each rasping breath. Berger stuffed two power bars into his mouth and downed a half bottle of water, fueling himself for the effort ahead.

He gathered his laptop, Coleman lantern, and backpack and took them to the car, leaving Ellen as the last item to be packed up. It was a starlit night, and outside, he was able to operate without the lantern. Inside, he shone the flashlight from his cell phone on the heap that was Ellen Klein.

"Come on, Ellen. Rise and shine. Time to get back in the trunk."

Ellen stirred, and Berger yanked the blanket away and tossed it onto the floor. At first, she was disoriented, but within seconds, her eyes locked on Berger, and the horror of her situation came flooding back. Berger took great delight when he saw her fear. He grabbed her by the arm and hauled her to her feet. She stood unsteadily, trying to gain balance. Berger smiled and offered a bottle of water, which he held while she gulped greedily with droplets rolling down her chin.

"Drink up; you need your strength. Here. Eat these," he said, unwrapping two more power bars. "You need to keep your energy up."

◆ ◆ ◆

Ellen didn't know who her abductor was. He didn't look or sound familiar. She doubted they had ever met before, so she was operating under the assumption she was a random victim. She didn't know what to expect, but while terrified, she hoped for the best. The alternative was unthinkable.

Over the years, she had seen many stories in the news of young women who were kidnapped and held by their captors for months or even years on end. Although not particularly religious, she prayed that was the case now. Being held for a prolonged period meant there would be ongoing opportunity for her escape or possibly even her release. She might suffer horribly and be abused, assaulted, and humiliated, but she would live.

The only other possibility was that her assailant was a crazed killer, perhaps even a serial killer. If that were the case, she would have to act sooner rather than later. She had a decision to make. If he intended to hold her long-term and keep her in some way for his own entertainment, then patiently waiting for a chance to escape might be the most prudent approach, she thought. As unpleasant as going along with him would be, a failed escape attempt might only provoke violence that would otherwise not have occurred.

On the other hand, if he was planning to kill her, there was only a small window of time in which to act, as desperate and impossible as that might have been. Ellen's hands were still bound by duct tape, so Berger fed her the power bars as if she were a young child. Ellen wanted to interpret that as a positive sign. Why would he have nourished her if he was planning to kill her anytime soon? She decided the best strategy for now was to play along and look for any discernible clues along the way that might point to his intentions.

When she was done eating, Berger took her hand and guided her outside.

"Where are we going?" Ellen asked. "What do you want with me?"

"You are going back in the trunk," Berger replied as he popped it open. "Then we are going for a ride."

"No, please," Ellen begged. "Let me ride up front with you. Please. No one will see the tape. I won't say anything to anyone. Please. I can't go back in the trunk."

"Yes, you can, and you will," Berger said calmly as he lifted her off her feet and forced her into the open trunk. There wasn't much Ellen could do to resist.

"Where are we going? How long is the ride?" she called out, hoping for any information before the darkness encased her again.

"Don't worry," Berger said, looking down at her. "It's just a short ride, a half hour or so, and then a little walk. We're going to a new location. It's beautiful there. I want you to be there for the sunrise."

He slammed the trunk shut. Ellen didn't know how to interpret his last remark, but she hoped it was part of some perverse, romantic notion the man had to win her over and brainwash her. She searched her mind for any hint or inkling of what his plan might be.

She wasn't sure how much time had passed since he'd taken her outside her apartment. He had been waiting in the hallway between the units of the two-family home off a quiet side street near Davis Square. Normally, she would have walked two blocks to the square and caught a bus to South Station, where she connected to a commuter train to Dorchester.

Pressed into a corner, he had stood perfectly still. She hadn't noticed him until she'd turned from locking the door, and he had been on her in an instant, holding a cloth over her face and pinning her against the door. Had that been yesterday, or had it been longer than that? She wasn't sure.

Whenever it had been, she first had awoken in the trunk. It had taken a while to figure out where she was. The darkness had made it difficult to calibrate her senses. She'd tried to cry out and realized there was something in her mouth. She'd reached to pull it away and realized her hands and arms were tightly bound together, and she could hardly move. She'd sensed motion and the rhythmic vibration of tires on pavement. The steady hum of a motor had seemed far away. She'd been unsure exactly where she was or how she had gotten there. The last things she had been able to remember at that point were the man in the hall and the smell of the cloth he'd clamped over her mouth and nose.

Now that she was back in the trunk again, her earlier uncertainty was replaced by the terror of anticipating whatever was to come next. If he'd wanted to rape her, wouldn't he have done so in the trailer home? She had caught a quick glimpse of the cement-block-mounted trailer, the clearing, and the long dirt driveway. If he'd wanted to kill her, wouldn't the isolation of where they'd just spent the night have been his safest bet? She wanted to believe that was true. She had to believe it was true. There was no other logical reason to take her elsewhere. The trailer home must have been a temporary stop on the way to someplace else, someplace he would keep her long-term.

Ellen had no idea what state they were in or how far they were from Somerville. Her body leaned slightly left, right, up, and down, as the road they were on curved, dipped, and rose. Maybe he was delivering her someplace else. Why had he chosen her? Was she a victim of human trafficking? None of it made any sense.

Suddenly, they made a sharp hairpin turn, and gravity forced her weight toward the back of the trunk as the car began a steep climb. The sound of the tires changed from the smooth pitch of rubber on pavement to the uneven crunching of a bumpy dirt road. The car came to a stop. This was it. Ellen held her breath, fighting back the panic that relentlessly surged to overwhelm her.

The trunk popped open, and once again, she could see the outline of the man peering down at her. It was still dark out. Ellen had no idea what time it was, but it must have been well before dawn, because the stars still shone brightly.

The man spoke. "Don't panic, Ellen. I took you to this spot because I want to show you something. If you promise to behave, I'll cut your feet loose so you can walk on your own. Can I trust you to do that?"

Ellen felt a ray of hope. Whatever he had planned, she couldn't fight back or run away with her feet bound. She had to stay calm and process each decision moment by moment. However poor her odds might have been, they were dramatically improved by getting out of the trunk and being able to move under her own power.

She nodded in agreement, and the man pulled a hunting knife from the back of his waistband and sliced through the duct tape around her ankles in one quick motion. He had not shown the knife before, and she tried to add that variable to her fluid calculus of what to do. The man replaced the knife in the back of his pants, reached into the trunk, and helped her out in a surprisingly gentle way, making sure she didn't bang her head—another piece of new information, another variable. He didn't want to hurt her. He was being kind and careful—but what about the knife?

Her hands were still bound. The man grabbed her by the forearm, not roughly, and guided her toward the tree line. He used only his cell phone flashlight to illuminate the ground. There were a few stone steps, followed by a steep path that rose severely amid the towering forest. As their eyes adjusted, only a trace of ambient starlight penetrated the canopy of the treetops, supplementing the light from his phone. The surface of the path alternated between heavily rooted forest detritus and exposed stone ledge. Some sections were so vertical that the man had to grasp a branch or small sapling to pull them up a few feet.

After five minutes of vigorous effort, Ellen's thighs began to burn. She was not a fitness enthusiast in the first place, and the ordeal exhausted her. She thought briefly of trying to break away and tumble back down the path to the car. Had he left the keys in the car or put them in his pocket? She had no idea. There was no way to overpower him. Her only options were to go along or make a desperate, futile rush back to the car in total darkness down what seemed like a virtual cliff.

Even if she could break free, he would be only a few feet behind, and he was the only one with a light. The chance of the keys being in the car was remote, and she'd be lucky if she had any time at all with him right on her heels. It really was not an option.

Thus far, he hadn't been unnecessarily physical with her as he led them on the climb to wherever. Ellen's body made a temporary decision for her as her legs gave out, and she slumped slowly to the ground, gasping for air.

"I can't go on," she panted, her butt planted on a stone outcropping. "Where are we going?"

Again, somewhat to her surprise, he didn't hit her or try to pull her to her feet. Was that another good sign?

"Take a minute to rest," he said reassuringly. "We're more than halfway to the top. It's not much farther. We need to get there before the sun comes up."

Ellen was grateful for the rest. She still had no idea what his crazy game was, but if he wanted to see the sunrise, maybe that was a good thing. After a minute or two, he reached out his hand and helped her to her feet. She smiled at him in the darkness, hoping he might see and somehow connect to her humanity.

Together they made their way forward slowly. He led with a firm grip on her arm. She made a couple of attempts at breathless conversation, but he just shushed her. Within minutes, the ground beneath their feet once again turned to ledge and seemed to level out as the woods thinned, and the stars came back into view. They drew deep breaths, apparently at the top of a mountain or at least a great hill.

There was no need for the flashlight now. It was a clear night, and the northern sky was sharp in its magnificent luster. Directly in front of them loomed the silhouette of a large stone tower.

"What is this place?" she asked.

"This is Douglas Mountain, the highest point of elevation for sixty miles. The top of this tower is the most glorious place in all of New England from which to view the sunrise. You can see all the way to the White Mountains of New Hampshire. Come." He gestured toward the dark opening of the tower entrance. "We haven't much time."

Ellen hesitated, but he nudged her gently through the entryway to the spiral stone staircase within. The man clicked his flashlight back on so they could navigate the narrow stone passageway to the top.

They emerged onto the observation deck. Ellen came out first with the man trailing slightly behind. She stood in the center of the small open space. The brilliance of the stars was again on full display. She wondered if she would see the sun rise.

The man came up behind her and put his arms around her waist. She couldn't see his face as he hugged her from behind with his cheek touching hers. She could feel his breath on her neck; it was sour and rancid, and his body odor was rank with sweat. The man whispered something softly in her ear. She wasn't sure she understood.

It sounded like "The truth shall set you free."

CHAPTER 11

Kendall Square, Cambridge, Massachusetts: Spring 2015

Susan Pearce looked at the raw data summary chart on her computer screen. In the time since PKC Group had been launched, they'd added two new researchers, several administrative people, and a CEO handpicked by the angel investors. They'd spent the first few months setting up the lab, hiring and training personnel, and refining protocol for the next round of mouse experiments.

The goal was to duplicate and, if possible, improve the original results from the work done at MIT. They were currently about halfway through that effort, and the early returns were encouraging but mixed. Susan was reviewing a preliminary summary of the data to date on trials she personally had supervised, as compared to the aggregate data of all the researchers as a group. There appeared to be a discrepancy, and she couldn't understand why. It was still early on, but her data showed no statistically significant difference in memory function between mice treated with any of the tau protein inhibitor compounds and those who were not.

The current project was larger than the experiments at MIT. There were now five scientists, including Susan, directly running groups of mice through different trials. There were also more moving parts as they sought to accelerate the research in an effort to speed up the commercialization process.

Susan was starting to have second thoughts about Berger. From her standpoint, he was less visible, no longer running individual trials and instead playing more of an oversight and liaison role. He circulated among, audited, and observed the five individual scientists doing the research firsthand. He compiled and analyzed their separate results, interpreting the aggregate data and reporting what it meant to the financial and business types in the organization. He split his time between the business side and the research side.

On the business side, he spent many hours with the CEO and his team, strategizing and developing a timeline, romancing the angel investors, and justifying the burn rate on their capital investment. On the research side, he wrote reports and documented their overall progress in summary tables and charts. He controlled and designed the experimental protocols and the incremental molecular modifications in the inhibitor compounds being introduced to the mice. He directed the researchers on what to run next and how to do it. Inherent in the process he'd designed was the independence of the five research scientists. The theory apparently was that a figurative wall between them would help control for any subconscious bias or influence they might have on one another.

Although there appeared to be a master plan, the individual scientists each ran different versions of the compounds at any given time. As a result, only Berger controlled the combined data.

He was also the sole disseminator of the information conveyed to the angel investors and their surrogates. When Berger distributed internal documents to the corporate hierarchy, only then did the other scientists see the aggregated data and resulting conclusions based on their combined efforts. Otherwise, from a research standpoint, they were all kept in their own separate silos.

Susan realized that for PKC Group to be viable, they had to have concrete forward progress. She hadn't been used to the concept of a burn rate when she was in the academic world. The angel investors might have been interested in curing Alzheimer's but only in the same sense in which they were interested in world peace.

Susan had no illusions: PKC Group was on the clock. The angels' primary and only relevant motivation was to turn over their capital and make money. When PKC Group burned through the initial $5 million of seed capital, they would be at a crossroads. Given adequate justification, there would be another round of funding. Spectacular results might even lead to a buyout offer from a major player, such as big pharma. The angels would have been happy to make a quick exit and a few-hundred-percent profit on their initial investment. The absence of such justification to continue would mean PKC Group would be defunct.

Susan clicked back on the latest internal progress report Berger had distributed earlier that morning. The tone was positive, indicating the early trend was supporting a range of 18 to 20 percent memory improvement for the most effective versions of the tau inhibitor compounds. That was below the level of improvement first shown at MIT, but the narrative indicated it was still early in the process, and the direction still was promising. Susan was not seeing a similar result in the data from the trials she was running, and she wondered why. She understood they were all working trials on different variations of the compound at different times, but it didn't seem logical that her result was so off from the group as a whole. Something was not right.

Susan got up from her desk, walked down the hall, and knocked on Berger's door.

"Enter," he said, not looking up from the papers on his desk.

"Hans," Susan said, "got a minute?"

"For you? Of course."

Berger quickly gathered the papers in front of him, slid them to the corner of his desk, and looked at her expectantly. He gave no indication for her to sit, and Susan made no motion toward the empty chair across from his desk. Neither spoke for several seconds, but it was obvious this was not a social visit. Susan was both agitated and perplexed at the same time, as if she had a puzzle she could not solve.

Finally, Berger broke the silence. "What is it, Susan? Do you have something on your mind?"

"It's this report," she replied, holding up that morning's progress report. "I don't think it's right."

"Not right? What do you mean by that? I don't understand."

"The overall data doesn't match up with what I'm seeing on my trials. How could I be looking at something so different?"

"Oh, so that's what's bothering you. I see. So what is it you think, Susan—that someone is cooking the books by altering the data?"

She looked Berger straight in the eye. "Well, is someone?"

Berger returned her stare. "And who do you think that someone might be? Me?"

"There's no one else in a position to do it, Hans. Are you altering the data?"

"No, don't be preposterous. I resent your implications."

"I'm not implying anything. I'm asking. Are you?"

"I've just told you. No. You do understand that all five of you are running different scenarios at all times. I designed that system purposefully to ensure independent verification of results. For all you know, Susan," he said patronizingly, "you've been running placebos a good portion of the time. That would explain any discrepancies right there, wouldn't it?"

"Possibly," she said, "but it doesn't feel right. Why have one researcher run mostly placebos? Why not spread it around over the five of us?"

"I think you forget your place here, Susan. Remember, it is I who started this project when you were a mere undergraduate, a sophomore. I design the protocols, the controls, and the modifications. You do your part and only your part. I gave you a chance; I took you along for the ride. If you want to stay on that ride, you will do things my way. Is that clear?"

"There's too much bottlenecked on you, Hans. Now that we're underway with research again, I can see it. If you wanted to, you could manipulate the data any way you pleased. We should make changes." Susan crossed the room and sat down in the chair. She crossed her legs and stared him down.

"That's not going to happen. I don't think you realize our position. We are not in the bosom of MIT any longer. We now answer to the god of capitalism. It falls upon me to satisfy that god. I am the bridge between what you all do in the lab and how it is translated to the investors and the outside world. Let me ask you a question, Susan. Do you want to keep the research going? Do you feel our concept has some validity, some possibility, or do you want to be shut down after all these years and go back to square one with no funding and no lab? That would set us back years, maybe permanently. How would that serve anyone?"

"Are you telling me the data is tainted?"

"No, I'm telling you to leave the integration of science and business to me. There are good reasons why I've designed the research protocols this way. You will just have to trust me. We are on the precipice of PKC Group possibly being acquired by a much bigger company for big money—many multiples of what the angels have invested. For that to happen, the results on our current research will have to justify it. We are headed in the right direction. We cannot afford to be distracted now."

"I'm not comfortable with this, Hans. It makes me want to question the original research we did back at MIT. Was anything done with that data?"

"You're not listening to me, Susan," Berger said. "You won't find anything wrong with that data. It's all buttoned up tight, documented, and published in several scientific journals."

Susan wasn't so sure. She made a mental note to dig up her notes from that time to check for any evidence of tampering. The only problem was that her notes were just that—her own personal journal of sorts. Berger had controlled all the official data storage and resulting conclusions. She didn't have any raw tables of thousands of mouse runs done years ago at MIT.

Berger shuffled in his seat uncomfortably and glanced at his watch. "I've got a meeting in five minutes. I appreciate your concern, but I need you to either be all in or all out. Everything is on the line right now. If our work is ever going to help anyone, we must keep going. Do you understand that? After all our years of work, it all comes down to where we are right here and right now. If there's any good to come of our efforts, we must move forward. Maybe our solution won't be perfect. Maybe it will only be the foundation for the next step. All I know is if we don't get funding, it's all gone. Zero good will come from our work. Do you understand that burden? Do you see the weight on my shoulders?"

"Are you telling me there is something going on?"

"No, I'm telling you I need you to get back to work. I know

what finding a cure means to you. This is your best shot. You play your role, and I'll play mine."

"Are you sure it's not the money? Is that huge payday too much of a temptation? Is that part of it? What if it's a house of cards? What if it all comes crashing down? What happens to all of us then? What happens to the work then?"

Berger stood behind his desk and picked up a folder. "I've got to go. You sleep on it, Susan. In or out? I need to know."

◆ ◆ ◆

Hiram, Maine: Present Day

The old Ford F-150 pickup truck pulled to a stop on the dirt turnaround area. Ignoring the No Parking sign, the young twentysomething behind the wheel switched off the engine and cut the lights. He took a draining chug from the Bud Light in the cupholder and tossed the empty can into the backseat.

His partner in crime in the passenger seat grinned and reached between his legs to retrieve a replacement from the bag at his feet. "Dilly, dilly," he said, popping the top and handing the beer to his friend.

"Dilly, dilly," the youth behind the wheel replied. He and his buddy had been up all night, partying hearty. The driver opened his door and fell to the ground. "Whoa!" he exclaimed, surprised that the ground wasn't exactly where he'd thought it was. "Recovery!" he yelled, quickly bouncing to his feet to demonstrate for his companion that he was fine.

"Dude, are you all right?" his partner cried, running around the front of the truck.

"Yeah, man. No worries. Let's do this thing." He brushed himself off, determined to show no weakness to his friend, and opened the tool box mounted in the bed of the truck behind the cab. He fished out two industrial flashlights and presented one to his companion, who was clutching a six-pack in his other hand.

"What time is it?" the passenger asked. "Can we still make it?"

"Yeah, we've got about twenty-five minutes."

"All right. Let's haul ass."

The driver thought about it for a moment and motioned for his companion to go first. Together they started up the stone steps and onto the trail with the beams from the flashlights playing ahead of them. Blessed with the resilience of youth, they rallied considerably despite having blood-alcohol levels that would have topped the charts. Apart from an occasional expletive, conversation was minimal; they focused their energy and breath on sucking it up for the climb.

Neither wanted to admit to being a pussy, so they pushed on at a rapid pace, stumbling, falling, and pulling themselves up the mountain with their lungs bursting and legs burning, until they were at the top. The driver bent over at the waist, fighting the urge to heave.

The passenger pulled out his cell phone to check the time. "Five minutes," he gasped. "Time to spare."

The driver straightened up. "What a head rush. Come on. Let's get up to the top of the tower."

It was already lighter out than when they'd parked the truck below, but the sun had not yet appeared. They clambered up the tower staircase to the top. The driver held the flashlight directly under his chin, producing a ghoulish effect. The passenger howled with laughter and pointed his cell phone to film the occasion. The driver pranced about pretending to be a drunken zombie while his companion filmed with one hand and opened beers with the other.

"Wait, wait, wait. It's time. Take a selfie of us with the sunrise in the background."

"Which way?" the genius with the phone asked.

"Over there, moron. To the east."

"Which way is east up here?"

"Okay, when I say, 'Go,' we both point to the east. Go!" They each pointed in a different direction and collapsed into each other's arms, giggling hysterically.

"This way. Come on." The driver pulled a joint from his shirt pocket and lit it. They each took a deep toke and slowly exhaled. They centered themselves with their arms around each other and their butts to the eastern wall. The passenger reversed the phone camera and extended his arm as far as he could to get them both in the frame. They held their beers high, and the driver held a bone in his other hand as the sun rose majestically behind them—a dream shot.

After a few moments, the film session was over, and they sank to the floor, sipping beers and passing the roach back and forth until the last of it was dead.

"Dude, what's that?" the driver said, pointing across the viewing platform to a large rope and two smaller ones tied off to the chain-link fence on the opposite wall.

"I dunno," the other replied. "Let's check it out."

They struggled to their feet and examined the ropes. Fatigue was setting in. It was almost bedtime for them. The passenger tried to tug at the ropes, but his fingers could not fit through the small square openings of the chain link. The driver climbed up to the shelf of the cement wall and leaned as far as he could over the higher protective fence.

"Holy shit, dude, there's a person down there! Oh fuck, man, I think it's a girl. I can't tell from up here. I think she's dead maybe."

◆ ◆ ◆

Douglas Mountain, Hiram, Maine

Five hours later, Dimase's police interceptor pulled into the same dirt parking area where the boys had parked their pickup truck just four and a half hours before. He got out, looked up at the steep trail crossed with yellow police tape, and cringed. He was in good shape, but he was in no mood for a hike. High up was the stone lookout tower where the murder vic had been found a couple of hours earlier. Various law enforcement vehicles were parked in the lot, including the coroner's van. A relatively young man in full police uniform but hatless, with calf-high black boots, stepped forward to greet them.

"Captain Warner, Maine State Police," he said, introducing himself. The men shook hands, and Warner continued. "I'm the one who called you. It's pretty bizarre up there," he said, nodding toward the trail head. "I've never seen anything like it, but I think it might be your girl."

"Have you seen her yourself?" Dimase asked.

"Yes, what made us look a little harder was the theatrics of the presentation."

"Theatrics?" Dimase said.

"Yes, our office was aware of the missing-person report you have out on Ellen Klein. I'm also aware of the information you put out that the murder of a woman in Cambridge and the stabbing of a woman on the Boston Common might be related to each other and in some way to Ms. Klein. I put two and two together and thought this might be her. You don't see something like what you're going to see up there every day. I took a good, close look, and I think it's her, so I called you right away."

"I appreciate that, Captain. What is it that is so different?"

"I think you'd better just see for yourself. It's about a

twenty-minute climb to the top. There's no other way to get there. I hope you're in decent shape."

Dimase self-consciously touched the pack of cigarettes he had earlier transferred to his pants pocket to keep them from view. "We'll manage, Captain. Let's get started."

"Okay." Warner smiled. "Follow me. It'll be pretty tough to talk until we get to the top. We've set up some staging and ladders, but other than that, we haven't touched a thing. You take a look, and then we'll figure out how to proceed."

"Thank you," Dimase said appreciatively. Warner not only seemed on the ball but also was not being overly territorial. With Captain Warner leading the way, Dimase, Rodriguez, and Coyne fell into line behind him and proceeded in single file up the stone steps and onto the trail. Dimase was confident he could handle the climb, although he knew a few fewer cigarettes would have made the task considerably easier. By the time the ground leveled off and the observation tower came into view, Dimase was covered in a thin layer of sweat and was focused on controlling deep, quiet breaths so he wouldn't appear to be out of shape in front of the others.

Warner, Rodriguez, and Coyne were all at least ten years younger than Dimase and were trim and fit. If the steep climb was challenging for them, they were doing a good job of hiding it. In the clearing at the top of the mountain, another dozen personnel were waiting for them, about half in uniform and the other half in civvies. Dimase silently looked at the tower as he bought a moment to catch his breath.

"She's on the other side," Warner said. "The kids who discovered her were on top to see the sunrise. They were half in the bag, but they didn't even see her for fifteen or twenty minutes after they got here."

Warner led them around the corner of the structure, stepping carefully over the rough terrain. Warner stepped back slightly, allowing the three detectives to line up squarely in front of the west-facing wall. Collectively, they stared at the scene in front of them. It was Ellen Klein all right. There was little doubt about that, although official identification would follow later.

The poor woman was hanging about four feet from the top of the tower with a thick rope tight around her neck. Her tongue protruded from her mouth—the sign of a gruesome death that probably had taken a minute or two. Her eyes were open, staring blankly into space in the direction of the White Mountains. Her arms were stretched out as if in crucifixion, held in place by smaller sections of twine placed around her wrists and tied off at the base of the chain-link fence topping the cement wall that surrounded the viewing platform. Her legs and feet hung straight down, bound together by duct tape at the ankles. A placard on a lanyard hung around her neck, but the message was not decipherable from where they stood. The police had placed extension ladders on either side of the body, and a small suspended platform hung to one side with an officer sitting, waiting for instruction.

"What does the sign say?" Dimase asked, the first to break the silence.

"*Veritas vos liberabit*," Warner replied.

"Meaning?"

"It's Latin for 'The truth will set you free.'"

CHAPTER 12

Cambridge, Massachusetts: Spring 2015

Berger stepped out of the shower, toweled himself off, and regarded his naked body in the bathroom mirror. He looked like a less-good-looking miniature version of Thor. His blond hair was slightly scraggy and not as long, and his face was more flawed, but his lithe torso was ripped, and his muscles were well defined.

He did his best thinking in the early morning, and the evening, after his workout and prepared meal, was his reset. He often caught up on world events on cable TV. Just as often, he read articles of interest, perhaps related to or as background for work. That particular evening, as he sat in a recliner with his feet up and a glass of wine at his side, he became annoyed with himself.

For the third time, he started to read the opening paragraphs of an article in the *Wall Street Journal* regarding the abundance of venture capital currently available in the marketplace.

Uncharacteristically, he found the words did not register, because some other yet undefined thought was subtly trying to force its way into his consciousness, chipping away at his focus just enough to make him read the words without processing the meaning.

He put the paper aside and took a contemplative sip from his glass of 2014 Duckhorn cabernet sauvignon. *Susan Pearce—that's what it is.* His confrontation with her was gnawing at him and now bubbled to the surface. She was going to be a problem. He could see that now. He had given her an ultimatum: in or out. Now he realized that in or out, she would continue to be a threat.

She was right, obviously. He had manipulated the data, and he continued to manipulate the data. He didn't feel bad about it. He looked at it as a necessary evil, an unpleasant duty to serve some greater purpose. The line of research they were pursuing held great promise. They'd achieved some good results both at MIT and now at PKC Group, just not as good as he portrayed.

Yes, Susan was right. The temptation in his days back at MIT had been too great for him to resist. He'd had no ill intentions when they embarked upon that last brain research project. Scientists around the world were circling the role of tau and amyloid beta protein buildup in brain synapses, but none had yet been able to put it all together to achieve that major breakthrough.

The mouse experiments at MIT had been both promising and intellectually puzzling. The truth, known only to Berger, was that some of the molecular compounds did have a positive effect on functional mouse memory but only a relatively small percentage of the time. That development legitimately had spectacular potential. The problem was that the same version of the compound used on similarly impaired mice from the same grouping also had produced many incidences of no significant memory improvement at all. That was not expected. Why? What could explain that discrepancy? Was the compound itself was the causative factor with the mice that improved, or was some other unidentified extraneous factor responsible? Clearly, they were getting positive results in some of the cases, but there was no way to consistently predict the outcome. Why would two mice from the same group, each bred for similar levels of brain protein, have such different and seemingly random results from the same compound?

Berger did not have an answer for the conundrum. To his knowledge, no one else in the world scientific community had yet developed any drug or compound with any positive result in reducing tau deposits in the brain. Whoever got there first would be richly rewarded, not only from a monetary standpoint but also, even more importantly, with recognition as one of the great scientists of his or her time, perhaps even of all time.

Berger had done it. He just couldn't do it all the time, and he didn't know why. It was maddening.

In his days back at MIT, he'd thought about his dilemma long and hard. An analytical man, he'd puzzled through all the options obsessively and come to the same logical conclusion each time: something was working some of the time. It must have been related to the compound, but he was at a loss to explain the inconsistency. With the MIT study coming to an end and the grant money running out, he had known the study would wind down with inconclusive results. He could have spent the next year or two developing new proposals and searching for more grant money, but that had not been an appealing option on any level, particularly because he did have something. Something was there. Something was working. He simply had not had enough time and money left to resolve exactly what and how.

Berger had done the only thing he could do: he'd given

the data a nudge. It had been easy enough. All the raw data and preliminary results had been funneled through him. He'd altered just enough of the information to make the summaries and resultant conclusions definitively support the efficacy of the compound. Those results in turn had supported the articles and publication effort that were now part of the official narrative.

Berger rationalized his deception as the only way forward—certainly the only way without a long delay of a year or more at least before being able to pick up the string again. Who would such a delay have served? Certainly not Alzheimer's patients waiting for a cure. What harm would result if he could secure funding for the next level and continue to pull at the thread of success they had discovered?

He was confident he'd covered his tracks well at MIT. Neither Susan nor anyone else was in a position to uncover his malfeasance at that point. He'd made the necessary adjustments, and it was all part of the documented record now. The current round of deception at PKC Group was more problematic. He was in deep. The more pressure had built, the more liberties he had taken, and now Susan was onto him. She didn't know specifics, at least not yet, but she was not the type to let it go.

Berger had temporarily repressed his confrontation with Susan, but as time passed, it continued to nag at him until it was front and center on his mind as a major problem he had to solve effectively and decisively. If she left, it wouldn't look good. If she stayed with PKC Group, she would continue looking at everything with a suspicious eye and likely would not be satisfied until she found the truth—and that truth would not be good for anyone, least of all him.

The same inconsistent results that had plagued the MIT experiments continued with PKC. Berger tinkered with the compounds, searching for the holy grail that thus far continued to be elusive. He had known what he was getting into when PKC Group was founded and funded. It wasn't as if he was a total fraud. They had a compound that worked some of the time on some of the mice. That had not changed. There had to be an answer buried somewhere in the science, if only he could hold on.

As he designed the experimental protocols and controlled the aggregate data, he knew it would be easy enough to continue his marginal manipulations. The best lies were built on a kernel of truth. He had more than a kernel; he just needed time and money to solve the problem. He knew it was a righteous decision—good for patients, investors, his colleagues, and himself. If they solved the riddle, everyone would benefit, and no one would be the wiser. It was a tremendous personal risk, but given the circumstances, he was convinced his path of temporary deceit was the only option. Now Susan presented a new obstacle, a risk he somehow had to mitigate.

It was a *Sophie's Choice* situation, but Berger concluded that any attacks she mounted from the outside could be effectively muted, delayed through denial and obfuscation, and written off as the rantings of a disgruntled employee. There was even an employment contract containing confidentiality and noncompete clauses. If need be, legal action could prevent any public comments or other disclosure of anything related to PKC Group.

Berger's analytical mind sorted and stacked all the alternatives and arrived at an inevitable conclusion: if Susan decided to stay, he would have to find a way to force her out.

◆ ◆ ◆

Cambridge, Massachusetts: Present Day

Dimase stepped off the elevator on the tenth floor, his mood darker than usual. As he strode down the hall to Elizabeth McFarland's suite, he wondered how he was supposed to tell her that another one of her friends had been brutally murdered. He hated notifying people about the death of a loved one. Sadly, though, such onerous duties were part of the job. He arrived at the door and knocked after hesitating for a moment to collect his thoughts.

"Ms. McFarland?" he said, knocking again.

"That you, Detective Augustin?"

"Yeah, you got a minute? We need to talk," he said through the door. Dimase heard the dead bolt turn, and a second later, he stood looking straight into Liz's eyes.

"Come in," she said, gesturing to him with her right arm. "I could use the diversion. Gets awful boring here, you know, what with only the tube to watch and magazines to read."

"Thanks," he said, following her into the living room.

"Come. Sit," Liz said. She sat down on the couch.

Dimase sat down across from her on a love seat, crossed his left leg over his right, and ran his hands down the front of his suit jacket.

"So what's up?" Liz asked. "You look like someone just shot your dog."

"I don't know how to tell you this, Ms. McFarland—"

"Liz. Please. How many times do I have to tell you to just call me Liz?"

"Liz, I'm afraid I have bad news."

Her face dropped. The smile and the slight playfulness in her eyes vanished in an instant. "What?"

"It's Ellen. I'm afraid she's been murdered. Last night."

Dimase watched the color drain from Liz's face and saw her hands start to shake.

"Murdered? Oh God! I knew it! I knew this was gonna happen!"

"I'm so sorry," Dimase said.

"How? How did she die?"

"You don't want to know, Liz. Let's just say we know, or we're pretty sure, it's the same guy who killed Gussie and Angela. MO is a bit different, but there are things that are similar in each case."

Liz buried her head in her hands and began to cry. "This is all too much. Too much. Why is this happening to me?"

Dimase remained seated. He fought back the urge to get up, sit next to her on the couch, and put his arm around her shoulders to comfort her. Distance in that case was his friend. He was already getting too emotionally involved. If he allowed himself to sink deeper into the darkness of the case, he knew he stood a good chance of getting swallowed up in it, as if he'd stepped in quicksand and had no way to get out of the trap.

"We're doing everything we can," he said. "We'll catch the guy. I'm pretty sure of that, and when we do, he'll have a lot to answer for."

"Yeah," Liz said, wiping tears from her eyes. "But it won't bring my friends back. They're gone. They'll always be gone from now on, and that just makes me so sad. So sad." She began to cry again.

"Can you think of any reason someone might feel they've been wronged by your friends, either the book club itself or maybe some of the members? Clearly, someone is angry about something. They feel wronged, and they are taking revenge or justice, as they see it."

"Why do you ask?"

"Because in all three cases, the killer left a message. You recall the ones left at the scene of Gussie's and Angela's murders."

Liz nodded.

"Well, in Ellen's case, the message was in Latin. '*Veritas vos liberabit*,' or 'The truth will set you free.' What truth, Liz? What truth would possibly set you free—any of you? What is this person's truth?"

"I don't know, I don't know, I don't know." She started rocking back and forth on the couch. "How did Ellen die? You have to tell me."

Dimase took a deep breath and plunged in. He described the murder scene while sugarcoating it as best as he could. "Does any of this mean anything to you, anything at all, even if it seems crazy?"

"No!" Elizabeth wailed, and her rocking intensified. "Seems crazy. Crazy. It's all insane. Why? Why? I have no idea why. I'm probably going to be next, and I don't even know why."

"You're not going to be next," Dimase said. "You are totally safe here. You are protected. I give you my word. We will find this person. There is some connection here. There always is. We will find it. I am sorry about your friends. I know you are suffering. I know you are frightened. We will protect you, but we must work together; we must help each other."

"What do you need me to do?"

"I want to set up a conference call with you and Susan Pearce as soon as possible. I don't know how much danger she is in while still in Switzerland. We need to make some decisions about her protection, but just as important, I want members of my team to freestyle with both of you. I'm also going to ask the departmental psychologist to sit in. I need you and Susan to play off one another. Maybe the psychologist can prompt each of you to recall some small fact that remains hidden right now. We need to go through everything. There is something there, something buried. There is some reason, something to do with justice and truth. It may be the smallest, most insignificant thing—I don't know. It will be very painful. We will go through every detail of all three murders if we have to. We have to talk about every aspect of the book club, no matter how intimate or private it might be."

Elizabeth stopped rocking and sat still with a mixture of fear, determination, and resignation painted on her face.

"Can I count on you to do this for me?" Dimase asked.

"Yes, yes, of course. I will do whatever you ask. I have to. I have no choice. I want to live. I will go crazy just sitting in this suite waiting—waiting for what, I don't know. Yes, let's talk to Susan; let's get your people together. I want to fight back. Please help me. Please protect me. Can we do it as soon as possible?"

"Yes," Dimase replied, "I've already set it up for 2:00 p.m. today; that's 8:00 p.m. in Zurich. Get some rest. Have something to eat. I'll send a matron up at 1:45 to bring you down."

Dimase offered his condolences once again, assured her she'd be safe in protective custody, and said his goodbyes. He felt a wave of relief wash over him as he left the suite. He also felt more determined than ever to catch the killer.

He passed the time by doing routine casework on the Klein murder and felt as if he'd gotten nowhere. Then he went to the conference room to get ready for the call to Zurich. A few minutes later, the matron escorted Elizabeth into the room. He didn't want Liz to feel overwhelmed by walking into a room full of people, so he intentionally had her come a few minutes early. She seemed more together than earlier, but Dimase wanted a few minutes to preview for her how the meeting would unfold.

Dimase rose politely to greet her as Elizabeth took a seat next to him. There were a dozen empty seats around the massive conference table, but Dimase guessed she felt safer in sitting as physically close to him as possible.

"I want to give you a little idea of what to expect before everyone else gets here. There will be about a dozen people, including you and me. You've met a couple of them, but most will be new faces. Just remember, no matter what anyone says, they are all here to help you."

Elizabeth nodded, and Dimase continued. "Some of the people are from the Boston Police Department and were originally assigned to Angela's case. The rest are colleagues of mine in Cambridge. There will also be a couple of detectives patched in from the Maine State Police, and as soon as everyone is here, we will connect with Susan on the speakerphone. This is not going to be easy for you or Susan, but there is no other way. We have to go over every little detail. Do you understand?"

"Yes."

Other officers and detectives began to arrive, carrying folders and notebooks, and somberly filled the empty seats. The detectives from Maine were conferenced in on the speakerphone, and at precisely two o'clock, Susan Pearce dialed a prearranged number and joined the meeting. After brief formalities, Dimase requested that the officers from Maine bring everyone up to date on the sequence of events and the details of Ellen Klein's murder.

Captain Warner took the group through the basics. "We believe the victim was most likely forced or somehow coerced to walk up the mountain trail under her own power."

"Why?" Dimase asked, interrupting. "Why do you think that?"

"Operating on the premise that we're dealing with one person, we don't think it's likely a normal person could carry a dead weight up that trail in the dark."

"Yes," Dimase said, "we now believe that the Watkins and Mancini murders were also the work of one perp."

The Maine detective continued. "Forensics found no significant bruises or broken bones on the victim to indicate she was beaten prior to the final act. It was masked by the impact of the rope around her neck, but there are smaller marks around Ms. Klein's neck that are consistent with manual strangulation. We think maybe the guy strangled her to the point of semiconsciousness and then placed the large rope around her neck and hung her over the edge of the tower to finish the job."

Dimase stole a sideways glance at Elizabeth, who maintained a neutral facade, her eyes downcast toward the table.

The voice on the phone went on. "There does not appear to be any sign of a struggle—no skin or DNA under her fingernails, no wounds, and no broken fingers or anything to indicate she had much time to fight back. Once they were on top of the mountain, he probably took her quickly. Hanging from the tower—the large rope around her neck—is what actually killed her in the end. The other stuff—the crucifixion pose—was done after the fact to maximize the drama for us, as was the placard around her neck."

"Thank you, Captain," Dimase said. "Regarding the placard, we have found a very similar message at each murder scene. The three victims were closely related—members of the same book club. The theme is consistent. It seems to be about justice. For Gussie Watkins, it was 'Justice is blind.' For Angela Mancini, it was 'Justice is swift.' Now we have a message in Latin, '*Veritas vos liberabit*,' meaning 'The truth will set you free.' Anybody have any ideas or any interpretation that might point us in the right direction? Why Latin all of a sudden?"

"I do." Susan Pearce spoke for the first time, her voice sounding distant and electronic over the long-distance connection, amplified over the speaker in the middle of the conference table. "The message was meant for me. I know who it is."

CHAPTER 13

Kendall Square, Cambridge, Massachusetts: Fall 2015

Several months passed after Susan's confrontation with Berger over possible data manipulation. During that time, he made her life a living hell. She thought about his ultimatum long and hard, but in the end, she realized there was only one course of action, at least for the time being.

If she left, she would be cut off from the work to which she had been dedicated since sophomore year at MIT. If PKC Group went on to achieve success, there would always be a question about why she had pulled out, a taint over her future career prospects. Leaving would mean, professionally speaking, going back to square one with no resources, funding, or track record. She may or may not be able to return to MIT in a teaching capacity, but her research days would be put on hold indefinitely. It could be years before she was back in a position to mount her own research effort, if ever. This was not an option.

The quest for a cure was her mission in life. She knew they

had been onto something back at MIT and now also were with PKC Group. The tortured blend of pure research colliding head-on into the unrelenting demand for commercial success had produced the current dilemma. The inability to meet artificially constructed financial deadlines did not change the fact that the underlying science held considerable promise. It seemed clear the business aspect was distorting the scientific component, hence her suspicions about Berger.

Susan was sure he was cooking the books to pacify the angels and the business side of the venture. She could not allow the research to be perverted, not when they were so close, not after all those years. The only way she could influence the eventual outcome, protect the research, and monitor what the hell he was up to was from the inside, so she told Berger she was all in.

After their confrontation and her acquiescence to Berger, for the next six months, every day he seemed dedicated to making her life miserable. It was subtle at first, a cutting remark here or a mild rebuke there. As time went on, she also noticed a difference in her lab results. Earlier in the study, she had seen evidence of memory improvement in some of the mice, just not at a level that reflected what Berger was reporting to the outside world. Now her results seemed to be completely random, with no noticeable benefit from any of the compounds she was testing. She came to the conclusion that Berger was further trying to isolate her, designing and assigning protocols for her that likely utilized a placebo compound 100 percent of the time, rendering her efforts and results meaningless in the big picture.

For the most part, Susan kept her discontent to herself, but as the months wore on, her frustration grew to an intolerable level. She had to confide in someone to blow off some steam and perhaps get a second opinion on what she should do. Each day at PKC Group had increasingly become an unbearable waste of time; she was alone, running useless protocols over and over again. Berger stonewalled any attempt to talk out the situation, typically reminding her that she was the one who'd declared she was all in and that the door was always there should she change her mind.

Susan wanted to confide in her fellow scientists and see what they really thought. She was superficially friendly with the two carryovers from MIT, but back then, they had been older male grad students, and she had intentionally kept their relationships professional, having no social interest in either of them. The new hires at PKC Group pretty much did their own thing. The structure of the workplace was designed to keep them all apart on a day-to-day basis.

Susan had a sense that most, if not all, of them were equally as excited about their own financial prospects as they were about finding a cure. That might not have been a fair assessment on her part, but she couldn't help but feel there was some truth to it.

Berger worked behind the scenes to keep her under wraps. When they had a staff meeting, Susan was afraid to be directly confrontational, realizing such an extreme approach would likely lead to her immediate dismissal, weakening her overall position and accomplishing nothing. She came to view such meetings as a chess match, one in which she was playing at a distinct disadvantage. Susan would attempt to ask nuanced questions designed to get the others to think about her issues without her specifically spelling them out. Berger would blunt her comments with a broad, dismissive reply and usually change the subject. If any of her fellow scientists picked up on the trial balloons she released, none seemed willing to pull the strings.

Over time, aided by Berger's subtle influence, the others came to see Susan as an outsider within the group, devalued her opinion, and quietly questioned her worth. The atmosphere at

PKC Group became toxic for her. She dreaded going to work in the morning. Sleepless nights were the norm. She became self-contained and withdrawn as she contemplated her next move.

Susan's only respite, an oasis of warmth and camaraderie, was her weekly book club meeting. The genesis for the book club had originated with her oldest and best friend, her old classmate at MIT, Elizabeth McFarland. Susan had come up with the original idea shortly after graduation. Once the crushing schedule of undergraduate academic life was behind them, Susan had thought it would be a great way for her and Liz to stay connected. They would alternate in picking a book for both to read and then meet over coffee or wine each week to discuss the topic du jour. Liz had been all for it. The only rule was that the books could not be directly related to their professional lives in any way. Everything else was fair game, the more interesting or controversial the better.

In hindsight, Susan realized the book club really had morphed out of the MIT study sessions she and Liz once had shared. When those sessions were no longer necessary, the club had been a natural progression. She and Elizabeth enjoyed each other's company and cherished the opportunity to maintain their friendship. The two of them had spent many entertaining hours together, debating, parsing, and pontificating on a wide variety of topics.

Eventually, there had been fewer meetings over coffee and more evenings over a glass of wine. As they'd gone about their separate professional lives, they had come to appreciate the weekly get-together. When Elizabeth had suggested they expand the group, inviting her friend Angela Mancini to join, Susan had agreed. Angela and Liz were also friends from MIT, but Angela had traveled in a different circle from Susan, and they had been only marginally acquainted. Nonetheless, the prospect of new blood had been exciting. Angela had a great analytical mind, and postgraduation, she had settled in as an independent code writer, contracting out to various software companies.

Angela, in turn, had introduced Cicely Blackwood, an English PhD candidate at Harvard she'd met some time ago through a networking event at the National Association of Professional Women. When Cicely had referred her friend Ellen Klein, a teacher at Dorchester High School, whom she knew through volunteer mentoring for disadvantaged kids, the group had been finalized, or almost finalized.

Five members felt like an ideal number—a small enough group to remain intimate and manageable. They'd voted and agreed to cap membership at five, but when Cicely had been offered an assistant professorship in Ireland, they temporarily had expanded to six women, pending Cicely's departure. The swing member was Gussie Watkins, Cicely's Harvard friend and the woman who would be taking over her apartment.

The way things had been going lately at PKC Group, Susan often felt the book club gatherings were her only anchor to reality and sanity. All the women meshed well; the intertwining connections that had brought them together had served as a good screening mechanism to ensure compatibility. Susan liked all of them, but at that point, there was only one person in the world she felt comfortable enough with to open up about her travails at PKC Group: Elizabeth McFarland.

As close as she and Elizabeth were, thus far, she had kept her suspicions about Berger to herself. Liz was loyal and trustworthy, but the possibility of data manipulation was a huge deal, a life-changing event for all involved. She didn't want to burden Elizabeth with it, and more so, instinctively, she felt as if PKC Group's dirty laundry should be kept in-house.

Now she was close to the breaking point. Depression was

starting to overwhelm her, gnawing constantly at her psyche, less willing to relinquish its black grip with each passing day. The burden was taking a physical toll. It was hard to laugh or even smile. There was no escape or solution. Susan was at the fulcrum of an ethical and practical dilemma, feeling as lost as she'd ever been, even worse than when her grandmother had slipped into dementia and eventually passed away. Each day she sank deeper into the depths, barely able to disguise her desperation from those around her.

Susan reached for her cell phone and impulsively hit Elizabeth's number on speed dial. It was time to give in. She had to share the weight with someone else, risks be damned.

Elizabeth's phone went to voice mail, and Susan left a message: "Liz, it's Susan. Can we meet somewhere tonight after work? It's important. I have to talk to you. Thanks, girlfriend. Call me back."

Later that evening, Susan sat alone at a corner table at Courtside, a cozy neighborhood bar in East Cambridge. She was early. Liz had been in meetings all afternoon but texted her back to set up the time and place. Susan repeatedly turned over in her mind what she should say to Liz, including how much to divulge and where to start.

Liz came through the front entrance, paused as her eyes adjusted to the dim lighting, and then spotted Susan in the back and moved to join her. "You okay?" Liz asked with a look of concern on her face as she pulled up a chair.

"No, no, I'm sorry, Liz. I'm not okay. I haven't been okay for a long time. I can't hold it in anymore. I have to talk to someone. You're elected. I'm sorry, but you're the only one."

"Stop saying you're sorry," Liz said, reaching across the table with both hands to reassure her friend. "This is me you're talking to. What is it, girl? What's wrong?"

"I'm lost." Susan started to cry, gently at first and then with escalating deep, purging sobs. She sucked in deep breaths and let them out again in successive staccato bursts rather than crying out. All Liz could do was continue to hold her friend's hand and wait. After a few minutes, Susan gathered herself and made eye contact. "I'm in trouble at work."

"You?" Liz replied incredulously. "How could you be in trouble? That's been your dream ever since I've known you, to work on a cure for Alzheimer's. You took it from the classroom to the real thing. I don't understand. What's wrong?"

"There's something wrong with the whole thing. I'm not even sure the results we had back at MIT were legit, and I'm certain the results we're putting out now are not real."

Once again, Liz looked shocked. "Not real? How could that be? I still don't understand. What's not real about them? I thought you had a breakthrough compound that was working with mice and that the next step in the real world was to take it to humans. Are you telling me it's all fake? How could that be? I know you would never be a part of anything like that. What's going on?"

Susan looked at her friend imploringly, looking for something. Forgiveness? Understanding? Sympathy? "No, no, it wasn't all fake."

"Then I'm really confused. What is it? Tell me."

"Some of it was fake, Liz. I know it now. I didn't know it then. We did have some good results. We had a compound that worked. It still does but not the way it's been represented."

"Represented? What do you mean? Represented by whom?"

"Berger," Susan said flatly, staring at her friend.

"Berger? Holy shit! How? What did he do?"

"I didn't know about it at the time, but I think he altered the data back at MIT to make things look better than they really were. Hell, I was just a sophomore, Liz. I'd never worked on any kind of major project like that before. He was the professor. He was like a god in some ways. It never even occurred to me that something like this was possible—that he would even consider such a thing. He was what I wanted to become. He held the key to my own success. It was an honor and a privilege to be selected to work with him. I never questioned anything. I had no background in how it should be set up, how it was documented and stored, how the flow of information was controlled, or any of that. I just did what I was told. I was thrilled to be a part of it."

"I always thought you and he had a thing," Liz said. "Did you?"

"No," Susan said dismissively, "but we were friendly. I trusted him. I looked up to him. I felt special because he let me into his inner circle."

"So what did he do?" Liz asked.

Susan lowered her voice and glanced around the bar to make sure no one was within earshot. "I think Berger fixed the data. Each of us ran separate trials. He's the one who put it all together. He's the only one who was in a position to change it. Now that I'm onto him all these years later, he's practically admitted it to me."

"Back up. Tell me exactly what happened."

"Bottom line, we had some promising results with a couple of variations of the compounds we were working with. It was very exciting—a breakthrough, really."

"Then what went wrong?"

"I didn't realize it then, but the grant money was running out. In hindsight, I think Berger was desperate. I think we had some good data, but it was very inconsistent, not enough to take it to the next level. There was something there, but it was only a hint, a possibility of a new direction. I know now that Berger inflated the positive results. I would never have considered that he could do that at the time, but that is exactly what he did."

Susan was on a roll now and was determined to tell Liz the whole truth—all of it. She continued. "I'm not sure what motivated him. It was probably a combination of things. I think he did believe we were onto something important, and he wanted to continue the work. I think there was also a financial factor and an ego factor. The temptation was too much for him. Maybe at first, he wanted success so much that he gave the data a little nudge here or there. I don't know how or exactly when he got started. He took the data from each of us separately and aggregated the results. He put it all together and constructed the narrative. We were all just thrilled that something good was coming from our work."

"Just asking," Liz said, interrupting, "but couldn't you all go back to that raw data now and find the truth?"

"It's more complicated than that. It was his grant money, his project. He took custody of all the raw data in the end. I'm sure if we could even get a hold of it, at this point, it's probably been changed to support his position. I have some journal notes, but they are a far cry from actual data and in and of themselves would mean nothing. Based on that data, he published several scholarly papers in various journals and went on the lecture circuit. Inevitably, he attracted a lot of attention and ultimately caught the attention of the angel investors. That brings us to where we are today with PKC Group."

"What happened?" Liz was wide-eyed at what she was hearing.

"We've been at war ever since. I questioned whether he did anything improper back at MIT, and he gave me a nondenial denial. I pretty much accused him of cooking the books at PKC Group, and again, he denied it but basically told me to mind my own business and leave his end of it alone. He didn't admit anything, but he gave me some garbage about how he now answers to the god of capitalism and asked if I wanted the research to continue or not. He gave me an ultimatum. He told me I had to be either 'all in or all out,'" Susan said, making quotation marks in the air with her fingers.

"Well, you're still there, so I assume you told him you were all in."

"Yes, I did. I had no choice."

"Why?"

"If I resigned, I would be back to square one. No one is going to give me grant money right now. I couldn't work on the same line of compounds; they are proprietary to PKC Group. I felt my only chance was to stay on the inside and maybe help get things back on track. I was wrong."

"How so?"

"Ever since I told him I was all in, he has done nothing but try to force me out. He's mocked me, isolated me, and worked at every turn to undermine my credibility with colleagues. He's changed the experimental protocols to render my work meaningless. He's crushing me—destroying me. If I blow the whistle, I'll be a pariah. What actual proof do I have? More importantly, if I succeed, I kill the research, the actual kernel of truth that has potential; shut that down indefinitely; and wall myself off from being able to work on it in any way."

A bunch of college kids drifted into the bar, all already in the bag. Susan paused, glanced over at the group, and wondered if she'd let life pass her by because of her obsession with finding a cure for Alzheimer's disease. For a moment, she felt sad and almost sorry for herself. She went on to sum up the situation for Liz and then went silent again, waiting for a response.

Liz shook her head and said, "You gotta get out of there, girl, before it's too late." Liz regarded her friend with sincere tenderness. "I believe in you, Susan. You are strong. We are strong. I'm with you, whatever you decide to do. You will get through this. I will get through it with you."

◆ ◆ ◆

Cambridge, Massachusetts: Fall 2015

The next morning, Susan was at her desk at eight o'clock, slightly hungover from an evening of commiserating with Liz but buoyed by the fact that she'd had an opportunity to let it all out and that the burden of truth was no longer hers alone. She realized there was nothing Liz could do to directly help solve her dilemma, but just having a confidante was liberating.

They had spent the better part of three hours brainstorming, considering different options and trying to game out each alternative to its logical outcome. They hadn't resolved anything, often repeating the same circular logic Susan had been practicing for months. If nothing else, Susan felt comfort that when the shit really hit the fan, there was another human being who could corroborate her story. It wasn't much, but it might be worth something.

Susan was making notes on a pad of paper, when an instant message appeared on her monitor screen: "Susan, are you there? I need to speak to you as soon as possible. Can you come to my office? Hans."

What the hell does he want now? Quelling her annoyance, she fired back a quick reply: "Yup."

Moments later, when she entered Berger's office, he was standing with his back to her, looking out the window at God knew what. Susan briefly wondered if he'd been standing like that since he messaged her, looking over his shoulder every few seconds to check for her arrival, wanting to maximize the dramatic effect upon her entrance. *How could I ever have been attracted to this guy?* she thought. *Even for a second just one time while caught up in the thrill of what then seemed to be a major scientific breakthrough.* All she felt now was revulsion. *What an asshole.*

True to form, Berger, although aware of her presence, continued to stare out the window as if she weren't there. Finally, he turned around with his hands folded churchlike in front of his body. "Susan," he said somberly, "I'm afraid I have some bad news."

"What might that be, Hans? Do you have some new series of meaningless experiments for me to run to keep me out of the way?"

"No, no, I'm afraid it's worse than that. There's no point in beating around the bush. Susan, I have to let you go—for cause."

"For cause?" she cried out. "What the hell are you talking about, Hans? I've run every useless protocol you've shoved down my throat since the day I asked you about the data. What more do you want? What are you talking about? For what cause?"

Berger slid around to the front of the desk and partially sat on the corner as Susan, incredulous, remained standing. The son of a bitch must have choreographed that moment all out, she thought, from the window to the folded choirboy hands to the corner of the desk and remorseful expression.

"Susan, I can't have you around here anymore. You're too much of a distraction."

"Distraction!" Susan exploded. "I barely have any interaction with anyone, thanks to you. You've locked me up and thrown away the key as far as the others are concerned. When we do have a staff meeting, you find a way to ridicule me or reprimand me."

"Exactly," Berger replied evenly, his voice purposefully calm, rehearsed. "You're not a team player. You don't have confidence in your colleagues. You don't have confidence in me. How can I tolerate that? It poisons the entire environment. Our work is too important, too urgent, and too sensitive to be jeopardized by a rogue team member."

"But you, Hans? What about you? You're the one who's a danger to the project. You're the one altering the data and building a house of cards that will come crashing down one day and take the research and everyone here down as well. It's you, Hans, not me."

"No, Susan. This is exactly what I'm talking about. I'm the one who's saving the research, giving it a chance to go on. You just don't see it. You can't contain your hostility toward me. Do you realize the personal risk I've taken on my shoulders? The responsibility I've assumed?"

"So you admit to changing the data?"

"I admit to no such thing, Susan, at least not to anyone outside this room."

They locked eyes on each other. Susan was so angry she could have killed him at that moment, while Berger remained infuriatingly calm and detached.

"Between us, yes, I may have made some adjustments here and there to put our best foot forward, but you and I both know we have something real here. We have the foundation for the next generation of worldwide research. The business types don't want to hear that it might take five more years to fully develop. They want results now—yesterday, if possible. I did the only thing I could do to produce both more time and more money. It's called backfilling, Susan, and I'm the only one in a position to do it, the only person in the entire world who may be able to spin enough plates on poles to actually pull it off—to actually save this project and guide us through to a cure. Then what will you say? What about that, Susan?"

"Hans, you are blind to the truth. Don't you see? You have

risked all of our careers without even asking us." Susan shifted in her seat, feeling weak, sad, strong, and outraged all at the same time. She struggled to keep her emotions in check. "You've sucked us all into a giant fraud. When it blows up, none of us will ever work in this field again. We don't deserve that."

"The truth, Susan? What are you saying? *Veritas vos liberabit*?" Berger sneered derisively. "The truth will set me free? I don't think so. At this point, the truth will finish me. No, Susan, my truth is that I'm all in, beyond the point of no return. We either find a major breakthrough, or I'm ruined. That's what I asked of you, Susan—to be all in."

"I can't do that, Hans. I can't knowingly be part of a lie, a fraud, a hoax you've perpetrated ever since we were at MIT."

"Yes, I understand. I know, and that is why we must part ways. You have to go, Susan."

"Are you sure you want to do that, Hans? You know what they say: 'Hold your friends close and your enemies closer.'"

"Are you threatening me, Susan?"

"Take it for what it's worth, Hans."

"Don't you think I've spent many hours thinking about this since the moment you came into my office and accused me of data manipulation? I'm not a fool. I'm an intelligent man and, in this case, a man who now has nothing to lose, so I've taken certain precautions."

"What kind of precautions?"

"I've gotten pretty good at nuancing the data. Your name, your efforts, and your suggestions are totally intertwined throughout all the changes that were made. Contemporaneous notes, altered reports, memos—I've assembled a customized evidence trail just for you that has you knee deep in anything improper that might have gone on around here. Your fingerprints, so to speak, are everywhere. Maybe they'll believe you, Susan. Maybe they won't. Is it the ranting of a disgruntled, unhinged employee or the heroic effort of a whistleblower? Either way, by the time they sort it out, you'll be approaching retirement age. I'm afraid I've built a pretty compelling case against you."

"You are a monster!" Susan said in a voice barely above a whisper.

"You have no choice, Susan, but I'll tell you what. I'll throw you a carrot." Berger turned, retrieved a prepared statement from his desk, and handed it to her. "Read this. If you sign this and resign for 'personal reasons,' I won't fire you for cause. You can save face and walk out the door with your head held high, and no one will be the wiser about the conflict between us. I'll even write you a recommendation if you want to go back to teaching at MIT or someplace else. A year of teaching, and you could even get back to research after the noncompete runs out. Refuse to sign it, and you'll be committing professional suicide. You will be finished. I will see to it, even if I am ruined myself. Your career will be DOA, the research will be in the toilet, and everyone here will be blown up, all thanks to you."

Susan regarded him contemptuously and took a moment to read the statement. She was more than ready to get the hell out after months of anguish at Berger's hand. She tried to do a quick analysis. Berger appeared to hold all the cards. She couldn't bear the thought of staying another day, especially now. He was right. If she fought him now, if she blew the whistle, she would likely collapse the whole thing, much of it on her own head.

On the other hand, she felt no moral obligation to Berger personally. To the contrary, she felt nothing but disgust and disdain for the man. She owed him nothing, certainly not personal honesty or loyalty. If she signed his statement, there was no moral issue in her mind with breaking the agreement at a later date if it served her purpose. If she didn't sign now, Berger was poised to attack on every front like a cornered animal.

She pulled a pen from the pocket of her lab coat, signed the paper, crumpled it up, threw it in Berger's face, and strode from the room.

◆ ◆ ◆

Cambridge Police Headquarters: Present Day

Everyone in the conference room stared at the speaker centered on the table, waiting for Susan to continue.

"You know who it is?" Dimase repeated excitedly. "Tell us, Susan. Who is this person? How do you know this thing?"

Dimase placed both hands palm down on the conference table, wondering what Susan would say next. He was certain that if anyone knew who the killer was, it was someone from the book club, and there were only two active members left. Time was of the essence.

Susan uttered a single word in reply: "Berger."

Elizabeth McFarland sat up sharply in her chair and exclaimed the name as well. "Berger? You think it's him?"

"It can only be him," Susan said, her voice sounding calm and detached over the long-distance connection. "It all makes sense now. I've been out of the loop over here in Switzerland. If I'd stayed in the States, I might have made the connection sooner. Remember, when I left to attend this conference, the only victim at that point was poor Gussie. It was tragic and devastating but random in my mind at the time. I didn't even know about Angela until you told me yesterday, and now Ellen. Obviously, someone's going after members of the book club, but none of us were in a position to put it all together until now."

"You really think it's him?" Elizabeth asked.

Susan paused and then said, "Yes. His latest message—*Veritas vos liberabit*—is meant specifically for me. He's mocking me, and he wants me to know he's coming. He used that exact phrase the day he fired me, only he turned it around and said something like 'The truth won't set me free; the truth will finish me.' He used the actual Latin phrase. Now he's speaking directly to me, saying, 'You thought the truth would set me free. Now let's see how you like it. Let's see if the truth will set you free, because I'm coming for you.'"

Dimase pursed his lips and blew out a long, slow stream of imaginary smoke. He had many questions and attempted to prioritize them in the moment. "Do you have any idea where this Berger person is now?"

"No, none at all, other than his being in and around Boston and New England, based on the location of the murders."

Dimase turned to Elizabeth. "And you, Elizabeth? When was the last time you saw this man?"

"I haven't seen him in years. I don't even know what he looks like now. The last time I saw him was on campus at MIT, when Susan and I were undergraduate students. I didn't even know him then—maybe I said a casual hello once or twice if I stopped by the lab to see Susan. Why would he want to kill me? Why would he want to kill all of us? Any of us?"

"Because of me, Liz." Susan's voice, suddenly emotional, emanated again from the speaker. "Everyone's dead because of me."

There was silence around the table. A few of the detectives scribbled notes on their pads. All eyes turned to Dimase. "Susan," he said, "you must take us back to the beginning. What happened between you and Berger? Why do you think he is coming for you? Why the other book club members?"

For the next forty-five minutes, Susan took them through all of it: her early excitement at being selected for the project at MIT, the origins of the book club, the potential compound breakthrough, the emergence of PKC Group as a commercial venture, and her suspicions and confrontation with Berger over data manipulation. When she was done with the general timeline and background, Dimase picked up the questioning once again.

"So after Berger forced you out at PKC Group two years ago, what became of them? Did they succeed? Did they get caught? Are they still in business? What became of Berger?"

◆ ◆ ◆

Cambridge, Massachusetts: Spring 2017

It took Susan a few months after her dismissal to reset. Free of the daily abuse at PKC Group, she felt her depression lift. Her departure from PKC Group had been abrupt but without incident, and her resignation had been portrayed as voluntary and for personal reasons.

Removed from the source, she didn't know what was currently happening within PKC Group, but she could only assume Berger was continuing his deception in order to parlay another much larger round of financing, perhaps even a sale of the entire enterprise.

Fortunately, Susan had applied and been accepted back as a teaching professor at MIT. It felt good to be back on campus and surrounded by bright, inquisitive young minds in all their wonder and innocence. Still, somewhere within, she was not at peace with herself. Whenever she was not occupied with her teaching obligations, the issue of Berger's corruption consumed her. She fantasized about different strategies to take him down but somehow preserve the viability of the core compound research.

It was a perplexing conundrum. Berger and the research were so intertwined that it was difficult to see any scenario whereby they could be separated without killing the project. Beyond that, there were the legal considerations. She was no longer bound by the noncompete now that a year had passed. More problematic was the confidentiality clause in her contract. There was no time limit on that. It always came down to a binary choice. She could opt for the traditional whistleblower approach and risk losing everything, including her own career and the research itself, or she could walk away.

It had been a good day as Susan returned to her apartment. There were a couple of kids in her class with real promise, and it gave her a sense of joy and deep satisfaction to mentor them. They had more or less self-selected themselves for her extra time and attention; they were always prepared, always inquisitive, and constantly came to her office whenever she was available for further discussion. Susan saw a little of herself in each of them and vowed she would never do to them what Berger had done to her.

She enjoyed their enthusiasm and appreciated their dedication. Finding a cure someday was still her number-one professional priority, but she was surprised and excited at how the act of teaching had renewed her. It was healthy to be able to look to the future with hope. In fact, as she thought about it analytically, she realized forward-looking hope and a purpose in life were probably the simple keys to mental health. Berger had taken that away from her, and now the kids were restoring it.

Her depression faded. She was able to look at her issues with Berger more objectively now that she was distanced from him. A satisfying solution still proved elusive, but her mind was able to contemplate the complexities without the despair that had plagued her while she worked at PKC Group. Sometimes consciously but perhaps more often subconsciously, she sorted through possibilities as if trying to solve an algebraic equation; her search for resolution was never too far beneath the surface.

Susan heated some leftover chicken and rice and plopped herself in the recliner to catch up on world news and see what the talking heads had to say. She was surfing channels, when a story caught her attention. It was a short retrospective updating viewers on the scandal swirling around Hollywood producer Harvey Weinstein. On-screen, Weinstein, unshaven and disheveled, was being escorted to a waiting vehicle. The voice-over recapped his arrest: "Five more women came forward this week to accuse famed Hollywood producer Harvey Weinstein of sexual assault. Once considered untouchable, the Hollywood mogul has been stripped of all interest in his production company, where representatives have said they will attempt to regroup and move on without him. In a stunning and rapid fall from grace, Weinstein has gone from the pinnacle of success to persona non grata."

Susan clicked off the TV. *That might be it. This could work.* She owed Berger nothing—not honesty, not moral equivalence, and certainly not compassion. He'd had her over a barrel, and he'd crushed her without remorse. He was amoral, ruthless, and dangerous. He needed to be taken out for the greater good. Could there have been an element of revenge in her thinking? So what if there was? He'd created a massive hoax and then falsified evidence to implicate her should she ever fight back.

It was the risk of losing the research that had held her back—that and the risk to her own career and those of the others at PKC Group, whom she presumed to be ignorant of Berger's actions. This idea could isolate Berger from all that. If she could take him down for reasons other than the fraudulent research, PKC

Group would still exist. They may or may not make it, but there was a chance they could fix it or sell the rights to the research to another group. Maybe she could even get back involved at some point. Every time she came back to the binary choice—blow the whistle or walk away—she defaulted to a wait-and-see position. There was no way to separate Berger and his corruption from the research and PKC Group. Now maybe there was.

Susan grabbed her laptop and started googling similar cases. There was a movement happening all across the country: newly empowered women were coming out of the shadows to seek justice from their abusers. Susan was well aware of the movement, but how she might use it hadn't clicked until that moment. Berger could be removed from PKC Group without the entire enterprise blowing up, and with a little luck, it might be done quickly and efficiently.

In case after case, previously untouchable men were being forced from powerful positions—in some cases, almost overnight. The momentum was so powerful and timely that targets were virtually defenseless. Company after company and board after board did not want to risk alienating half the population. At the mere perception of abuse or any credible accusation, boards were taking the path of least resistance, summarily forcing the accused perpetrator out. Bill O'Reilly, Roger Ailes, Matt Lauer—the list went on and on. There were hundreds of such cases. Many involved famous men, but most involved relative unknowns.

In that environment, companies were quick to cut their losses, wanting to move on as soon as possible and put any controversy behind them. Perception, not a court of law, ruled. If Susan could orchestrate what she had in mind, there would be no multiyear court battles, no discovery, no questioning the research, and no other careers involved. Berger could not counterattack her in regard to the research without compromising himself.

Undoubtedly, most of the men caught up in the maelstrom deserved what they got, but that was beside the point for Susan. She was looking for a mechanism, a tool, and this could be it. One thing she'd learned from Berger was that the best lies were always based on partial truth. She thought back to her sexual encounter with Berger in the lab office at MIT all those years ago. Though it had been consensual at the time, she certainly regretted it now—or maybe not. After all, stepping back from the immediacy of that moment, any objective person would have had to acknowledge that the power dynamics had been totally inappropriate.

He had been the authority figure; she had been the intern. He'd held her career in his hands and had the power to move her ahead or cast her aside. Indeed, he had promoted her career by taking her along to PKC. He'd been the professor and mentor, ten years her elder. She had been the innocent. It was similar to the Clinton and Lewinsky scandal. It might have worked for the former president then, but even he wouldn't have gotten away with it now. The world had changed.

◆ ◆ ◆

A few days later, Susan found herself once again back at the same rear table at Courtside, waiting for Liz. This time, she was intentionally early, working on her second glass of Santa Margarita pinot grigio in an attempt to screw up her courage. Unlike during their meeting eighteen months ago, when Susan had spilled her guts to Liz, her mood that day was upbeat, a mix of trepidation and excitement.

Susan had made a decision, and she needed to enlist Liz's support. She realized that despite her own moral clarity, what she was about to do was, on some level, both unethical and illegal, but she had weighed all the facts and was committed. In this case, the old adage "Two wrongs don't make a right" was outweighed by "The end justifies the means."

Berger deserved what was coming his way. The fact that Susan might have to bend a few rules to get there was mildly troubling, but she quickly dismissed that as being of no real consequence. Berger had done far more than bend rules; he had broken them, and he had made it personal.

Susan's greater concern was how deeply she should involve Liz. After considerable internal debate, she concluded that the best approach in order to protect Liz would be to mildly deceive her old friend as well. Again, she recalled the bromide of the best lies being based on a kernel of truth.

There was no need to inform Liz of the real truth about her sexual encounter with Berger. Such knowledge would have made Liz a willing accomplice in a complete fabrication, as justified as it might have been. She knew Liz would accept at face value whatever Susan told her. She also knew Liz would do anything to support her and do whatever she asked. Despite all that, it was more comfortable to ask Liz to bend the rules to support something she believed to be true. There was no need to go deeper than that.

Liz made her appearance, sliding into her seat, as Susan downed the remnants of her wine, clearing the deck for another round with Liz.

"Hey, girlfriend, trolling the neighborhood bars now?" Liz said, keeping it light.

"Yeah, I'm becoming a regular here." Susan laughed and raised her hand to signal the waitress.

They each ordered a glass of wine, and after some initial banter, Liz said, "You seem in good spirits. You doing okay?"

"I feel great," Susan replied. "Thanks for being there for me. It means everything to me. You're a lifesaver, honestly."

"Hey, that's what friends are for—you know that. I've got your back, baby girl, just like I know you'd have mine. Sisterhood."

They clinked glasses, and Susan smiled at her friend. "I've got something else to unload on you. Sorry it's been me doing all the unloading lately. It's not like before, though. It's a good thing. Actually, I feel great about it. I feel excited. Looking back, you know, I was feeling depressed. I'm past that now—way past it—thanks to you. I'm taking back control."

Liz beamed back at her friend. "What is it? What else do you need to get off your chest?"

"Something bad happened to me, Liz. Something bad I've been carrying around for a long time. But you need to understand: don't feel sorry for me. Feel happy. I feel happy. I really do because I'm taking ownership, and I'm going to do something about it."

Liz was puzzled but smiled encouragingly. "Well, enough of the suspense already. What is it?"

"You know how you keep hinting around that there was something sexual between me and Berger?"

"Yeah," Liz replied, all ears.

"Well, it's true. We did have a sexual encounter, only it wasn't consensual on my part."

"Holy shit," Liz said, drawing out the words slowly and with emphasis. "Why didn't you tell me?"

"I don't know. A lot of reasons. I was embarrassed. I didn't know how to react. I was still excited about the project. I didn't want word to get around and have people think less of me. I didn't want to get kicked off the team. Back then, I didn't want Berger to get kicked off the team. That would have killed the project for all of us. I mean, he had all the power; I was just an intern. Who was going to believe me? What good would have come of it?"

"I would have believed you," Liz said earnestly.

"I know you would have, Liz, but where would it have gone from there? I eventually got it under control. I think that's one of the reasons he hates me so much—because I shut him down."

"Tell me what happened," Liz said.

Susan pulled her chair forward closer to the table and spoke in low tones. "It started innocently enough. He would just flirt with me, especially when no one else was around. I mean, I probably flirted back a little, but I didn't mean anything by it. I just wanted him to like me. I wanted this powerful guy in my life to be my friend, my advocate—to be on my side for whatever lay ahead." She spun the story to make it sound as if Berger had forced himself on her, which was patently false, and Susan didn't care. As she'd said to herself over and over again, she owed it to the world to shed light on the falsehoods that Berger was shunting onto the scientific community.

Liz gasped but said nothing as Susan rushed to get it all out.

"I was so ashamed. From that moment on, working there was never the same again. The next day, he acted as if nothing had happened, but it felt as if this great distance had opened up between us, a detachment on his part that hadn't existed before. The banter and flirtation stopped. For a few weeks, it was all about work—nothing extra. Then, one day, we were alone in the lab again, and suddenly, he pulled me into his office and said all he could think about was having sex with me, and he exposed himself. That time, I managed to run out the door, and I just kept running. After that, he never showed any interest in me, not sexual interest anyway."

"Oh my God, Susan, I can't believe it. I mean, I do believe it, but I can't believe the guy was such a scumbag. How could you stay working there with this guy?"

Susan rehashed all the reasons she'd felt both trapped and compelled to remain silent at the time.

"I'm going to fight back," Susan said triumphantly. "I'm going to take Berger down, and I've figured out how to do it without having to confront him about data fraud or taking down PKC Group or the others along with him."

"How?" Liz asked.

"The only way to give PKC Group a chance to stay alive and maybe reinvent itself is to take Berger out for reasons that have nothing to do directly with the research or PKC Group itself. The cause of his removal must be something specific to him, with no ill reflection on the research. I think I have something—something so powerful and possibly so swift that it will blindside him and destroy him. And it will happen in a vacuum with no impact on anything else. That's why I'm excited, Liz."

"Okay, okay, girl. What in the hell are you talking about?"

"Have you watched the news the past few months, Liz? It was right in front of my nose, and I didn't see it. Now I do."

"What, Susan? What do you see? What is it?"

"All across the country, powerful, untouchable men are being taken down almost overnight and removed from businesses or positions of power, with their reputations ruined and their careers crushed. The men are gone, but the companies continue on, at least in most cases. They continue on without them, as if they never existed. That would be the perfect scenario for Berger. Think of it, Liz: Bill O'Reilly, Harvey Weinstein, Matt Lauer, and there's hundreds more. I've researched it. I'm going to take Berger out for sexual assault. It's the perfect scenario. The climate is ripe for it. The angel investors will run in the other direction. They'll move quickly to dump Berger if a credible claim is made in this environment. They're not going to run away from their investment. They're not going to run away from

PKC Group. They'll probably find someone else to run it, but Berger will be gone. I might even be able to get back involved in the research again at some point and help straighten things out."

Liz had to hand it to Susan; it was a brilliant, ballsy strategy. "Do you think you can mount a credible accusation?"

"Yes, if you help me."

"Me? How so?"

"Look, Liz, like I said, I've looked into a lot of these cases. They're mostly 'he said, she said.' The very nature of the situations are that no one else is usually around, just the abuser and the victim. Can I provide a viable case in a court of law? Probably not, but I don't have to. Can I mount a credible case in the court of public opinion, with the board of PKC Group, and in the MIT community? You bet your ass I can, and I will. Will you help me, Liz?"

"Yes, of course, I told you I'd always have your back, but how?"

"All I need is supporting evidence—enough to make my claim believable. It doesn't have to be proven beyond a shadow of a doubt; it just has to be possible and more believable than not for the PKC board. They are the judge. They are the jury. I just need you to support the fact that we had multiple conversations about this at the time it was happening. Like I said, there's almost never an eye witness. What I need is a corroborating witness. Someone who was around at the time and talked with me about it—my dilemma, the leverage he had over me, the assault, and unwanted advances. You might just have to sign a statement to that effect and maybe do an interview or two with an investigator or the PKC board. Would you do that for me, Liz?"

"Of course I'd do that for you. We did talk about it at the time," Liz said, already starting to convince herself. "You just didn't want to admit anything. We can change that part."

"We have to change that part," Susan said. "That's the only

thing we have to change. Everything I just told you, you have to pretend I told you back then. Are you okay with that?"

"Of course. What difference does it make if you told me then or you tell me now? It happened; that's the important thing. I'll back you up, Susan. You can count on me, baby girl."

"What about the others?" Susan asked. "Do you think they would back me up as well?"

"You know they would," Liz replied. "I'll cover it with them. You don't have to ask. They don't have to say they had direct knowledge of the actual rape. All they have to do is say they were aware that some sort of abuse was going on—that you talked about it a couple of times at our meetings. Not rape, just that you were harassed by your professor, who later became your boss."

"You think that would be okay?" Susan asked.

"Most definitely," Liz replied. "They will just be supporting cast. I'll do the heavy lifting. We'll just have them put out a statement of support and corroboration—you know, strength in numbers type of thing."

Susan smiled appreciatively. Berger was going down.

CHAPTER 14

Cambridge, Massachusetts: Present Day

Dimase sat at his desk as Joe Bucci was shown into his office. As Bucci was no longer a suspect, there was neither reason nor justification to hold him any longer. Dimase smiled without getting up and waved Bucci to a seat. "Your big day has finally arrived, my friend. You are going to be released."

"Thank you, Detective. I'm sorry for my crazy story; it was a stupid thing to do. I'm just glad to be getting out of here."

"That's fine, Joe. There's just one thing. That fifteen minutes of fame you were looking for—I'm afraid you have to wait, at least until this is all over." Dimase slid a document across the desk to Bucci. "This is a court order—a gag order. You are not to discuss anything regarding this case with anyone at any time. Is that clear? No media, no friends, no tenants at the building—no one. When the crime is solved, if you wish, you may tell your story then. Anything before then, and you will wind up right back here. Capisce?"

Bucci nodded vigorously in agreement. "Totally clear, Detective. You have my word. I don't want to be coming back here again ever. I'm sorry for any trouble I caused."

"That's all right, Joe. We enjoyed having you. I have one more task I must ask of you, and then someone will escort you downstairs, process you out, and give you a ride home if you want." Dimase pushed a manila file to Bucci's side of the desk. "Open this, please. There are several photographs of a man we believe may be involved. Think hard, Joseph. Have you ever seen this man before?"

The file contained several shots of Berger, including an old driver's license, an MIT ID card, and headshots lifted from reprints of scientific articles. Bucci studied them carefully, and sudden recognition flooded his face. "Yes. Yes, I do remember this guy. You think he's the one?" he asked excitedly. "You didn't show me his picture before, right? All those pictures you made me look at—he wasn't one of them, right?"

"That's correct, Joe. We didn't have his picture then. When did you see him?"

"He was dressed different, with longer hair, but it's definitely him. He came by the building one day maybe six months ago—maybe a little more. He said some friend or relative or someone told him a unit was going to turn over and asked if he could look at either that one or a similar one. I tried to turn him down, but he was on a tight schedule, leaving town or something, so I helped him out. I told him usually we have a Realtor do stuff like that, but he was asking a favor, and I didn't see any harm, so I showed him around. You think he did it?"

"Let's just say he's a person of interest. Did you ever see him any other time?"

"No, I don't think so, not that I remember. Who is he?"

"He's a former college professor. We are just trying to rule him out."

"Wow, that's crazy!" Bucci exclaimed. "Why don't you just bring him in for questioning?"

"We would if we could, but we don't know where he is at the moment. It's unlikely, but if you should ever run into him around the building or anything, contact us immediately, and mum's the word, Joseph."

Bucci stood, shook Dimase's hand, and rejoined the escort waiting for him in the hallway.

Dimase continued sitting at his desk, tapped a cigarette out of the pack in his suit coat pocket, and began subconsciously rotating it through his fingers. It was obvious now that Berger was their man. The fact that Bucci could place him at Gussie's apartment building prior to her murder was just one more piece of circumstantial evidence.

Unfortunately, knowing it was Berger and locating and arresting him were different things. The man had vanished from the face of the earth several months ago. He was gone without a trace, surfacing only long enough to commit brutal murders before disappearing once again.

Dimase had the task force digging into every aspect of Berger's life. They had a good picture of his upbringing, rise through academia, and transition from MIT to PKC Group. He had no siblings, his parents were deceased, and he had no lasting friendships. At MIT, he had been known by many but involved with few—an intellectual loner dedicated to his work. That pattern had continued at PKC Group—that was, right up until his fall from grace. And what a spectacular fall it had been.

Detectives from the task force had already completed preliminary interviews with all his coworkers at PKC Group, as well as the primary angel investors. They'd learned that PKC was still afloat despite Berger's dramatic departure but had scrapped all his protocols in an internal overhaul and restructured the research effort entirely. Berger's leaving had been a shock to his colleagues, but in hindsight, under a new scientific director, they now saw it as a blessing in disguise. As far as they were concerned, PKC still had the basis of a promising compound, but it turned out that the protocols designed by Berger had been flawed, ultimately deemed unacceptable, and discontinued without prejudice.

New leadership had made great strides to tighten up the science. The angels were convinced the best strategy to protect their original investment was to float another round of capital. With Berger's removal, they accepted the fact that the path to human trials and eventually a marketable drug would be much longer than originally thought, but the smart move was to keep going.

Berger, for his part, had fought vehemently against the accusation of sexual assault. The board had tried to keep the controversy quiet, but the victim, Susan Pearce, a longtime colleague of Berger at MIT and coworker at PKC Group, had proven to be persistent and thorough. She filed a formal legal complaint not only with the PKC board of directors but also with the board of overseers at MIT. She presented a compelling case: she'd been only a nineteen-year-old student at the time of the alleged abuse. Susan had a sterling reputation of her own, which helped her cause. Her age at the time, the imbalance of power in her relationship with Berger, and the fact that she'd been forced out of PKC Group after months of harassment for no specific, documented offense all played in her favor. She claimed she had been forced out because she continued to refuse Berger's sexual overtures.

Susan was credible and believable. A huge factor in the board's decision was that Susan also had sworn statements from multiple witnesses who corroborated her accusations through contemporaneous conversations at the time. At the time of the alleged rape and subsequent harassment, she'd had numerous spontaneous discussions with several people concerning how distraught she was over the abuse, how to handle it, and what to do next. Berger didn't help his position any when, at the eleventh hour, in a desperate attempt to save himself, he finally admitted to sexual contact, but he claimed it was consensual. Neither board was sympathetic. Susan had brilliantly placed Berger in a position in which he could not raise any issue regarding the tainted research for fear of further damaging himself. If he tried to raise the data manipulation as a motive for Susan to set him up, he would only be cutting his own throat. It was advantage Susan and then checkmate.

From start to finish, it was all over in a week. The board of overseers at MIT censured Berger and banned him from campus. The PKC board fired him for cause, citing violation of the morals clause in his contract and conduct that reflected poorly on the company. Berger denied any malfeasance but was not given a choice. To expedite the process, under threat of full prosecution, he agreed to a settlement. Berger's interest in PKC was bought out at a relatively modest sum, and any legal implications for the company were dropped in return for his signature on an exit document.

Within weeks, Berger was not only gone from PKC but gone completely. He was off the grid, nowhere to be found, and all but forgotten by his former colleagues and coworkers. He left his apartment with no forwarding address. He cashed out his bank accounts and retirement funds. There were no financial records, phone records, credit cards, vehicle records, or internet presence. His driver's license was still valid but irrelevant; his whereabouts were totally unknown.

In addition to the legwork being done by the detectives, Dimase had immediately put out a nationwide BOLO on Berger. Every law enforcement member in the land would be on the lookout for the psycho, and they'd pick him up for suspicion of murder if they could grab him. Dimase also had alerted Interpol, noting that Berger could show up in Zurich. He'd alerted the media as well, and the papers had run headshots and stories on Berger and his possible connection to three murders. Getting the picture out there would hopefully make it more difficult for Berger to operate without being seen, and putting him on notice that they were on to him might scare him into changing plans or force an error on his part. It was a calculated risk but one Dimase felt he had to take.

The other aspect to consider was the safety of Susan Pearce. With Liz McFarland safely stashed away in the protective custody suites at Cambridge Police headquarters, Dimase asked Susan to stay in Zurich for the time being, and she agreed. Arrangements were made to hire private security to watch over her at the Baur au Lac Hotel.

Dimase also coordinated with Homeland Security. If Berger were to make an attempt to get to Susan while she remained in Switzerland, the only practical means of getting there was to fly. He'd obviously have to use a fake ID. That would be difficult to do on an international flight in that day and age, particularly if TSA was on the alert. Putting nothing past Berger, hopefully they would be ready for him if he attempted to get on any plane headed from the USA to Europe.

Dimase stared at the photo of Berger in his hand. *How does someone go from being an esteemed professor at MIT to being an internationally wanted criminal, a butcher? Well, the shoe is on the other foot now. You wanted Susan to know you were coming for her. Now everything is in the open, and we will be coming for you. The hunter is about to become the hunted.*

◆ ◆ ◆

Somerville, Massachusetts: Present Day

Hans Berger stepped from the shower and sat on one of the two chairs he'd brought in from the kitchen, glad to be back at his new digs, the apartment near Davis Square in Somerville. Halfway through his master plan now, like any great strategist, he had to make some halftime adjustments.

Up to that point, neither the authorities nor the book club victims had had any idea whom they were dealing with. Now they did. It had taken them three murders to make the connection, but make it they had. He had known they would put it together sooner or later. It was pretty obvious if one was paying attention. He was a little surprised they hadn't figured it out after the second murder. Susan Peace's disappearing to Switzerland had been the main reason for that. If she had stuck around, she would have known as soon as Angela went down.

Berger had fully anticipated reaching this stage. He had lost the element of surprise partially but not completely. They now knew who he was, but that was it—big deal. They had no idea where he was or what he might do next. They didn't know he could still monitor Susan Pearce's emails and texts. His extensive network of hidden cameras was now obsolete, as the targets were either already dead or, in the case of Liz and Susan, holed up in different locations.

Surprise, he thought. *What a tactical advantage in a fight.* He would show them a surprise that would rock them to the core and shatter any confidence Susan might have been feeling that she was safe beyond his reach now that they knew who he was.

After days of inactivity, email and text traffic between Liz and Susan resumed at a brisk pace. Understandably, they talked only about their friends' murders and their own safety. Their three fellow book club members—coconspirators, in Berger's mind—were all gone, and Liz and Susan knew they were next in line.

It quickly became apparent from the content of their conversations that Liz was being held in a protective custody suite for her own safety at Cambridge Police headquarters, while Susan was being kept in Zurich with private security put in place as an extra layer of protection. Each of the women felt safe for now, but all they could talk about was where Berger might be and what he would do next. They openly speculated with each other about how long the ordeal could possibly go on and what the duration of their confinement would be. As secure as they felt in their current locations, it was clear they were already chafing at the restrictions. They were virtual prisoners for their own good.

Susan seemed to have it a little better than Liz, as she was an ocean away and had a two-man security detail assigned to be with her 24-7. She pretty much had the run of the hotel grounds and, accompanied by the security personnel, was allowed to make short, random trips into town.

Liz was confined mainly to her suite on the tenth floor of Cambridge Police headquarters. There were three suites in all, and she complained to Susan that the other two had been empty since her arrival. Liz was not allowed outside the building, and other than the occasional meeting with Dimase or some of his team, she spent her days in relative isolation. She appreciated the feeling of safety and security afforded by the arrangement and was in no hurry to leave until Berger was apprehended, but she admitted to a bad case of cabin fever. She passed her days watching TV, reading, and texting or emailing extensively with Susan.

Berger was pleased at the way the sequence of murders had played out and that the field was considerably narrowed. Susan and Liz were his primary targets now, but to satisfy his obsession with order and proper sequencing of his murder protocol, he had to kill Liz first.

He had a grudging admiration for Susan; she was a bright kid, and their relationship had certainly gone through an unforeseen transformation. She had gone from teacher's pet to lover to obstacle to nemesis. She had played her cards perfectly and exactly at the right time. He had never seen it coming, a two-pronged attack at both MIT and PKC Group. She'd lied about their sexual encounter, calling it rape. That bitch Liz McFarland had also lied and backed Susan up. He hadn't even gotten a chance to confront his accuser. It all had happened behind closed doors, with an emphasis on protecting his accuser and sparing her the trauma of having to see him in person.

The first time he'd heard anything about it had been when they called him into the office of the PKC CEO and informed of the complaint. Of course he'd denied it, but to no avail. He also had been told of the concurrent complaint filed at MIT. Under the circumstances, he'd been suspended immediately, pending the outcome of an investigation. Despite his protestations, he had been unceremoniously escorted from the building, never to return again. He still couldn't believe it, even now, and as he thought about it further, the rage boiled over. It would never leave him, not ever, but the best way to calm the beast was to feed it.

As the permanency of his exile had become evident, Berger's mind repeatedly had turned to one line of thinking: justice, revenge, and retribution. Susan was smug in her superiority and her success in taking him down; he would show her a brilliant plan, and she would suffer. Her callous, casual supporters would suffer also. They would suffer themselves, but even more importantly, their pain would enhance Susan's own misery. She would watch them fall one by one, knowing she was responsible and knowing he was coming for her. She would know terror. He would see to that. She would see what it felt like to lose everything one piece at a time until she suddenly realized she could never get it back.

She wants to match minds? Bring it on, he thought. He had nothing else to do. *Satisfy the monster. Feed the beast.*

Berger raised his legs, first one and then the other, onto one of the chairs and covered them in shaving cream from midthigh to each ankle. Carefully, methodically, and almost ritualistically, he shaved the hair from his legs. When satisfied, he crossed to the sink, lathered up his arms and chest, and repeated the process, staring at his own image in the mirror, mentally and emotionally getting into character. Lastly, he took scissors to his head and crotch, cutting down the ragged blond locks and curly pubic hair, and used the razor to shave himself bald.

When he was done, there wasn't a hair on his body. Still naked, he was surprised at the difference in appearance. He probably could have thrown on some clothes, walked right past police or former colleagues, and not drawn a second look, but he wasn't done yet.

He took a bag from his shopping spree earlier in the week, returned to the two chairs, and took a seat on one. He emptied the contents of the bag onto the second chair and sorted through them, selecting a package of women's panties. He slipped a pair over his feet and up to his waist. *Not bad*, he thought. *Cherry red.*

Next, he removed a set of sheer nylons, sensually rolled them up, and pulled them to the middle of his thighs. He removed a garter belt from the bottom of the bag, put it on, and attached the nylons. A push-up bra with inserts completed the foundation. He crossed to the bedroom and removed a short red-print dress from the closet. It fit his medium frame perfectly, and the long sleeves disguised the lightly rippled muscles in his arms. He slipped on a pair of matching high heels. His wiry runner's build, defined legs, and ropy muscles transformed well to women's clothing. The high heels made his calves pop but not too much. He had the makings of a sexy woman. Hopefully the final touches would do the trick.

He stood in front of the bathroom mirror and applied foundation all over his closely shaved face. He shaped, shaved, and plucked his eyebrows and applied false eyelashes, blue shadow, a layer of skin-toned makeup, and some blush. He applied two coats of red polish to his meticulously manicured fingernails and waited patiently for it to dry as he quietly meditated, realigning his mind and body for the task ahead. He pressed his lips together to smooth the matching red lipstick and used a Kleenex to touch up the corners of his mouth.

The final act was to remove an expensive medium-cut blond wig from its box. The professional piece fit perfectly on his shaved head. He pushed at the edges with a brush, regarding the finished product once again in the mirror. He looked great, not beautiful but not bad—perfect for his purposes. He looked like a midthirties blue-collar babe who was a little hard around the edges but street-smart and sexy in her own way.

He moved around the apartment, practicing a feminine strut and working on mannerisms. The biggest challenge was his voice. A little rasp would fit—perhaps she was a heavy smoker. He worked on softening his voice, gliding from room to room, catching glances of himself in the mirror as he went about his metamorphosis. The more he practiced, the better he came across. He willed himself to become a woman physically, mentally, and emotionally.

Finally, he was fully satisfied. He was ready for his afternoon appointment at Cambridge Police headquarters. It was an appointment the police knew nothing about, an appointment only Berger had put on the schedule, and he was looking forward to it with great anticipation.

CHAPTER 15

Somerville, Massachusetts: Present Day

Fully transformed into a woman in outward appearance, Berger grabbed a pocketbook from the counter and set out for the bus stop two blocks away. Inside the pocketbook were several items he'd spent some time accumulating, among them a couple of fake IDs for Rachel Boudreaux.

Berger had developed several identities for different contingencies, and he had taken great pains to make one of his options a woman, Rachel Boudreaux. The real Rachel was a dead prostitute from Manhattan. For his purposes, Berger had assumed her identity and moved her to Boston, where police would be less likely to be familiar with her.

Also in the pocketbook were various other feminine items: sunglasses, a pack of ultralight cigarettes, and a tiny black notebook Berger had carefully constructed to hold the names and dates of encounters with several local gangster types as well as a number of other fake johns. A woman like Rachel didn't have a driver's license or carry a credit card. He also had a burner phone he'd purchased some time ago, on which he'd listed fake contacts and phone numbers to match many of the client names in the black notebook. However things went, however deeply the police probed, he was prepared to be flexible and keep the charade going for as long as possible.

Berger exited the bus near the Middlesex Court Building and entered a small luncheonette nearby. Without stopping, he quickly entered a single-stall unisex bathroom in the rear. He checked his makeup in the mirror, pulled out and lit two cigarettes, and puffed vigorously on both of them, filling the small space with a cloud of smoke.

He took out some cheap perfume and sprinkled it generously on his neck. He hoped the stench of cigarette smoke mixed with a little too much perfume would enhance the illusion. He practiced his voice and mannerisms one last time. The voice was low and gravelly, not necessarily off for the character he was portraying.

His last touch was to remove a small plastic bag containing a freshly chopped onion mixed with black pepper. Taking great care to not overly mess his makeup, he rubbed small amounts of the mixture around the corners of his eyes and in the tips of his nostrils. His eyes began to water and turn red. He sneezed a couple of times, and his nose became a runny mess. Berger discarded the baggie in the trash, made one more mirror check, and headed out the door. A couple of nearby patrons cast dirty looks in his direction when a small cloud of smoke escaped along with him as he made his exit, but no one said anything.

He walked three blocks to Cambridge Police headquarters, talking to himself, willing himself deeper into character. He walked haltingly, as if conflicted, up the front steps of the headquarters, realizing he was probably on camera. He proceeded through security to the far side of the metal detector. One of the officers asked him the nature of his business.

"I want to turn myself in," Berger said, his voice low, his eyes wet with tears, and his makeup slightly smeared.

"Okay, ma'am, step over here, please," the officer said professionally but with a note of sympathy in his tone as he directed her to the side. "Tell me exactly, ma'am—what is going on?"

"I'm in danger," Berger replied in his best semihysterical voice. "They're gonna kill me. I need protection, and I have information. Please help me."

The officer suddenly seemed more interested in what Berger had to say. "Who's trying to kill you?"

"Them."

"Who?"

"I told you."

The officer looked frustrated. "Okay, I'm going to help you. You're safe here."

"Salvi Terrazinni," Berger blurted out, using the name of a well-known local hood, and he broke into soft sobs. "I saw him kill someone. Now I know he's going to kill me. I want to turn state's evidence. It's my only chance. He's expectin' me to come to his place this afternoon. I know how this works. If I show up there, I won't be leavin' again. He's a client. He's actin' like there's nothin' wrong, but I've seen this before with other people. He's not going to let an eye witness go on breathin', not unless it's part of his inner circle. I'm not. I'm just a hooker. He's not going to risk it. I'm a dead person if I stay on the street. If I don't show up, he'll just send some guys out to pick me up. Please help me."

"Okay, okay. Slow down. We're going to help you. I'm going to call Sergeant Coyne. He'll know what to do. He'll take you upstairs and get all the information. Don't worry. He'll take care of it."

"Thank you, thank you," Berger repeated, regaining his composure.

"You wait here for a moment," the officer said. "I'm just going to call him on that phone over there, and he'll be right down in a few minutes. Sit tight. It will be okay."

Berger leaned up against the wall while the officer crossed the lobby and picked up a red wall phone. After a few words, he returned to assure Berger that Detective Coyne would be right out to take her upstairs and process her statement. Berger thanked him repeatedly and remained against the wall as the officer returned to his post near the table beyond the metal detector. A tiny smile creased the corners of Berger's mouth. He was in.

Within minutes, Detective Coyne stepped off the elevator and greeted Berger, a.k.a. Rachel Boudreaux. Together they went up to the seventh floor, where Coyne secured coffee for both of them and invited Berger into a small conference room. "Okay, Ms. Boudreaux, suppose you tell me what's going on, and let's see what we can do about it."

Berger launched into a rehearsed story about how Rachel had been in a motel room in Revere with the gangster Salvi Terrazinni, when three other men had arrived, and Terrazinni had ordered her into the bathroom. One of the men had been first interrogated and then beaten to death. The entire fabrication was convincing. The detective bought it hook, line, and sinker.

"Why did you come here? Why not Revere Police or FBI?"

"I don't even know where the FBI is, and I ain't goin' nowhere near Revere. It was an impulse. I had a meeting with my probation officer at the courthouse, and you guys were nearby, so I came. There's no way he's gonna let me hang around long-term after what I seen."

"How well do you know Salvi Terrazinni?"

"Well, you know, just on a professional basis, so to speak, but everyone knows who he is. You don't mess with him. He's connected."

"Yes," Coyne replied. "We know him. A real scumbag—that's for sure."

"That's what I'm talkin' about," Berger said, starting to manufacture some emotion. "I might as well be a dead girl walkin' after what I seen. He ain't gonna let that stand. If you don't help me, I probably won't even make it through the weekend."

"Do you have any ID?" Coyne asked.

Berger fished in his pocketbook and produced the fake Social Security card and a voter registration ID he had purchased online. "I don't have a driver's license. Ain't no need 'cause I ain't never owned a car. I can get a birth certificate later if you need one; I just don't carry it around."

"These will do for now," Coyne said, examining the items and then returning them. "Ms. Boudreaux, I'm going to have to refer your situation to the FBI. We know they're building a federal case against him. I'm sure they'll be very interested in what you have to tell them. We'll talk to them. Cooperate, and I'm sure it will work out."

"Okay, if you say so. What choice do I have? When do I talk to them?"

Coyne glanced at his watch. "I don't know how fast we can set it up with the right people. It might not be until sometime tomorrow—in the morning, hopefully."

"Well, you can't put me back out there. I can't be walkin' around like a dead duck. I have to stay here. You get me a meeting with the FBI. That's fine, but I ain't goin' nowhere by myself, not until I'm safe and sound with some kinda deal. I'll stay right here in this conference room if I have to."

"Don't you worry, Ms. Boudreaux. We have temporary protective custody suites upstairs. I know a couple of them are open. I'll get a matron, and we'll set you up for the night. Tomorrow we'll get you connected with the FBI. Deal?"

"Deal," Berger replied.

Fifteen minutes later, Berger was in the elevator, accompanied by the matron, on his way to the protective custody suites on the tenth floor. The matron was a short, wide-bodied black woman in her midthirties. She wore a light blue uniform shirt with tight black pants and matching shoes. When she spoke, she seemed out of breath, as if talking were an effort for her. She pushed the button for the tenth floor and looked Berger up and down.

"You sure are one hot mess, honey, but don't you worry none. Whatever it is, you'll be okay here."

"Thank you," Berger mumbled.

The doors parted, and the matron said, "I'm gonna give you the tour and just a few guidelines. Okay, honey?"

"Of course," Berger said, stepping into the hallway to join her. There were secure doors to their left and right.

The matron pointed to the right. "That down there is a secure area. You can't get in there. It's for evidence storage, records, and such—nothin' you'd be interested in anyway." She turned to their left and held the ID card hanging from her neck against the code reader. The door clicked open, and they entered a long hallway. "These here are the suites. There's three of them. We have one other customer right now. She's nice; you'll like her. She's down at the end. You can take this one here." She opened the first door on the right.

The room looked like a luxury hotel suite. It had a bedroom, living room, and bathroom, along with a large closet. On the desk was a coffee machine, next to a half fridge and built-in drawers. There were writing materials on the desk, and on the shelf above was a neatly arranged collection of paperback books. The bedroom had two double beds, and the bathroom featured a double sink. Berger imagined they must have had couples or even families who needed protection from time to time.

He opened the fridge and noted it was stocked with soda, water, and a few candy bars. He walked to the window, took in the view toward the Charles River, and then turned, smiling, and thanked the matron.

"Come this way, honey," she said, motioning him back to the corridor. "This whole floor is secure. The windows don't open, not that anyone would be climbing in or out up here." She laughed. "This here is the empty suite, and this last one is our other houseguest. We use first names only up here. Her name is Liz. You'll probably see her soon enough. Down at the end here is the common area, so you won't feel so cooped up. There's an officer on duty here 24-7 whenever we have any occupants."

The duty officer, a middle-aged Hispanic woman with dark hair and a toothy smile, gave a slight wave, and Berger waved back. Her uniform was identical to that of Berger's tour guide.

"You can come here anytime you like if you want to get out of your room," his guide said. "You can't leave this floor without an escort, but you can come here and watch TV, read, or even play board games and such if our other guest is up for it. There's no talking about anything to do with why it is you're here, and like I said, it's first names only, but other than that, you guys can socialize if so inclined. Fair enough?"

"Fair enough," Berger rasped quietly.

"If you have a problem of any sort, you can talk to the duty officer. There are no kitchen facilities up here; your meals will be delivered from the cafeteria. If you are hungry or need something else, just use the phone on the desk in your room. There's a menu there as well. That's pretty much it. Any questions?"

Berger shook his head.

"All right then. I'll be leavin' now. Officer Fernandez here can answer any other questions, and don't you worry, honey; you'll be safe up here. That's what we're here for."

The matron gave Berger a reassuring smile, which he reciprocated appreciatively. He walked with her back down the corridor to his room and watched as she again waved her ID card in front of the door to the elevator reception area and left.

There was no sign of Elizabeth McFarland. Berger assumed she was either in her room or perhaps in a meeting with detectives in some other part of the building. No matter—she would surface sooner or later. His mind raced, running through different options. His plan to gain access to the tenth floor had worked beautifully, but he really hadn't had a clear idea in advance of how he would complete the mission once there. He'd had no idea what the setup would look like, and now that he did, he had to improvise the rest of the way.

He walked back down to the common area, where Officer Fernandez sat at a table, reading a book. She looked up as he reentered the room. "Quite a fancy place," Berger said in his soft, low tone. "Much nicer than I was expectin'. I was wonderin', though. Anytime I'm in a hotel high up, I'm always afraid of the same thing. What do we do if there's a fire?"

"Don't worry," Fernandez replied. "We would get you out."

"How?" Berger asked.

"It depends on the nature and severity of the emergency. We might just go back down the elevator the way you came in. That's probably the most likely thing."

"What if we can't do that? I'm always anxious about that type of thing."

Fernandez smiled again. "This is a government building, sweetie; we've got procedures and backup procedures and then more procedures. Don't you worry. You see that door right there?" She pointed behind her. "That's plan B. We go out there and down the concrete stairwell. Highly fireproof."

Berger walked over as if trying to assuage his anxiety and tried the door. "But it's locked," he said, turning back toward Fernandez. "How do we get out if it's locked?"

Fernandez held up the pass key hanging from the lanyard around her neck. "No worries. I've got it right here."

"But what happens if something happens to you? We'd be trapped."

"Nothing's going to happen to me or whoever's on duty at the time. We'd be right here with you guys. What do you think? I'm going to keel over with a heart attack or something? You worry too much, sweetie. That's not going to happen."

"You'd worry too if you seen the shit I seen. Crazy shit happens."

"All right, all right, so if something happens to me, which it won't, they've got us on security cameras. They'd send someone up from the outside to get us out."

"That's good," Berger said. "Does that mean they're watchin' me in my room too, like if I'm gettin' dressed and stuff or takin' a shower?"

"No, you're not a prisoner. You're here for your own protection. The security cameras are in the hallway and common area, not to spy on you. You have privacy in your room."

"So that's it?" Berger said, continuing to act like someone afflicted with extreme anxiety.

"Sweetie," Fernandez said, "you are wound up way too tight about this. You're totally safe. I promise you."

"I know, I know. I'm sorry. I just can't help it. I'm petrified of heights. I'm scared to death in tall buildings."

"All right, sweetie, we've got to put this conversation to bed. You need to relax. I told you we're all safe. If it helps to put your mind at ease, there is a plan C to go up, so we have options. We can go up or down. Okay?"

"Go up?" Berger asked.

"You see that closet over there?" Fernandez said, gesturing toward a corner of the room. "This is the top floor. In the closet, there's a ladder to a roof hatch. If a fire alarm goes off, it automatically unlocks the hatch, and if we can't go down, then we just climb up to the roof. Simple as that. Lots of options. You feel better now?"

"Yes, I suppose," Berger said hesitantly, "but how do we get off the roof if the buildin' is burnin' up?"

"Sweetie, if we finish this fairy tale and I get you safely to the ground, can we be done with this conversation?" Fernandez was getting exasperated.

"Yes, I promise. I just want to know that we can get out whether we got to go down or we got to go up."

"You ever hear of the stocking of life?" Fernandez asked.

Berger looked puzzled for Fernandez's benefit, but in reality, he had read about the device as an escape mechanism from rooftops.

"The stocking of life is like a big, huge women's nylon—big enough for you to get inside. Most likely, if there were people on the roof, they would just pick them up with a helicopter. If for some reason they can't do that, then you fire the stocking of life, like setting off a cannon, and the stocking, like a long tube, shoots out to the ground, and you get in and slide down."

"Wow, ain't that somethin'," Berger replied, signaling his satisfaction. "What will they think of next?" He wondered if

Fernandez was simply making up the story about the stocking of life to shut him up or if it really existed on that particular roof. If push came to shove, he might find out.

◆ ◆ ◆

Dimase was at his desk when Coyne raced into his office.

"Chief, we may have another problem."

"What might that be?" Dimase replied.

"There may be another woman on Berger's list. Someone we haven't thought about protecting."

Dimase was alarmed. "Who? How?"

"Cicely Blackwood," Coyne fairly shouted. "The professor in Ireland!" Coyne sat down, leaned back in his chair, and told Dimase he'd found a second version of the statement the four ladies had signed that corroborated Susan's assertion that Berger had raped her. The newly discovered statement had five signatures, with Cicely Blackwood's added at the bottom.

"I was wondering about Cicely myself," Dimase said, clasping his hands in front of him. "But I dismissed her as a possible target because she was long gone before any of this happened. Why do you suppose her name was on this second statement?"

"Dunno. But it is," Coyne said.

"The real question is whether or not Berger saw the second document, and if so, is Cicely Blackwood on his list? Let's talk to her and see what she knows, but my guess is she'll be as surprised as we are. We'll let her know what's been happening. Warn her to keep her eyes open for anything suspicious," Dimase said, thinking that the odds of Cicely Blackwood being in danger were probably low. "Berger can't be everywhere at once. He can't be here and in Ireland and in Switzerland. We at least have that going for us. Three possible targets spread out across the globe."

"Right, Chief. Put yourself in Berger's shoes, if he even knows where they all are. Come to think of it, how would he know where they are? We have Elizabeth locked up tight in here. He doesn't know that. How would he know Susan's in Switzerland? He probably doesn't know that either. From his standpoint, they just disappeared, and he has no idea where to find them."

"When you look at it that way, Cicely Blackwood might be the only one he does have a location on," Dimase said. "That is, if she's on the list at all. If that is the case, he has two choices: he either lays low here in the States, waiting for Liz and Susan to surface, or he somehow finds a roundabout way to get himself to Ireland and go after Professor Blackwood."

"That seems like a long shot to me, Chief. First, we don't know for sure that she's a target, and even if she is, the logistics are overwhelming. I think it makes more sense for him to wait it out over here for his shot at Elizabeth or Susan."

Dimase stood up from his desk. "Let's go upstairs and see what Ms. McFarland knows about this."

Dimase left his office with Coyne in tow. They went to the elevator and took it up to the tenth floor. Dimase held his ID against the code reader, and they walked down the corridor, past the suites, to the common area, where they found Liz McFarland playing checkers with the new arrival Coyne had told Dimase about earlier. Officer Fernandez sat at her duty table and acknowledged the detectives.

"Officer Fernandez," Dimase said, nodding in her direction.

"Detective," she said.

Dimase approached the table and looked down at the woman who'd been processed into protective custody earlier in the day. He thought she looked pretty rough around the edges, but life on the streets was hard, especially for hookers. He nodded and introduced himself.

"Nice to meet you too, Detective," Berger said.

"Everyone getting along well?" Coyne asked.

Berger smiled and nodded.

"It's nice to have company," Elizabeth replied. "It makes the time go faster."

"That's good. Elizabeth, I wonder if we might have a word with you in your suite. There's been a new development, and I'd like to get your take on it."

"Of course." Elizabeth looked alarmed. "Do I have anything new to worry about?"

"No. Come." Dimase motioned with his hand. Elizabeth excused herself and followed the men into her suite. Dimase closed the door, and they all took a seat in the living room.

"Elizabeth, when is the last time you heard from Cicely Blackwood?" Dimase asked.

"Oh my God, is she all right?" Elizabeth cried out.

"Yes, yes, she is fine as far as we know. She was not a signer of the statement of support you showed us from your phone. You and I have never talked about her as a potential target. Do you feel she could be a target?"

"No. I mean, she wasn't a part of it, and to answer your question, I haven't really heard from her since she left the club and moved to Ireland. Well, except, of course, when Gussie died. I sent Cicely an email of condolence. I know they were close. She sent me back a short thank-you. That was it. We were friendly when she was in the club. I knew her from MIT, but we drifted apart when she moved. I mean, you know, it had been a couple of years. We just didn't keep up on a daily or weekly basis, and then our contact just fell off from there. We both had our own lives. Why are you asking me this?"

"Did you know there was a second statement of support, the official version on file at both PKC and MIT—a version Cicely Blackwood signed?"

"No, I had no idea. How did that happen?"

"We're not sure," Dimase said. "We were hoping you could tell us."

"I don't know. I mean, I guess the only way would be if someone sent it to her, and she added her name and passed it on to the boards."

"Who do you think might have sent it to her?"

"It had to be Gussie. She's the only one, I think. They were close, as I've said. They definitely kept in touch. It had to be her."

"So the question is," Dimase said, pondering out loud, "which version is Berger working with—your list or the list on file at the two boards?"

"I don't know," Elizabeth said, "but if I had to guess, I'd say it's the statement Cicely signed, if that's the one on record. The one on my phone is the one we sent to the boards. If another version exists, it had to have been sent to them directly, probably by Cicely herself. Can't they tell you where it came from?"

"Yes," Dimase replied. "I'm sure they can, and we will confirm that right away. I just wanted to see what you could tell us. I think we have to assume that Berger was shown the statement with all five signatures, the one including Cicely Blackwood."

"If that's true," Elizabeth said, "that means she could be a target also."

"That's what we think," Dimase said. "We will take steps right away to bring her up to speed and let her know what's going on. Precautions will have to be taken."

"What do you think Berger will do next?" Elizabeth asked.

"I wish we knew," Dimase said. "I wish we knew."

CHAPTER 16

Cambridge Police Headquarters, Tenth Floor

Berger was sitting in the common area, reading a magazine, when Elizabeth returned.

"Hey, Rachel," Elizabeth said. "Sorry about the interruption."

"No problem," Berger said.

"You wanna take up the game where we left off?" Elizabeth asked.

"Maybe a little later," Berger replied, glancing at the wall clock. "I thank you for the company and all. It's been a really bad day—you know, stressful and all that. I just suddenly feel wiped out, like a truck run right over me. You know what I mean?"

"Of course," Elizabeth replied politely. "Maybe later then or in the morning?"

"That might be best. I think I'll take a little nap and maybe order some food. I'll poke my head out later an' see if you're around."

"That's fine. I'll probably be out here if it's not too late."

Berger rose, nodded to Fernandez, and said to both of them, "See you all soon." A makeshift plan was starting to form in his head. At first, it seemed like a long shot, but the more he thought about it, the more he felt there was no reason it shouldn't work. It was bold, but Berger could see the steps clearly. *One, two, three. A + B = C. It will be a matter of focus, full commitment, timing, and execution.* He smiled momentarily at the irony of his word choice. *Yes, a matter of execution—literally.*

In his mind, he pictured what was soon to happen as a sophisticated dance routine, like the fight scene in *West Side Story* or something similar. Once he started the action, the choreography had to be perfect, with the sequence exactly on time and as he envisioned it. He didn't have the benefit of countless rehearsals; to the contrary, he had just improvised the plan in the last five minutes and would have to get it right the first time.

Berger opened the door to his suite and sat on the edge of the bed. To compensate for his lack of rehearsals, he visualized every detail of what he would do, step by step, over and over again, playing it out to the finish. He realized he had to act soon, but he had to exercise patience.

In the morning, they would transport him to a different location, most likely the local FBI office in the Saltonstall Building, near Government Center in Boston. He had to pull the trigger before then. There was no assurance they would return him to Cambridge Police headquarters. In a situation like that, he imagined, the feds would probably take custody.

More problematic was the fact that with each passing hour, the illusion of his disguise would start to fall apart. He had a little makeup in his purse, but he hadn't dared to try to get a razor through the metal detector in the lobby. From the beginning, his goal had been to get to the protective-custody suites for a few hours, take care of Elizabeth McFarland, and freelance his escape.

In the morning, stubble would begin to appear on his face. As the day wore on, his appearance would start to look bizarre. The window of opportunity was the next several hours. He had to be gone by dawn.

As anxious as he was to get started and then get out, the situation called for discipline. The best time to strike would be in the wee hours of the morning, around two o'clock, he thought. He guessed there would be fewer overall staff on duty in the building, and reaction time might be a bit slower. His target would be sleepy and in a state of disorientation. Officer Fernandez would luck out because she would be off duty by then. The first order of business would be to get her unfortunate replacement out of the way.

Fernandez had told him the security cameras only covered the hallway and common area, not the individual suites. That was good. He would require privacy to set things up. She also had told him that if the fire alarm went off, it automatically unlocked a roof hatch in the closet in the common area.

When Berger first had come up with the idea of infiltrating the security suites, he'd figured his most likely escape route would be down. He wasn't sure how he'd do it, but he thought of taking a hostage, although the odds of that ending well were not high. If all else failed, he figured an all-out dash down a stairwell or fire escape in the middle of the night might have a chance. He didn't know for sure. He hoped the element of surprise and creation of as much confusion as possible would present an opportunity at the time. If not, so be it—he would get his target whether he could get out or not.

He had always been prepared for the possibility of capture. It was not his ideal plan, but he was prepared to pay the price, and if he managed to take out the entire book club except for Susan, that would be spectacular payback. She would feel the weight of responsibility for the rest of her life, and who knew? If he was lucky and still inclined, maybe he would get his chance in the distant future.

Of course, there was the woman in Ireland. She had signed the statement as well, but given the logistics, she was always on the back burner. She had not been around for a couple of years. It wasn't possible to construct the same level of surveillance and preparation in her case. She might have drawn the lucky card by being so far away. It was a bit of a compromise on his part, but Berger had determined early in the game that he would be satisfied if he could take out all the current members of the book club, ending with a face-to-face with Susan Pearce. Now only Elizabeth McFarland stood in the way of that moment.

Berger used the desk phone to order a meal. Veal parm, green beans, and mashed potatoes—not something he normally would have eaten, but it was one of the few items on the menu that would require a knife of some sort. He wanted the calories for energy, but more than that, he wanted the utensils. Even though he was in a secure facility, he was a guest, not a prisoner, so he was hoping for a real knife and fork, not a spork.

There was a knock, and Berger opened the door to find a service worker with a covered tray. Berger indicated for her to put the meal on the desk and stepped into the hallway to get a peek at the common area. Officer Fernandez had been replaced by another duty officer, who looked to be middle-aged, white, and of a normal build, with a butch haircut. Elizabeth was nowhere to be seen. He returned to the room as the service worker exited, and he was pleased to note that the utensils were indeed metal—a good sign. Things were breaking his way.

Berger took his time, chewing slowly, running the

choreography through his head, rehearsing in his brain. When he was done eating, he unplugged the coffee maker and used the knife to remove two screws and pry off the plastic backing. Inside, he found a heating coil made of copper wire. The tight coil was wrapped into a narrow, grooved metal tube through which water passed as it was superheated before it dripped through the coffee filter.

Berger chipped away at the plastic and used the fork to pull at the wiring until at last it was freestanding within the shell of the machine but still connected. He plugged the cord back into the outlet and observed as the coil heated up and slowly turned bright red. He unplugged the cord and waited for the coil to cool down. Once it was cool to the touch, he tore out several of the thin, fine paper pages from a paperback book on the shelf. He took the cigarette lighter from his pocketbook, removed the cap of the lighter fluid compartment, and carefully soaked the corners of several of the pages. To add an element of sturdier fuel, he crumpled up several pieces of writing paper from the desk and intertwined them with the thinner paperback pages. He placed the papers delicately around the exposed coil, taking care not to pack them too densely, leaving room for oxygen to feed the flames.

He repositioned the plastic backing on the back of the machine and reinserted the bottom screw but not the top, leaving a small gap for ventilation. Everything was ready to go. The first objective, when the time was right, was to get the night duty officer into his room and away from the security cameras. Taking her out in the privacy of his room would buy precious extra time. The coffeepot should do the trick.

The next step was to get Liz out of her room. The fire alarm should accomplish that. By then, there would be no further need for secrecy. Help would be on the way. It wouldn't matter. Berger was unsure of security response time to the fire alarm, but he couldn't imagine it would be under seventy-five seconds from the time of the alarm, and by then, he would be gone.

◆ ◆ ◆

The alarm on the clock radio went off at precisely 2:00 a.m., but Berger was already awake and alert. Anticipation had kept him from sleeping; nonetheless, he felt rested and primed. Meditation and focus had taken the place of sleep. The hardest part had been forcing himself to wait until two o'clock. He'd once read an article on hostage rescue suggesting the wee hours were the best time to attack due to a natural dip in the human biorhythm cycle at that time of day. He hoped the article was accurate.

On the wall beyond the half fridge and built-in drawers was a full-length mirror. He had been thinking about what message to leave at the scene and considered using lipstick on the mirror. Unlike with the previous three murders, when he'd had all the time in the world to stage his dramatic theatrics, this time, he was on the clock. He didn't want to disappoint, but he could work only with whatever he'd been able to bring in the pocketbook and whatever resources he could find in the room.

Worse yet, once smoke started filling the room, he had maybe thirty to forty-five seconds before the fire alarm went off and maybe seventy-five seconds from the time it started to kill two people and make his escape.

He weighed the pros and cons of using the lipstick on the mirror to scrawl his taunt. The size and location of the mirror made it the most impactful location, large and noticeable. Bright red lipstick would make the message pop. His main concern was that it might be too noticeable if the duty officer wasn't preoccupied enough with the smoking coffeepot when he lured her into the room. He didn't want to let the cat out of the bag before he got the drop on her.

He couldn't afford the time to write the message after he set things in motion. He toyed with the idea of using the bathroom mirror instead, but just as quickly, he rejected that thought; it just didn't feel right. It was too far removed from the action. He wanted to invoke a maximum "Holy shit!" factor the moment responders and, later, investigators entered the suite.

Berger noticed a white bathrobe hanging in the closet and got an idea. To deal with the duty officer, he needed to get her in the room, distract her momentarily, and take her by surprise—to create maximum confusion just for an instant.

He pulled out the built-in drawers one at a time as far as they would go. There were six of them. They were not designed to be fully removed, but when they were extended, he could easily apply enough leverage to force them out. Temporarily, he threw the drawers onto the bed nearest the mirror. Using red lipstick, he went to work putting his message on the mirror. He smiled, thinking about what a surprise it would be when Dimase Augustin learned that Berger knew who he was and knew he was the lead investigator on the case. Berger had picked that tidbit up in a couple of email exchanges between Liz and Susan—the same way he'd discovered that Liz was being held under protective custody in Cambridge. After that, it had been easy enough to research online all he wanted to know about Augustin.

Berger was euphoric as he applied lipstick lettering to the full length of the mirror: "Dimase, don't step on Superman's cape. Truth, justice, and the American way."

It was the most fun setup yet. What the scene might have lacked in theatrical staging it would more than make up for with emotional punch. He wished he could see the look on Dimase Augustin's face when he realized Berger not only knew who he was but also had walked right into the heart of Dimase's own headquarters, seen him personally, and taken what he wanted while Dimase and his minions were powerless to stop him. They were impotent. They would be incredulous that he had pulled it off, chastened that he was always one step ahead of them, and terrified of what he might do next and how and where he might do it. He would be a phantom to them. Berger didn't take drugs, but he was as high as a kite; the endorphins in his brain were on full release, and his senses were heightened. It was like a runner's high on steroids.

He stood back, admired his work, and felt immensely satisfied. It was almost time. He felt as if cosmic energy had infused his body, making him capable of anything, yet in a surreal way, he was completely calm. Everything slowed down for him as if it were frame by frame on a video replay. He watched the replay over and over again. He could see every detail in slow motion as it would happen.

Berger stacked two of the drawers vertically end to end against the mirror and hung the bathrobe over the drawers to obscure most of the writing. He tossed a couple of the other drawers onto the floor near the entryway, where the duty officer would have to step over or around them as she rushed into the smoky room to get to the coffeepot. He ripped blankets and sheets from the beds and tossed them in clumps about the room and also scattered paperback books everywhere. The room was in total disarray. Disorientation and distraction would lead to hesitation.

Berger took one last long, contemplative look at himself in the mirror, his gaze locked on the reflective image of his own eyes staring back at himself, assessing, approving. He was unrecognizable from the professor who had once roamed the halls at MIT. It was time.

He plugged in the cord of the coffee maker and waited patiently for the coil to heat. Wisps of white smoke curled from the gap at the top of the plastic backing. Within moments, the smoke turned darker, and the stench of burning plastic filled the air. A tongue of flame licked out the back of the machine. Billowing, smelly smoke began to fill the room. The alarm would go off any second. Berger knew the flames would likely burn out quickly once the mix of paper was consumed.

He opened the door and burst into the hallway, calling for help. A small cloud of foul smoke escaped into the corridor. "Help!" Berger screamed. "Fire! Help me!"

The duty officer was momentarily startled, but her training kicked in, and she responded quickly. She ran down the hall toward Berger, pausing only to pull a fire alarm on the wall in the common area. Berger had hoped she would come to the room first to check things and then determine whether the situation warranted an alarm or was easily controlled. The choreography had just accelerated. The clock had started, and Berger's window of operation was smaller.

She rushed toward Berger, who was still screaming near the door to his suite. The officer was the same white woman with the butch haircut he'd seen earlier. "Hurry!" Berger cried, motioning her into the suite. "I think it's an electrical fire. I was sound asleep. I think it's the coffeepot!"

Berger held the door open for her as she rushed past him and immediately tripped on a drawer on the floor just inside the entryway. Berger slammed the door shut and pounced on top of her. Totally surprised, the woman reacted instinctively to being attacked as Berger was on top of her in an instant. Berger worked to secure a grip around her neck with his right arm, but the woman was stronger than he'd anticipated and well trained.

She dipped her right shoulder and grasped Berger's wrist,

trapping his arm tightly to her chest, as she rolled. Berger's weight was too far forward. She used his own weight and leverage against him, breaking free as he rolled over the top of her.

Berger reacted instantly, punching her hard in the face before she could get her hands up. She was stunned, and Berger, catlike, was on her once again, placing his hands around her throat. They were both on their knees, facing each other. The officer tried to drop and roll again, but this time, Berger was ready for her with his weight back, counterbalancing her effort, keeping his hands viselike on her throat. The woman desperately threw her forearms against Berger's arms but could not break his grip. She was fading fast.

Berger couldn't control her arms and keep both hands on her throat. Their bodies shifted in the struggle, and the officer was now on her back. Berger straddled her in a wrestling hold with a leg on each side of her torso, his short dress hiked up around his waist. The officer flailed her arms, but Berger's weight and strength were too much to overcome. In one last desperate surge to survive, she plunged her right hand beneath Berger's skirt, between his legs, and grabbed him by the balls. She squeezed, pulled, yanked, and squeezed some more as hard as she could, digging deep with her fingernails, penetrating the soft tissue of his scrotum and doing serious damage.

Berger willed himself to ignore the pain and finish the job. It was a battle of mental toughness and willpower at that point. The officer's eyes fluttered. The door opened, and Berger looked up. The fire alarm must have automatically prevented it from locking. There in the entryway stood Liz McFarland, holding a small towel to her face in order to breathe through the smoke. Their eyes met, but Berger could not release his grip on the officer, nor did she release him.

◆ ◆ ◆

Liz stood still for a few seconds, paralyzed by incomprehension at the scene before her, not able to process what was happening. Everything was out of context. Why was Rachel on top of the duty officer? Nothing made sense. Then it did.

Berger's blond wig was half off his head. He had a maniacal look on his face as he rocked back and forth over the fallen officer, trying to free himself of her grip and force his weight on her throat. Liz didn't know who he was or why this was happening, but she understood she had to act, or the duty officer would die.

Berger's head was an open target. Liz turned sideways and delivered her best sidekick straight to Berger's nose. He buckled but maintained his grip on the officer. Blood streamed down Berger's face; his nose obviously was broken. Liz wound up and delivered a second blow. Berger's head snapped back, and his hands slid off the officer's throat. He grabbed the officer's arms and pulled them away from his crotch. Liz attempted to deliver a third blow, but Berger anticipated it and grabbed her by the ankle, pulling her to the floor.

◆ ◆ ◆

The fire alarm continued to blare in the background, a rhythmic, alternating horn. Berger tried to calculate in his head how many seconds had elapsed since it first had gone off. Too many—he knew that. Responders would burst into the corridor at any moment. He dragged Liz across the floor toward the desk as she thrashed and kicked, trying to escape. The duty officer lay gasping for breath on the floor.

Berger's head throbbed, and his crotch was on fire. Blood trickled down his legs, streaking his nylons, and also covered his face. The euphoria was gone, replaced by rage. Things were no longer happening in slow motion. Panic began to set in as the seconds ticked away. He was starting to feel dizzy from the blows he'd absorbed and the toxic smoke.

Berger still held Liz by the ankle as his free hand swept across the desk, feeling for the dinner knife. His vision was impaired from the blood in his eyes and the thick smoke concentrated in the area of the coffee machine. He couldn't find it, but his fingers touched something else—a pencil. Desperately, he released his grip on the one ankle and jumped on Liz with both knees, attempting to grab her by the hair and pull her head into striking position. He yanked her head up with one hand and swung the pencil down in a wide, sweeping arc toward her ear. Liz turned her head at the last second, and the tip of the pencil embedded at an angle in the side of her skull before snapping in two.

From across the room, Berger could see the incapacitated officer struggling to her feet, still trying to suck oxygen through her damaged throat. In a few more seconds, she'd be on him again. More panic bubbled up. Liz was bleeding profusely from her head wound but still fighting for her life. The duty officer put the radio on her belt on open mic and started across the room toward Berger and Liz. "Officer down. Code six. Tenth-floor suites," she said, coughing. "Repeat: officer needs assistance. Tenth floor. Code six. Security lockdown."

Although she could barely stand, she launched herself at Berger. The two women joined forces and battled ferociously. Berger knew he was out of time. He broke away and stumbled from the room, taking deep breaths of cleaner air as he made his way to the closet in the common area. He yanked open the closet door and started up the ladder to the roof hatch, praying the officer's call for a security lockdown had not caused the hatch to be relocked. Behind him, he heard Liz and the officer coughing in the hallway, and then he heard other voices.

Berger emerged onto the roof. Visibility was good between

the emergency lighting and the stars. Near the edge of the roof was the apparatus he was looking for. Fernandez had not been making it up. Large yellow lettering on the side provided operating instructions. He pulled a release lever and removed the protective cap from the front of the cannon. The cannon cylinder was about four feet in diameter. On the rear of the platform was a glass-covered control panel. Following instructions, he pulled the handle to break the glass and pushed the firing button. A loud whoosh exploded from the cannon, and the tubing shot out about fifty feet before gravity, aided by the weighted front tip, pulled the tube gracefully to the ground.

The tube was fully deployed, held in place by the same weights that had controlled its arc to the side street below. There was a cutout in the fabric through which to enter, and Berger wasted no time. Inside the giant stocking, small built-in handles were spaced every three feet to help control one's descent. Berger was in a great deal of pain but managed to slide to the pavement in a controlled free fall.

The streets were deserted. He was ahead of them but probably not by much. Whatever the response to the fire alarm and the officer-down call might have been, for a few minutes, they were likely to focus on the tenth floor. Berger sucked it up and jogged down the street. His only thought was to put as much distance as possible between himself and the Cambridge Police Department. Speed and distance were his first priorities, and then he had to figure out a way to get back to his apartment in Somerville without being traced.

Within minutes, Berger was several blocks away. He made his way across the McGrath and O'Brien Highway, moving away from the Charles River. He was searching for something, but he didn't know what.

He needed transportation, and he needed to get cleaned up.

He couldn't stay out in the open, walking down the street in the middle of the night. Whatever was going on back on the tenth floor, they were sure to call the state police and mobilize some kind of search effort. He had to go to ground somewhere and wait until the hustle and bustle of the morning commute, when he could blend in with a couple of million other people.

Even that would be a challenge. The point was to travel unnoticed under the radar and have no one remember him. He couldn't just climb onto a bus or jump into a taxi barefoot, wearing a women's dress and nylons, with a shaved head, broken nose, and blood everywhere.

The city at night was not as silent as one might have thought. The faint whine of cars on the highway, the hum of electricity, and an occasional out-of-place sound, such as a dog barking or a door shutting, punctuated the stillness. He heard the new sound before he saw them. *Helicopters*, he thought. *At least two of them.* Suddenly, the cones of light appeared several blocks away, piercing the night in a crisscross search pattern, flying low to the ground. One was moving away back down Memorial Drive near the river. The other was heading in his direction, although he figured it might take several minutes to reach his location if it maintained the current grid pattern. Patrol cars driving up and down each street, expanding the search radius block by block, couldn't have been far behind.

Berger was now in a blue-collar neighborhood. He wasn't sure of the time. It couldn't have been any later than four o'clock in the morning. He thought of breaking into a home, but in his weakened condition, depending on whom he ran into, that might have been a bad idea.

There were no underpasses in sight. He might have been able to press up against the side of a house or find some decent bushes, but where would that have gotten him? There would only be more searchers as the night wore on toward dawn and beyond. He'd have been out in the open with no means of hiding for long or procuring transportation.

Four blocks away, he saw a car turn slowly onto the street with a spotlight playing from side to side, proceeding at a snail's pace and examining each clump of bushes and space between houses. Ahead of Berger, cars were parallel-parked in front of homes for as far as he could see in the ambient light.

The beam of the spotlight was not trained straight ahead in Berger's direction, except for the fleeting moment when it swept from side to side. He had maybe a minute before he could either roll under a car and hope they passed or be caught in the glare. Desperately, Berger shuffled sideways, grasping at door handles, searching for one that might be unlocked. One after another, he had no luck. He cursed the fact that no one trusted his or her neighbor anymore.

The slow-moving spotlight was five cars away. He tried to anticipate each time the arc of light would swing to the other side of the street, crouching between cars to avoid being detected and then leaping out to try five or six more door handles before being forced to retreat again. The next sweep would surely capture him. After one last handle, he would have no choice but to dive under the nearest vehicle and hope for the best.

Click. The handle gave, and the door popped open. Berger dove into the backseat of the dark car, pulling the door closed behind him. He had no idea what make or model it was; he was just grateful the owner had not locked the doors. His head throbbed, and his lungs burned, but they were no match for the intense pain in his crotch. He curled into the fetal position and waited. The top portion of the car's interior briefly lit up as the patrol car passed, and then the lights were gone.

Berger's options were still limited. It was too far to walk back to his place in Somerville, and the odds of his being caught if he abandoned cover before dawn were unacceptably high. He did a quick recalculation and determined his best shot was to stay put right where he was and wait for the owner of the car to show up. If he stayed rolled into a ball on the floor, he thought there was a pretty good chance the driver wouldn't notice him as he entered the vehicle. He could surprise the person and figure it out from there.

He hoped the owner was male. He needed men's clothing. Maybe then he could get dropped at a bus station—nowhere near Somerville; make a couple of changes; and walk the last few blocks to his place. There were many variables he couldn't control. What if the guy was on vacation for a week and wasn't coming? No, surely he wouldn't have left the car unlocked for a week. What if it was a woman? How would he get men's clothing? He couldn't just send her back to get some. He'd have to stay with her at all times. What if she didn't have a man in the house? What if she did? It was a problem either way. What if multiple people came to the car at the same time—a family or neighborhood commuters—or a guy Berger couldn't handle in his present condition?

Berger was frustrated. He prided himself on his superior mind and his problem-solving ability. In addition to revenge and justice, that was what his operation was all about: demonstrating his intellectual superiority over those who'd taken him down and their protectors. He'd meticulously planned each detail, and when facing choices, he'd gamed out all the options. In the face of some unforeseen variable, he'd had total confidence in his brainpower and felt he would react clearly and decisively in the moment with the right move.

That was not what had happened this time. Nothing had gone right. He was blowing in the wind, beaten, crippled, his mission a failure. He couldn't reason his way out of his current predicament. He had to rely on pure, blind luck and give himself up to fate. He hated it, but he vowed to learn from his mistakes.

Presently, as they always did, the variables became more defined. The morning sun was low in the sky when he heard the driver's-side door open, and a person slid into the front seat. From his position on the floor, Berger couldn't tell if it was a man or woman. The key turned in the ignition, and the engine sputtered to life. Time for his bluff. Berger rolled to his knees, fighting the pain and being careful to stay out of sight behind the seat. He shouted, "I have a gun to your back!"

The startled driver showed no overt reaction whatsoever, so Berger shouted, "Hands up where I can see them!" The driver complied. They looked like male hands—so far so good. "Tilt the rearview mirror straight up so you can't see me." Again, the driver complied. "Listen carefully. I give you my word you will not be harmed if you do as I say, but know this: I have killed several people, and I will not hesitate to kill you if you give me even the slightest sign of resistance. Do you understand?"

The driver adjusted the mirror as instructed and nodded in understanding. Berger's head was above the seat now, and he could see that the driver was an overweight and docile-looking middle-aged white male. Berger immediately felt better about himself and his ability to overcome any obstacle. "This may sound strange to you, but remember what I said, because if you hesitate even for a moment, I will kill you. I can get what I need just as easily off your dead body as I can by your giving it to me. Nod your head if you are clear."

The man nodded.

"I need your pants, your shirt, and your shoes. Take them off."

The man immediately began to remove his shoes. Berger was pleased at his compliance. When the man gave Berger his clothes, Berger got dressed, noting that the man had left his wallet in the back pocket of his pants. He'd need money for bus fare, so he was glad about the wallet.

"Now, drive!" he said.

They rode in silence as the streets around them began to fill with morning commuters. Forty-five minutes later, they pulled into the long access road to Market Basket, and Berger directed his captive to the farthest corner of the huge lot, where cars were few and far between.

The man's pants were so big around Berger's waist that if he removed the belt, he couldn't keep them up. Being a man of his word, at least in the tortured world of his own moral construct, Berger searched for a tool to bind the man's hands behind his back and eventually settled on a shoelace. It would be easier and far more natural to walk the several hundred yards to the bus stop with one loose shoe rather than having to use one hand to keep the tent-sized pants from falling to the ground.

Berger tightly bound the man's hands and warned him one last time to keep his eyes shut for at least five minutes and sit quietly in the car until he was discovered later in the day. The man nodded once again, and Berger made his exit.

The sheltered bus stop was back down the access road and a couple of blocks away on Route 20. Berger covered the distance at a leisurely, casual pace in about twenty minutes, and shortly after that, he was in the rear seat of a bus headed to Watertown, where he could make a change to Arlington and a second to Somerville. No one paid any attention to him. He kept his head down and pretended to be snoozing as the bus slowly filled to capacity over the course of several stops.

By nine thirty in the morning, he was back in his Somerville apartment, damaged but not defeated. He was confident his return to Somerville had not been tracked by the authorities or noticed by anyone who would recall him later. Of course, the driver at Market Basket would eventually be identified, and the bloody nylons and dress discarded in his backseat, along with the location and time of his abduction, could only point to Berger as the culprit. That changed nothing.

They already knew who he was. Their problem was they didn't know where he was.

CHAPTER 17

Greater Boston Area: Present Day

Dimase shuffled his notes in front of him as he waited for the last members of the task force to arrive at the meeting. He thought about Liz McFarland and Brenda Clark, the duty officer Berger had ruthlessly attacked. Liz had simply needed stitches to close up the head wound, whereas Clark's larynx had been crushed, and one of her lungs had collapsed. Both of them would recover. Dimase was grateful for that. Sometimes small blessings were all one got.

In addition to the usual group of detectives, there were now two representatives from the FBI. After the latest episode of Berger infiltrating the Cambridge PD and attempting two murders, including that of a uniformed officer, the feds would be all in from then on. The FBI contingent included John Smith, number-two man in the Boston office, and Bill Larson, an FBI psychologist and senior investigator. Larson and Smith sat next to each other. The attendees around the table were assembled by tribe, with Boston cops on one side, Cambridge on the other, and the two FBI guys next to Dimase, sending a not-so-subtle signal that they were part of the command structure. Even though it was still Dimase's investigation to run, the FBI was now on equal footing and poised to take over if there were any more screwups.

The overall mood was grim. Seventy-two hours removed from Berger's attack, Dimase and his group were embarrassed and chagrined at how easily Berger had walked right into their own facility and penetrated one of the most secure areas of the building. Dimase realized how close they had come to losing two people on his watch.

The intended victims had saved each other's lives. If Liz McFarland had not intervened when she did, the duty officer would have been dead within seconds. If Brenda Clark had not miraculously rallied to her feet and then half fallen and half thrown her body at Berger, he surely would have murdered Liz with a second and third blow within moments.

Dimase opened the meeting with a statement of facts and concluded by saying, "We obviously know who he is. Our challenge now is to find out where he is and to protect the remaining targets while we do so. There are a number of open questions we must resolve. We have a pretty clear idea of how he got to the tenth floor, but how did he know Liz McFarland was up there in the first place? This was not public knowledge. No one outside this room knew we were holding Ms. McFarland in protective custody. I can't believe it would be true, but is it possible we have a leak?" Dimase looked around the room, knowing that what he'd just said couldn't have been true but nonetheless showing the angst he felt through his facial expression. "Think about this, people, because there must be some explanation."

His colleagues shifted uncomfortably in their seats, but no one spoke. The amplified voice of Susan Pearce coming from the speakerphone in the center of the conference table broke the silence. "I have an idea on that," she said. "It might be a long shot, but it's plausible—more plausible than the possibility that someone on the inside is somehow, for some reason, sharing information with Berger. That makes no sense. Why? Toward what purpose? No, I think there is a simpler explanation. What if Berger has managed to hack my email? If that's true, it would explain a lot. He would be privy to every communication I've had with Liz—or anyone else, for that matter. He would have learned she was in protective custody, specifically right there on the tenth floor. That's the only way it makes sense. Berger is a highly intelligent, tech-savvy individual, but more than that, at one point in time, he had access to all kinds of personal information about me: DOB, Social Security number, family history, and whatever else. He knew it all. I'll bet anything he's been reading my emails, and that's how he knew where Liz was."

Dimase clapped his hands. "That makes sense. If that is in fact the case, maybe we can use this knowledge as an edge against him—plant some false information at some point to draw him out. I'll contact Interpol and have them send a tech to analyze your computer. If it's been hacked, we need to know."

There were looks of hope and relief that the leak theory was unlikely. Dimase continued. "We must give some thought to that approach. It may be the best shot we have. Along those lines, I've asked Dr. Larson to join us today. He is one of the FBI's most noted experts in profiling serial killers. The more we understand about how Berger may be thinking, the better opportunity we have to predict his behavior. If we combine that with the fact that we can possibly feed him false information through Susan's email, perhaps we can come up with a strategy to make him show himself. Dr. Larson, what can you tell us?"

Larson looked briefly around the table and dove right in,

providing a brief overview of possible characteristics to look for in a psychological profile of Berger. "Ms. Pearce, did you and Elizabeth reference Dimase Augustin by name in any of your emails? Might you have mentioned the fact that he is in charge of the investigation?"

"Yes," she replied. "More than once, I'm afraid. We talked often about the case, the other girls, and how long we would be confined. We thought it was a private, secure conversation."

"Further circumstantial evidence that Berger was monitoring your email. Not only did he know that Liz was in protective custody, specifically on the tenth floor of this building, but he also knew that internally, Dimase was the individual heading up the investigation, hence the taunt on the mirror. How else could he have known those two things?"

"Susan," Dimase said, "we must do a total review of your emails so we can put together an outline of everything Berger may have learned if he was monitoring you. Liz's emails also. Once we understand the scope of that outline, we can then construct a plan to draw him out."

"Of course," Susan replied. "I'll give you the username and password."

Larson resumed his overview. "There are some other points we should discuss about Dr. Berger. If I had to guess, based on what I've read about his background, as well as his flair for the dramatic in these homicides, I'd say he has some form of narcissistic personality disorder, referred to as NPD. These individuals exhibit an extreme lack of empathy for other people. They don't look at victims and see human suffering. They only see them as objects. There is also an exaggerated need to be admired by others, which leads to a tendency for grandiosity. We've seen all these traits in Professor Berger. People with NPD can be so self-centered that from their perspective, the entire world revolves around them, their needs, and their fantasies and desires. They believe in their own superiority and are convinced that the rules don't apply to them and that they deserve special treatment. If we place Berger in this category, it may provide a prism through which to view his behavior and possibly anticipate how he may act in the future."

"Who do you think he'll target next?" Dimase asked.

The agent paused, obviously giving the question some thought before he answered. "Hard to say right now. Depends on the path of least resistance and the highest probability of success in carrying out his plans. People, regardless of mental state in most cases, take the easy way out nearly all the time. Berger will too, if I had to guess. Have you advised Cicely Blackwood as to the potential danger?"

Dimase nodded. "Sure we did. Right away when we found her name on the statement."

"Good," Larson said. "Because she might be the easiest target of the three he has left."

"That's not good," Susan said over the speakerphone.

"No, it isn't," Dimase said.

"Of course, he could, and probably will, surprise us," Coyne said. "I mean, hell! Who'd've thunk a dude would dress up in drag; brazen his—uh, her—way through security; and get outta Dodge through the sock of life? Come on, man! You just can't make this stuff up!"

Dimase smiled despite his fatigue and frustration. Coyne was one of a kind.

"Collateral damage will not be a hindrance for him," Larson said. "If there's one thing I can assure you of, it's that."

There was silence as the import of Larson's words sunk in. "His pattern also indicates that he won't be satisfied with killing from a distance. He wants to be with his victims up close—personal and intimate. He also wants to impress his audience. That would be us. He wants to come out of this with two things. He wants Ms. McFarland and Ms. Pearce dead. He also wants all of us to think he's amazing—a phantom, a ghost. That is why he made it personal by taunting Dimase in the message on the mirror. He wants us to recognize his superiority."

"So how can we use all this to our advantage?" Dimase asked.

Larson looked directly at Dimase and smiled. "You were exactly right with what you said earlier. We have the potential advantage of the emails. We know what drives him. We know what type of thing will trigger him. We have to devise a trap so irresistible that he can't help himself. We use the emails to bait that trap. In this way, we remove the element of surprise that he has used so well. In setting the trap, we control the time and place; he does not. We will have the element of surprise; he will not."

◆ ◆ ◆

Greater Boston Area: Present Day

Dimase awoke earlier than the alarm clock. He yawned, stretched, and got out of bed, glancing toward the window as he did so. It was still dark outside. He cursed softly, annoyed that he was awake when he should have been asleep. He stalked into the bathroom, took a leak, and turned on the cold water. He cupped his hands under the faucet and splashed his face with water.

He got dressed, went into the kitchen, and put the kettle on to make some instant coffee. He slumped into a chair at the kitchen table while he waited for the water to boil.

It had been quite the week since the attack on Liz McFarland. He and the rest of the team had been busy laying a trap for

Berger. He hoped the advantage they now had in knowing where Berger got his intel would make a difference. They had set up a separate encrypted email account for the two women, as well as Dimase and Larson, to use for real communication. They made the flow and content of Susan's old account look as realistic and natural as possible. They crafted the messages to discuss Liz's healing process, Susan's probable travel to other European cities, and the efforts to catch Berger. It was all a grand show. Liz was out of the hospital and in an FBI safe house, and Susan wasn't going anywhere. She was, in fact, taking a liking to life in Zurich.

The shriek of the kettle whistle jolted Dimase from his thoughts. He got up from the kitchen table, poured the boiling water into his coffee mug, stirred, sipped, grimaced, and sat down again. He pulled out a cigarette and twirled it unconsciously through his fingers. It was the start of another day—a day he hoped would bring him one step closer to catching Berger.

Dimase and Larson spent a month attempting to lay the groundwork, creating and maintaining a natural sequence to the exchanges on Susan's email. They decided not to include Cicely Blackwood on any of the fake emails. There was no point in bringing her to Berger's attention, in case she wasn't already on his list. If she was on the list, they believed the distance and security put in place should be adequate. There was no point in including her and giving Berger any ideas.

As the weeks passed, there was no sign of Berger. He had disappeared completely, despite the fact that his image had been well distributed throughout all of law enforcement. The trail dead-ended in the Market Basket parking lot in Waltham. Dimase hoped that Berger was monitoring Susan's emails and that the pattern and content seemed real to him. It was time to bait the trap.

Offline, they had another conference call with Liz and Susan.

The gambit would be that Gussie Watkins's parents had finally decided to come to Boston to host a memorial service for their daughter. In reality, the Watkinses knew nothing about the plan and would remain in California. The challenge was to make the return of Susan and the temporary exposure of Liz credible and at the same time create some vulnerability that Berger could possibly exploit.

They decided the general itinerary would be for Gussie's parents to fly in and stay at the Long Wharf Marriott in Boston. A memorial service would be held the next afternoon at the Harvard Memorial Church in Cambridge, followed by a small reception at Fay House on the college campus. Susan and Liz debated online about how safe the overall situation would be and lamented the fact that they didn't want to make Gussie's parents uncomfortable by an overwhelming presence of uniformed police and military-type security personnel. As the false narrative developed, they would concoct a scheme to slip away, ditch their security for a couple of hours, and take a cab to Courtside, the neighborhood bar where they used to meet.

In truth, they had never been to Courtside with Gussie Watkins, but Berger wouldn't have known that. The idea was to make him think it was a defiant, courageous, quick trip to a nostalgic place of special significance where they had spent many happy times with Gussie. The storyline was that after many weeks of being kept isolated and surrounded by security people, they wanted to escape, even if only for a couple of hours. After all, how dangerous could it have been? No one would know of their plan in advance. They could sneak out after the reception and take a cab to Courtside before anyone was the wiser.

They drafted, deconstructed, and rewrote a long sequence of emails designed to be released over the course of several days. First, they revealed and discussed the memorial service invitation. Each day or two, they added a little more detail to the itinerary. They hoped Berger would recognize that day as the only chance he might have to get at the two women before they returned to the obscurity of some form of witness protection. They knew Berger was driven by a singular purpose. Whereas most people would have seen long odds, they hoped Berger, in his arrogance, would see a chance to show off.

Still, they had to make some part of the schedule seem more attractive than all others. That was the only way Dimase and his team could try to control the time and place Berger would strike. Once the schedule was fully established over the course of a few days, Susan and Liz began to cook up their little escape plan. At first, the idea was couched as some sort of whimsical wish by Susan: "Wouldn't it be cool if we could ditch these guys, just for a couple of hours, and do something that would have been meaningful just to Gussie, you, and me?"

So it went. They fleshed out the escape plan. The trap was set.

◆ ◆ ◆

Somerville, Massachusetts: Present Day

With each passing week, Berger grew stronger. He dared not leave his apartment yet and venture out in public, which turned out to be only a minor problem. For the first several days, he did little but sleep and subsist on peanut butter, protein bars, and ramen noodles. When he started to run low on supplies, he found an online delivery service that would leave food and other sundries at his door whenever needed. There was never a need for face-to-face encounters.

Berger had never interacted with any of his neighbors, so there was nothing unusual about their not seeing him now. The outside world couldn't tell if he was home or not. Frankly, no one was looking, and no one cared. There was no mail buildup because Berger received no personal mail. The mailman had long ago stopped delivering junk mail after realizing it was never picked up from the small overstuffed box by the front door.

As he began to sleep less and move gingerly about the apartment, he resumed his old habits of reading, watching cable news, and surfing the internet. He was pleased to note that the authorities were completely baffled as to his whereabouts. When he last had spent time in his apartment, he had been a complete unknown to them. He'd been able to plan and execute the first three murders in total anonymity. Now his face was everywhere.

The media had been in a frenzy, but as time passed, the story lost its luster and got less ink and screen time. Besides, the talking heads didn't know the entire story. The murder of Gussie Watkins had been front-page news, albeit only for a couple of days before it was eclipsed by the sensational murder of Angela Mancini on the Boston Common. When the two murders had been linked, the talking heads had loved it, at least for a little while. But the news cycle being what it was, the story got fewer mentions on the nightly news as time wore on.

As his wounds healed, the panic and disappointment of his failed attempt at Liz also faded away, replaced by excitement and the familiar thrill of constructing a plan. He didn't have any specifics yet. At that early stage, his mind spiraled through different fantasies, an orgy of possibility without any requirement of realism. Whatever he came up with, his field intelligence was the most limited yet. In the beginning, he'd had his extensive hidden-camera network. He had known exactly where each victim lived and worked. He'd been able to monitor Susan's emails and sign in to her text account at will. He had operated in a veil of secrecy, watching each of their movements and reading much of their communication.

Now most of those advantages had been taken from him. He had no idea where Liz was, and Susan was in Switzerland, out of reach for the time being. Everyone in the world knew what he looked like. His one remaining edge was being able to monitor Susan's communications.

He spent the first few weeks of his recuperation watching Susan's emails, looking for any indication she may have been aware of his surveillance. All appeared normal. She had taken a leave of absence from MIT and was apparently going to stay in Europe until the crisis was over. As she was without a work connection and lacked any remaining family, the level of traffic on the account was low. Her primary correspondent was Liz McFarland. From the emails, it was apparent Liz was still recovering in one of the Boston hospitals, although it was unclear which one and for how long. Berger was still far from feeling 100 percent himself. He needed more time to physically heal and regain his old form. In the meantime, he was content to follow the emails, looking for an opportunity, waiting for the variables to better define themselves.

Berger still retained the ability to sign in to Susan's cell in order to overview her texts, but each time he did, he found no activity. The account was still open but apparently dormant. There were old texts related to work and some others between various book club members, but there had been nothing new in recent weeks. Liz was her only daily contact, and it seemed that email, rather than text, was their preferred method of keeping in touch.

Berger scanned an email from Gussie Watkins's parents. It was addressed to Susan and cc'd to Liz, inviting them to a memorial service for Gussie. They hadn't determined a date but were thinking of doing something on the Harvard campus, the site of Gussie's undergraduate studies. *This could be the opportunity I've been waiting for,* he thought.

Over the course of the next several days, there were multiple exchanges. Apparently, the Watkinses did not realize Liz and Susan were being kept on ice. Within a couple of weeks, details began to fall into place. The Watkinses would fly to Boston on March 1 and stay at the Long Wharf Marriott. They scheduled a three o'clock memorial service at Harvard Memorial Church for the next day, Saturday, March 2, followed by a reception at Fay House. The Watkinses planned to return to California on Monday. Susan purchased tickets to fly back from Switzerland that same Friday. She would fly with a security escort and also stay at the Long Wharf, where the feds would take over her security coverage. The plan was to meet the Watkinses the next day at the church and attend the service.

Liz hoped to be discharged earlier that same week. She too would attend the ceremony with a security detail and would meet them at the church. There were numerous exchanges about how excited the girls were to see each other again and how sad it would be to see Gussie's parents. Eventually, the idea of Susan joining Liz in protective custody crept into the conversation. There were no specifics, just references to the fact that they would be reunited and placed at a secret location together after the ceremony, most likely a safe house in some other part of the country.

Berger knew this had to be it. He had waited weeks for them to come out of hiding and was prepared to wait until hell froze over if he had to, but realistically, this might be the only chance he would get for the foreseeable future. If his targets disappeared back into protective custody after the ceremony, he knew he may or may not catch up with them later in life, and if he did, it might not happen for years.

During his confinement to the apartment, Berger's beard had grown out two or three inches. His strength gradually had returned, and he decided it was time to venture out of the building. He had not yet settled on a plan, but one way or another, he had to change his appearance so he could have freedom of movement. He needed at least two entirely different looks, and to accomplish that, he needed some supplies he couldn't simply order to be left at his door by the grocery delivery service.

He still had the oversized pants and shirt taken from the man who'd driven him to Market Basket the night of his attack at the Cambridge PD. He put them on and used towels and paper towels to fill out his stomach, arms, and legs. His face was a little too thin to go with the inflated body, but the beard disguised that fact fairly well. It was not the best clothing to move around in, but it was a good first step toward rebuilding confidence and going out in the neighborhood. He didn't expect to have to do anything too athletic, just a little shopping. Once he was able to do that, he could then gather whatever materials were required to create the look or looks that would best suit his yet-to-be-developed plan.

He had two weeks left before the memorial service at Harvard. The self-imposed pressure was starting to build, and with it, the excitement built. He went over every aspect of the itinerary from Susan's emails. He viewed her receipt for plane tickets and knew exactly which flight she would be on and when she would arrive from Switzerland. He knew Susan and Liz, accompanied by security details, planned to meet at the church just before the ceremony. He looked at Google Maps to plot their likely course from the church to the reception at Fay House. He did the same for the route from Fay House back to the Long Wharf Marriott, where apparently they would stay for one night after the ceremony before being whisked off to some unknown government safe house.

From all appearances, even Liz and Susan didn't know where they were going after the ceremony or how they would get there. They speculated they might travel on a government plane of some sort, because to their knowledge, no commercial reservations had been made. Berger searched over and over again for the most vulnerable point in the itinerary, the time and place for his greatest chance to take them out and maximize the wow factor. There was no obvious solution, and the risks to him were high. He ran through dozens of possibilities but couldn't settle on the optimal plan. No matter—he was confident it would come to him, and as the hours and days ticked away, the anticipation and challenge thrilled him.

Berger checked his appearance and was satisfied that he was unrecognizable, particularly for a short foray around Davis Square with quick stops at a few local stores. He pulled on a stocking cap and sunglasses, and his blond beard and wide girth gave him the appearance of an off-duty NFL tackle.

Two hours later, he was back in the apartment, having successfully completed his shopping trip. He packed the items away, fired up Susan's emails, and was surprised to see a new development. There was a lengthy exchange about sneaking away from their security escorts for a couple of hours to hit some bar where they'd used to hang out with Gussie. It was too good to be true. Was it too good to be true? Berger wondered if it could be a setup. He would have to wait and watch. The variables would eventually sort themselves out.

With one week to go, the variables had indeed further defined themselves, as they always did. Berger had a plan. Susan and Liz had convinced each other it would be perfectly safe to temporarily ditch their babysitters as one last expression of free will before being shipped off indefinitely to places unknown. In all likelihood, it would have been safe if Berger had not been able to follow their emails.

It would be the most difficult mission yet. It would be impossible to do the staging and dramatic messaging he'd produced for the earlier murders. Nonetheless, it would be spectacular for his audience if he could take out both women at once. It would shock and titillate the public and the authorities. He could still leave a message behind; it just wouldn't be on a mirror or on a placard around the neck of a woman hanging from the top of an observation tower.

The method of message delivery would have to be more along the lines of the Angela Mancini murder: a note left behind. The words would have impact, but the value would be in the sensationalism of the double murder of two women who were supposed to be untouchable under tight security with the police. They would be the last in a complete set. He'd have accomplished his mission.

Berger ramped up his mental preparation, repeatedly playing in his mind the video of what would happen. He would be in a disguise no one would recognize. He knew the exact time and place to rendezvous with his victims: the Courtside Bar at about six o'clock on Saturday, March 2.

There was still a chance it was a setup, but how? No one should have been aware that he had hacked Susan's email, although that was always a possibility. Knowing Susan as he did, he felt it was in character for her to want to make a statement, assert her independence, and exercise some degree of control by sneaking away. Berger had little choice. He had to play the odds.

On a whim, even though it had been inactive for weeks, Berger decided to sign in to Susan's cell phone and check her texts.

> Susan, Cicely here. Just FYI. The Watkinses have invited me to visit them in California, and I decided to take them up on it. I'm on semester break, so I'm going to fly to Cali on March 1 and spend a week with them. It must be terrible for them, but they reached out, so I feel like it's the least I can do. I'll let you know how it goes. Love, C.

What the hell is this? March 1? That was the same date the Watkinses were flying to Boston for the memorial service. Obviously, they couldn't be in two places at once. It was a trap after all. There was no memorial service at Harvard, at least not a real one. Susan had set him up again. *Unbelievable. And I almost fell for it. The little bitch.* Most likely, his precautions would have sniffed out the trap, and he would have aborted. Still, this changed everything.

Susan and the Keystone Cops must have figured out he'd hacked her emails, and they'd been feeding him a bunch of garbage ever since. It was not that big of a surprise. She was a bright kid. He had to admit the way they'd gradually introduced the idea of the memorial service and then later woven in the subtext of Susan and Liz slipping away without security, creating a perfect opportunity custom-designed to flush him out if he was watching, had been clever. Berger had been conscious of the possibility of a trap from the beginning. Now it was confirmed.

He looked again at the text. It was marked as unread, and he quickly erased it, hoping Susan would never see it. He would have to monitor her texts constantly from then on in case Cicely sent a follow-up. He would erase the texts as fast as they came in. The emails were fake, but the texts were real. That was why there hadn't been any until Cicely had sent one out of the blue. That was why Susan wasn't checking them. She wasn't expecting any. Cicely obviously didn't know about the memorial service scheme. She'd just randomly sent a text to update her old book club friend about her unexpected trip to visit the Watkins family.

This called for a new plan, advantage Berger.

CHAPTER 18

Cambridge, Massachusetts: Present Day

Dimase assumed Berger had seen his picture and was familiar with his appearance. In light of the personal taunt on the mirror in Liz's room on the tenth floor, it was logical to figure that Berger had also researched him online. For that reason, even though he would have loved to be on scene at Courtside, Dimase was relegated to the rolling control and command center situated two blocks away with an accompanying FBI SWAT truck and team.

The task force members debated long and hard about whether to actually place Susan and Liz in harm's way inside the bar or use female officers to impersonate them. Normally, protocol prohibited ever putting members of the public at risk, but this case was different. Susan and Liz were already at substantial risk, and given the circumstances, they would remain so until Berger was captured and incarcerated.

Berger knew his targets well. Chances were he would spot

replacements the moment he walked through the door. Some argued he could still be grabbed at that point without putting the protectees at risk. The bottom line for Dimase was that there was more risk to the women if Berger remained at large. The deciding factor was Susan and Liz's insistence on being the bait. They felt it was the best way to protect themselves in the long run. If Berger was spooked, he might just turn around and walk out. Given his penchant for disguises, if it was crowded, they might not even know he was there at all. That was not a chance Susan and Liz wanted to take. Ultimately, Dimase agreed with them and made the call.

He realized he was sticking his neck out, but in the end, his overriding concern was for a positive outcome for Susan and Liz. They had to be authentic if this was going to work. Dimase might not have another clean shot like that at Berger for a long time. Who knew how much damage Berger could do in the interim? The long-term exposure of having Berger out there was more than the short-term risk of a tightly controlled situation.

In the interest of realism, the FBI actually flew in two agents posing as the Watkinses and put them up at the Long Wharf Marriott. Susan also flew to Boston on Friday, March 1, and was sequestered under heavy security. The next day, an actual ceremony was held at the Harvard Memorial Church at three o'clock. As planned, Susan and Liz met in the vestibule before entering the church.

The assumption was that Berger would strike at Courtside. Nonetheless, every attempt was made at realism. After the ceremony, the participants were escorted into two waiting limousines and driven to the front door of Fay House for the reception. No detail was overlooked. The only false piece of the entire arrangement was that the Watkinses knew nothing about it, and the FBI decoys took their places.

It was predetermined that the same limos would return Susan and Liz to the Long Wharf Marriott, along with the pretend Watkinses. Once there, Susan and Liz would slip their security, exit a side door, and meet a cab driven by an undercover FBI agent who would take them to Courtside.

Everything went off without a hitch. There was no sign of Berger, nor did they expect there to be until sometime after the two women arrived at Courtside. Earlier that afternoon, the task force had paid careful attention to laying out the final details in and around the bar. They'd selected a table far removed from the exit and restrooms for Susan and Liz, wanting to lengthen the distance for anyone approaching. Dimase didn't want a potential assailant to be able to make a quick entrance or exit near the women, nor did he want restroom traffic passing close by.

The table for Susan and Liz was up against a side wall toward the back of the bar. To their left, two undercover female agents sat at an adjacent table, apparently engrossed in an engaging conversation. Eight to ten feet to their right was a young couple—also undercover officers. A substitute waiter hovered nearby, patrolling back and forth between the bar, the kitchen, and the three tables with no possibility of a real customer to distract him. Additional plainclothes personnel were positioned at tables near both exits as a well as a position behind the bar as one of the bartenders.

Inside the kitchen were four more agents ready to deploy as needed. Outside the bar, six undercover operatives were positioned, two on foot and two pairs in separate unmarked cars. Dimase monitored communication in the mobile command center adjacent to a SWAT team truck. It might have seemed like overkill, but to Dimase, too much was preferable to too little. He couldn't recall an operation like this one, wherein the bait was actually the intended victim. Berger had already proven himself to be clever and unpredictable. If things went south, there would be hell to pay, especially in the court of public opinion.

Dimase watched nervously via remote security cams as Susan and Liz entered the bar and were shown to their table. The game was on. He wasn't certain if Berger would show, but if he did, they would be ready for him.

◆ ◆ ◆

Susan sat at the table with Liz. She tried to make normal conversation, but neither of them had much to say, despite the fact that they hadn't seen each other in what felt like ages. As the minutes ticked by, the tension became unbearable. Instead of feeling calmer, the longer they sat, the more anxious Susan became. Each time a new customer entered the bar, Susan couldn't help but stare intently for a moment too long before turning away. Every time a patron walked anywhere near them, Susan recoiled involuntarily and watched the person's hands to anticipate in what manner he or she might launch an attack.

She was just about to jump up and call the whole thing off, when she heard a faint buzz and felt a slight vibration on her phone. The ringer was off, but she took it from her pocketbook and realized she had just received a text: "Hey. Landed in Cali yesterday. Is sad, but Watkinses were glad to see me. Going well so far. Did you get my text last week? Love, C."

Susan quickly searched through her texts, but there was nothing else. She texted Cicely back: "You okay? Didn't get your other text."

To her surprise, she got an immediate reply: "Fine. Yeah, was wondering why you didn't get back. Watkinses say hi. Having an early dinner."

Susan was starting to panic. An undefined fear percolated

in a back corner of her mind. She wrote, "How many times did you text me?"

"Twice, actually. Are you okay?"

"Yes. What did you say?"

"Told you I was flying to Cali this week to stay with the Watkinses. Why?"

"Do you have security?"

"Yes. A local guy. Why? No one knows I'm here."

"He knows. Berger knows. You are in danger."

Susan suddenly realized the cause of her welling terror. Berger not only had hacked her emails but also was somehow reading her texts. He knew it was a trap. He'd known since last week. That was why he hadn't shown up. He knew the Watkinses were still in California. He knew everything.

◆ ◆ ◆

Albany, California: Present Day

Berger was getting close. He wondered how the sting operation was going back in Cambridge. He could just picture the bar full of undercover cops waiting for him to show up. He glanced at the time on his phone: 11:00 p.m. California time, which made it 8:00 p.m. at Courtside. He smiled at the thought of Dimase finally calling it a night, realizing once again that Berger was always at least a step ahead of him.

The drive cross-country had been a challenge, but Berger had known he could do it. His original estimate had been forty-six hours nonstop, and there he was, at a rest stop no more than ten minutes from the Watkins home. The old Volvo had held up well. Despite infrequent use, it was always in good repair, ready for action should the need arise.

He remembered reading years ago about a lady astronaut who put on a diaper and drove a thousand miles nonstop to Orlando in order to confront a rival for her lover. He'd found it amazing—one of America's best and brightest had thrown away her life over some silly romantic notion. At least she'd had a choice. Berger had not consciously chosen to toss his life away. The destruction of his life had been forced upon him, not a result of some foolish decision he'd made for himself. They had done this to him. He'd fought, but resistance had been futile.

They'd created him, at least what he had become now. So be it. He would make them all pay, and at the same time, they would have to admit to his superiority. They'd turned him dark to the world, but they had not stolen his competitive nature or creative mind. They'd changed the parameters of the game and the parameters of his life. Now he was stimulated beyond anything previously imagined, and he embraced it.

Berger wondered what Dimase and the others would think when he didn't show up. Maybe they would rethink the idea that he was monitoring Susan's emails. The most logical explanation for his not falling into their trap would be that he hadn't known about it. Of course, the second most logical explanation would be that he had known about it.

Unlike the lady astronaut, Berger had had to make a couple of stops for gas, but that was it. He kept four extra fifteen-gallon tanks of gas in the car, two in the trunk and two on the floor in the backseat. It hadn't been enough to get him all the way to California, but it had stretched his range to about fifteen hundred miles between stops. He also had stolen the diaper idea from the lady astronaut. He no longer had pain in his crotch, but the duty officer must have inflicted some permanent damage, because he found he had to urinate frequently, sometimes an hour apart but occasionally as often as every twenty minutes. The diaper solved that problem.

The journey had been tiring. Now that he was in the vicinity, he could hit his victims at any time. Given that he'd been awake for forty-eight hours straight, he'd thought it would be wise to pull into the rest area to take a thirty-minute power nap just to make sure he was sharp for whatever lay ahead.

He set the alarm on his cell and reclined the seat, when it occurred to him he hadn't checked on Susan's communications in more than an hour. Throughout the trip, he consistently had signed in to review both emails and texts, ready to erase any texts and keep updated. He was dying to know what their reaction was to the failed setup at Courtside, but realistically, since both women were together at the scene, they probably wouldn't be emailing about it, at least not until long after the fact. He was not surprised to see there was no email activity. He was surprised to see a series of texts.

Damn. What shitty timing. He'd just checked no more than ninety minutes ago, and there had been nothing. Now there was a whole series of texts, and it was too late to erase them. Susan not only had seen a text from Cicely but also had responded, and the two of them had had a real-time conversation. *Damn. Damn. Damn.*

They were onto him again—well, not totally. They finally had figured out he was watching Susan's emails and texts. The obvious conclusion was that he had known about the trap in advance, and that was why he had not shown. They also knew now that he was aware Cicely Blackwood was in California with the Watkinses. However, they didn't know he had just made it across the entire width of the United States and was now parked around the corner from Gussie's childhood home.

◆ ◆ ◆

Courtside Bar, Cambridge, Massachusetts

Just to be safe, Dimase ordered the cab and unmarked cars to pull up and make a quick transfer of the women to the rolling command center two blocks away. He wanted to debrief immediately, even as the mobile operations vehicle drove back to the subbasement at Cambridge PD.

Inside the cramped space, Dimase, Larson, Smith, Susan, Liz, and three other support personnel huddled around a small counter protruding from a wall of electronic and communication equipment.

"How could this happen?" Dimase asked, not accusing anyone in particular.

"I think we were right in surmising that Berger hacked my email," Susan said. "The basic plan was good. What we didn't consider was that he also had access to my texts. Why would we have? Not only has the account been totally inactive since I left MIT, but it is also completely separate from my emails. Even though it hasn't been used for weeks, I would have assumed it was secure."

"I suppose so," said Dimase. "It's no one's fault; I just wish I would have thought of it before. So we are back to square one. We must assume Berger knows everything, not only our operation at Courtside but also the fact that Cicely Blackwood is in California. The big question is, where he is now, and what will he do next?"

"Put yourself in Berger's shoes," Larson said. "He's probably pissed that what he thought was his last best chance to get Susan and Liz was nothing more than a mirage. He knows the emails were false. If he's read that last text exchange between Susan and Cicely, he's also deduced that we know about his ability to watch texts as well. If he didn't know before, he knows now that Cicely is at the Watkins home in California."

"Right," Dimase said. "So now Susan and Liz go back into hiding, presumably someplace totally unknown to Berger, a location impossible for him to determine. The two of you don't even know where you are going, so from Berger's standpoint, you are now totally off the table. The next most logical path for him is to go after Cicely."

"Yes, maybe, but to do that, he'd have to get all the way across the country. She's only going to be there for five or six days," Susan said.

"I don't think he could fly," Dimase said. "He knows there's a BOLO out on him. Even with a false identity, he'd be at significant risk. He could be exposed to facial-recognition software. TSA is on the watch for fake IDs. It's not impossible, I guess, but I'd say unlikely that he'd be stupid enough to fly."

"Or take a train," Coyne said.

"I think he would drive," Larson said. "He must have access to a vehicle, or else how did he get to Maine with Ms. Klein? He could make it in four or five days with a couple of stops at motels for a few hours—maybe even less if he pushed it."

Dimase put his hands behind his head and leaned back. "So how long has he known about our trap, and how long has he known the dates Professor Blackwood would be in California? He could have left a week ago and already be there for all we know."

"I've got to call Cicely right away. She's got to get out of there," Susan said. She took out her cell phone, ready to call.

"You can't text her without further alerting Berger. Could he be tapping phone calls as well?" Dimase said. "Don't ask me how, but it seems like anything's possible with this guy. He's a real freak show, but he's obviously also pretty smart about tech."

"Let's not chance it unless we have to," Larson said. "It's after midnight there now. Let's see if the Watkinses have a land line and try that first."

One of the support guys tapped a few keys on his pad and accessed the number. He handed Susan a phone and put it on speaker. The phone rang at least twenty times before Susan hung up. The tech support officer got an outside operator on the line and asked her to put the call through. After several attempts, she came back and said the line appeared to be out of order.

"Shit," Dimase muttered. "Try Cicely's cell phone."

The tech guy keyed in the number as Susan fed it to him. The call went directly to voice mail. They tried again with the same result.

"All right, the hell with it," Dimase said. "Susan, send her a text. If he sees it, he sees it. We've got to get word to Cicely and the Watkinses to get the hell out of there. See if she'll respond. Meanwhile"—he nodded at one of the techies—"you get the local police department on the phone, and have them send a couple of guys over there right away."

"Right," the tech guy said, pulling up the first number as he spoke.

"What has she got for security out there?" Dimase asked. "I thought she was still in Ireland."

Susan said, "She hired her own guy. At least that's what she said—a local guy."

"That's great!" Dimase exclaimed. "Do we have any way to get in touch with this guy? Any way to even know who he is or who he works for?"

"I don't know," Susan said. "I didn't even know she was going to California. I just found out when I got the text at Courtside. When I asked her if she had security, she said, 'Yes, a local guy.'"

"So Berger not only knows where she is but also knows her

security situation, and he could have left a week ago to get there. How are you doing on getting the local police?" he shouted at the techie.

"Right here, sir," the man said, handing the phone to Dimase.

Dimase filled the Albany police captain in on the situation. "Get some uniforms over there right now!" he said. He ended the call, turned to the team, and said, "They'll be there in a few minutes."

"Great," Susan said.

"Are you ready to send that text?" Dimase asked.

Susan nodded.

"Don't say that we have people on the way. Just tell her it's urgent, a matter of life and death, and she should call you right away."

Susan did as she was asked and typed out a message: "Cicely, Susan here. Please call me immediately. It's a matter of life and death."

They all looked at her phone expectantly, hoping for a reply. A moment later, the phone pinged, and Susan held it up so they could all read the text: "Sorry. Cicely can't come to the phone right now. Can I help you with anything?"

CHAPTER 19

Cambridge, Massachusetts: Present Day

Susan stared down at the text on her cell, horrified that Berger was with Cicely. Images of unspeakable torture flashed through her mind, and she had to will herself not to scream. Suddenly, Susan's phone rang. She picked up the call but couldn't speak; her brain seemingly was frozen, and her systems were on hold. She simply stared straight ahead.

Dimase gently took the phone from her. "Hello? Who am I speaking to?" he asked.

"Detective Augustin, is that you?" a voice replied. "What an honor and privilege to speak with you. I hope you had a pleasant evening. Did you go out for drinks at Courtside? Perhaps we will meet someday. Actually, we may have already met briefly when I tried to kill Liz, although I'm afraid formal introductions weren't made at that time. Be that as it may, Dimase—oh, may I call you Dimase?"

Dimase remained silent.

"Well, as I was saying, I do have a message for you—for you, Susan, Liz, and all my fans: 'Justice prevails.'"

Susan leaned against the desk. She felt as if her knees had turned to jelly. For a moment, she was afraid she might hurl.

The line went dead.

"Shit," Dimase said.

"Oh God," Susan said. "This can't be happening. Not again!"

"It's going to be okay," Dimase said. "The locals will be there any minute." He turned to Larson. "Call the field office out there. The FBI is going to want in on this too."

"On it," Larson said.

"I think we should get out there right away," Dimase said. He shook his head and sighed. "I'm sorry to say I think we're too late. Berger's gonna be in the wind before the local cops even get to the house. Bet on it."

"Sucker bet," Coyne said.

Dimase shot him a look.

"I can get us an FBI jet," Larson said. "Gimme a few, okay?"

"Got it," Dimase said.

◆ ◆ ◆

Dimase surveyed the crime scene at the Watkins house. He tried to keep from getting angry and tried not to blame himself for always feeling a step behind this guy. He was starting to hate the psychopathic Hans Berger.

From what he could see, the deal had gone down like a horror show. They found the security guard lying on the ground next to his vehicle parked in front of the Watkins home. The driver's-side window was smashed, and the man's head had been beaten to a pulp, probably by a crowbar or similar instrument. He was armed but never had managed to get his gun out of the shoulder holster. The door was ajar. Forensics' best guess was that Berger had gotten the drop on the unfortunate security guard and caught him completely by surprise. He might have been snoozing due to the time of night. It had been strictly amateur hour. The guy most likely had not expected any action; he probably had thought it was a routine detail just like a thousand other details. He might have thought his mere presence parked out front would scare off any would-be intruders.

It looked as if Berger had snuck up on him, suddenly smashed the window with a crowbar, and maybe landed a stunning blow before opening the door and pulling the guy into the street, where he'd pummeled him. Chances were the encounter had not produced much noise. It probably had been much quieter than a gunshot and not noticeable to anyone inside the house, unless they'd been looking out the front window.

The neighborhood was strictly residential, with no known security cameras oriented toward the street. The scene inside the house was worse. Although the bodies were now gone, Dimase could see where the killings had gone down. It looked as if Berger had taken the crowbar with him and gained entry through the back door. The first vic was Mr. Watkins. The blood pool and spatter indicated a kill zone about ten feet from the door. Speculation was that he might have heard something and come to investigate. Then Berger had moved on, murdering Mrs. Watkins in her bedroom. He also had gotten Cicely Blackwood in her bedroom, but he hadn't killed her in the same way.

"I wonder why he posed her like that," he said.

Larson sighed. "Who knows?"

Dimase examined the crime-scene photos in the folder an agent had given him. The young woman had not been bludgeoned to death, as Mr. and Mrs. Watkins had. In fact, she didn't seem to have a mark on her. She was posed angelically on the bed with her hands folded, with decorative pillows fluffed up all around her. The bed was neat and made. She was on top of the sheets and barefoot, wearing a nightgown. There was no obvious sign of trauma. It was almost as if Berger had been respectful to her in some way.

"What do you think?" Dimase asked.

"I'm not sure," Larson replied. "But I can tell you one thing: he's escalating. He didn't have to kill Mr. and Mrs. Watkins, but he did anyway. Because he got his jollies off on it. You might say Dr. Hans Berger has graduated to a full-fledged serial killer capable of doing basically anything."

Dimase closed the folder and kept looking around, hoping he might find something in the Watkins house that would give him what he needed to catch the bastard.

"If we don't stop him, he'll find other victims—other causes to motivate him and keep him sharp for the big climax," Larson said.

"The big climax?" Dimase asked.

"Susan and Liz," Larson replied. "He's not on a timetable. That's the problem. He could go to ground for years before he strikes again, but I don't think he'll do that. I think if we make it easy for him, he won't be able to resist trying again soon."

"We're back to bait, eh?" Dimase said. "It didn't work out well for Cicely Blackwood. I'm not sure we should tempt fate with Susan or Liz."

"We may not have a choice."

Dimase stepped outside through the back door. He stood in the yard and tried to clear his head. Larson joined him.

"What's the deal with Professor Blackwood?" Dimase said. "Why would he pose her like that? And how did he kill her?"

"As to the posing, I think it comes back to his flair for theatrics and his desire to show us he's in control. I don't know how he killed her. If I had to guess, I'd say he injected her with some kind of fast-acting poison. Tox'll be back soon enough. The autopsy might turn up an injection site. In any case, like I said before, I think he's escalating. There will be more killings. Of that you can be sure."

◆ ◆ ◆

Eureka, California: Present Day

Berger was back in the Volvo, six hours and hundreds of miles north in a Holiday Inn Express in Eureka, California. This time, he was in no hurry. On the contrary, he was ready for a vacation of sorts.

His plan was to continue over the border to Vancouver and then across the width of Canada to Montreal and finally Toronto before reentering the United States. He was pleased about his latest accomplishment. With success came freedom. He gave himself permission to relax. The all-consuming drive to prosecute revenge on Susan and Liz had abated, if only temporarily.

There was no schedule and no pressure. He knew Susan and Liz were gone. When his brain was ready again, it might subconsciously come up with some means of finding them. There was no rush. Eventually, something would migrate to his conscious mind. As always, the variables would better define themselves. Time was on his side.

He knew he was mentally stronger than all of them. They probably thought it would frustrate him not to know where Susan and Liz were going to be kept. He looked at it in a different light—a superior light. Susan and Liz had also had their lives taken away from them. It was an appropriate and satisfying interim step. It would be fine with him if they spent the next fifty years in misery and isolation, always looking over their shoulders. He doubted it would come to that. More likely, at some point, they would make a mistake, and he would get another opportunity.

No, the greater frustration must have been with Dimase Augustin and his friends. He had bested them once again. They were the ones who didn't know what to do next. As long as he could stay invisible, that in and of itself demonstrated his superior abilities. They knew who he was and were powerless to find him. That alone put him in elite company and gave him legendary status, like D. B. Cooper jumping out of a plane with a million dollars never to be seen again or Whitey Bulger being on the lam for decades.

There was no rush. For starters, he planned to spend a month or two in Canada, working his way slowly east, taking in the sights, and spending whatever time he liked wherever he liked. What better way to stay invisible than to remain out of the country for a month or two?

◆ ◆ ◆

Time passed. Dimase continued to work the Berger case but came up with nothing. The trail was cold, and he knew it. The monster had slunk away into the darkness. He was still out there watching and waiting no doubt. The FBI had placed Liz McFarland into witness protection. No one but the US Marshals knew exactly where, but he figured she was somewhere out of the way, working in a nondescript job of some kind. She had lost her normal life because of what Hans Berger had done and could do if given the chance. The outcome wasn't fair, yet it was much better than the alternative of being a dead woman walking.

Susan, on the other hand, had rejected long-term witness protection. She wanted desperately to get back into research, and she'd convinced the FBI to place her temporarily under a false name as a research associate at Feinberg School of Medicine, an affiliate of Northwestern University. She would do no teaching and technically be under the wing of the head of her department, but she would be allowed to conduct her own research. She would keep a low profile, and that was fine with her. She'd had enough excitement for a lifetime.

The foundation of knowledge she'd acquired in the Alzheimer's field during her time at MIT uniquely positioned her. There were a number of real possibilities she wanted to pick up and pursue from that time. It was not publicized, but as part of the package, the government provided a secret grant of $250,000 to fund her operation. As far as Feinberg School of Medicine was concerned, she was a government researcher whom the government wanted affiliated with a top-notch institution for a joint special project.

Dimase felt cautious satisfaction as he thought about that. Susan, it seemed, had landed on her feet. The only problem was that Berger was still out there. He was still a threat that had to be neutralized.

CHAPTER 20

Chicago, Illinois

In the lab, Susan peered through the microscope at a slide with a smear of brain tissue on it. The cells were clearly distorted, ravaged by the poisonous touch of Alzheimer's disease. How she wished she could find a way to treat the illness, the source of too many long goodbyes for too many people. She sat up straight and rubbed her eyes.

She thought of Berger and of Liz and the others multiple times every single day. Her responsibility for the deaths of her friends weighed heavily on her. If she hadn't made up the false story about Berger raping her, they all would have been alive that day. Now only she and Liz survived, but Susan alone knew the truth about that part of the story. Her plan to take down Berger had been stunningly successful, but she never had envisioned the fallout. In her mind, she more than anyone was responsible for creating the monster Berger had become. Of course, intellectually, she knew Berger was responsible for himself and his own actions; however, emotionally, as much as she tried to rationalize, she could not escape her own guilt. Although she hadn't realized it at the time, she now understood that Berger had been dishonest and self-absorbed from the start. Yet there was no escaping the fact that she had been the trigger. She had set all this in motion with one innocent, well-intended lie. She could never escape that truth, and worse, she could never share it with anyone. The research was her only salvation, and every day she wondered if that would be the day when Berger came for her.

◆ ◆ ◆

Cambridge, Massachusetts

The search for Berger had been stalled for months. The analysis of the Blackwood murder scene in California had turned up nothing useful, except the autopsy had revealed that Cicely had been injected with cyanide, a major shift in Berger's typical MO. The lunatic generally liked dealing with sharps.

As he sat at his desk, mulling over the case, Dimase suddenly wondered if Berger still checked the text account on Susan's old phone. Berger was astute enough to realize that by now, Susan and Liz had both been given new identities and placed beyond his reach. Part of that process would have involved Susan surrendering her old cell phone. Still, if he ever checked it again, even once, it could open a line of communication. Maybe Dimase could stir the pot.

He called the evidence room and asked them to retrieve the phone and send it to his office. He charged up the phone and called Coyne into his office. "Do you think he still checks?" Dimase asked.

"Only one way to find out," Coyne replied.

Dimase tapped out a message: "Hans, Dimase here. It occurred to me this might be a way for us to talk. Interested?"

"That should do it," Dimase said with satisfaction. "If he sees it, I bet he can't resist saying something in response."

"There's no way to trace him even if he does, right?" Coyne asked.

"No, I don't think so. He used to sign in to her account remotely. He could do that from any computer anywhere. I'm just thinking if we can communicate, maybe he'll give us a clue by accident, or, as unlikely as it may be, perhaps we could even negotiate something."

"Good luck with that," Coyne said. "Have you asked Larson what he thinks?"

"No, but that's a good idea."

Dimase kept the phone in his office and got in the habit of checking it a couple of times each day. It was a long shot, but at that point, the trail was cold, and any possibility was worth trying. Larson agreed there was a good chance Berger would respond if he saw the message.

◆ ◆ ◆

Davis Square, Somerville, Massachusetts

Berger finished his last set of push-ups and toweled off as he admired his naked torso in the mirror. He'd given some thought to relocating elsewhere but ultimately rejected that idea. He remembered the hunt for Osama bin Laden. The United States had spent most of its time looking in the mountains of Afghanistan, when he actually had been right next door to a major Pakistani military installation, hiding on the outskirts of a city. The Pakistanis were supposed to be US allies, yet they'd claimed to know nothing about the world's number-one fugitive living right in their midst, hiding in plain sight. Bin Laden had been caught only because his identity was known to a courier, and he also had allowed himself to be seen out in the open once or twice on the grounds of the compound, caught by satellite imagery. Nothing like that was a threat to Berger.

Still, he admired the brilliance of bin Laden in remaining hidden for years and occupying the biggest house in the neighborhood right under the noses of his would-be captors. Berger derived pleasure from being able to do essentially the same. It was just another indicator of his superiority that he could maintain his base of operations a mere cab ride away from the headquarters of the Cambridge PD. He never went out in public as himself anymore. He was a master at changing his look as well as his persona when assuming different identities. If he had moved anywhere else in the country, there would have been a level of risk to getting reestablished. Neighbors could have become aware of someone new in the area. That could have sparked curiosity. He'd have had to find a new place to keep the car and deal with a new landlord.

When he analyzed it, the best choice was to stay embedded right where he was. He had everything set up just the way he wanted. He could leave the apartment and move about as he pleased as one character or another. His vehicle was readily accessible. If he didn't get caught in the act of committing a crime somewhere out in the world, there was no reason he couldn't stay for years or even decades in the Somerville location. The only real risk would be when he decided to murder again, and he controlled that risk. He could turn that risk on, or he could shut it off.

That was his dilemma. He could remain passive, and his

chance of getting caught was almost nil, but the itch was starting again. It became more of an irritant with each passing month. Physically, he was back to peak strength, in better shape than ever, fully recovered from all his wounds with the exception of the urination problem. Mentally, he was sharp, filling his days with voracious reading on innumerable topics and keeping up with current events on TV and online. Emotionally, he was roiled; his urges were becoming unbearable and impossible to ignore. He was like a young man at the peak of his libido who hadn't been with a woman in a long time and had the thought of copulation enter his mind every minute of every day. Only with Berger, it wasn't sexual desire that consumed him. It was bloodlust. He had to kill again.

The desire was overpowering. He missed the challenge of creating a plan, the thrill of carrying it out, the power it gave him, and the notoriety that followed. Susan and Liz were not a consideration. He had no idea where they were. He would have to find a substitute. For the time being, surrogates would have to do. It was time to plan a field trip.

◆ ◆ ◆

FBI Headquarters, Saltonstall Building, Boston, Massachusetts

Dimase Augustin, Bob Coyne, and Bill Larson huddled around the small table in Larson's office at FBI headquarters in the Saltonstall Building in downtown Boston. Larson had summoned Dimase to discuss a report that had surfaced the previous day, and Dimase had asked Coyne to tag along. All three of them read it twice through.

"Do you think it's him?" Dimase asked.

"I think there's a pretty good chance," Larson replied. "It

could be a copycat, but the reference to truth, along with the posing, is what caught my eye."

"That's a fair point," Dimase said, "but the reference to truth is in a different context. Remember, with Berger, the message wasn't always about truth. It started out about justice. Only the attempt on Liz at Cambridge PD had a message involving truth: 'truth, justice, and the American way.'"

"You're right. In the beginning, Berger's message was about justice for Susan and her friends. He sought revenge against those he felt had wronged him, but we all know that changed. He expanded his targets to include anyone in the way—anyone in the wrong place at the wrong time. 'Truth, justice, and the American way' is a reference to Superman. I think he was telling us that he sees himself as Superman, perhaps in a mocking way toward us. He was telling us two different things. First, he is like Superman and can do anything he wants, and we are powerless to stop him. Second, life isn't fair. There is no justice, not for him and not for anyone in his path. There is only truth—the truth of death. What started as a revenge tour has evolved into his becoming a full-blown serial killer. If he did these girls on the Appalachian Trail, that's what he's telling us. He's saying this is his truth now. This is what he has become. This is what we have made him: a killer with no purpose other than to kill. His truth now is that he kills for the thrill of it and all that entails for him."

Dimase sighed and read the report again. "Two female hikers in their late twenties were found on a remote section of the Appalachian Trail near Ashby, West Virginia, with their throats slit, their heads shaved after the fact, and their faces painted with excessive makeup and lipstick. They were posed in a mutual embrace, sitting upright on the ground with their backs against a fallen tree. Each held one corner of a poster board positioned like a sign between them. Their hands were stapled to the poster board to keep it in place. Written on the board was the simple message 'My truth.'"

Larson continued. "I think it's significant there are two of them."

"How so?"

"They could be taking the place of Susan and Liz. He can't get to them, so he did these two girls in their place. Fantasy maybe? He knows it's not them, but he pretends. He gets the same thrill, and he gets some sort of dry run. At the same time, he satisfies his growing need to kill."

"So you actually do think it's him," Dimase said.

"I think there's a pretty good chance. They're processing the scene today, looking for DNA, fiber, and anything else that could help us. If it's someone else, there's a pretty good chance they left something behind. If it's our guy, my bet is the sight will be clean. They won't find anything."

Dimase had a thought. Weeks ago, he'd set up his own phone to access Susan's old text account in order to make it easier to consistently check for communication from Berger. He kept his message on the site and periodically refreshed the date in the hope that if Berger did visit, he would realize Dimase's attempt was relatively current.

Dimase explained to Larson what he'd been up to. "I've been fishing for a couple of months, knowing he has access to Susan's texts. I realized if he ever went on and looked at it again, it might open up a means of communicating with him."

Dimase pulled up the account, and his eyes widened. He turned the phone slightly so Larson and Coyne could read his text: "Hans, Dimase here. It occurs to me this might be a way for us to talk. Interested?"

Then he scrolled down with his thumb to show them what he had just seen: "Dimase, how nice to hear from you. I've seen your message for some time but really didn't have anything to talk about until now. It wasn't Susan and Liz, but it will have to do for the time being. You wouldn't know how I could get in touch with them, would you?"

"Holy shit!" Larson exclaimed. "It was him. He's known you were trying to reach out to him the whole time."

"The man is everywhere," Dimase said, "from Maine to California and now West Virginia. Do you think he's living in that area?"

"Possible, but I doubt it," Larson said. "He's obviously got wheels, and we have no idea what they are. He probably picked that location to throw us off because it's not near any of the other murders. He could be set up anywhere at this point, but he's obviously mobile. I don't think we're going to solve this one by drawing circles on a map to see where they overlap."

◆ ◆ ◆

Davis Square, Somerville, Massachusetts

Berger, safely ensconced in his Somerville apartment, grinned at the article in the *Boston Globe*. The story was about the murder of two young women on the Appalachian Trail in West Virginia. He thought back on doing the deed, including how excited he'd been as the girls begged for their lives. Now it was all over the media, and somehow, the reporters had rightly put it together that he, the Phantom Professor, had done it. They portrayed him as being invisible to the authorities, untouchable, and an evil genius. The police were out of their depth, outsmarted, and overmatched at every turn. They were no closer to catching him now than they had been after the first murder. His superiority was obvious. When, in the long history of serial killers, had there ever been such a diabolical mind? He appeared and disappeared without a trace. In that age of technology, why couldn't the police find Dr. Hans Berger? Where would he strike next, and whom would he choose for victims?

Berger wanted to stay active. He loved the game. He lived for it now. Ultimately, he still wanted his shot at Susan and Liz. It was one thing to avoid capture by going underground and staying hidden. It was quite another to evade the authorities while still putting oneself out there. That was exclusive territory—legendary territory. That was Berger's legacy now.

Berger's subconscious mind had been working on the Susan and Liz problem all along. Recently, he'd started to get some conscious ideas about how to possibly flush them out, particularly Susan. Two concepts came to him specifically. Until now, they had been kept out of the public eye. He was about to change that—and in spectacular fashion.

It was an inspiration. When he developed and executed his project, Susan and Liz would become household names. Everyone in the country would know who they were and that they had been members of the book club. His fan base would go wild.

Berger still wouldn't know their new names or locations in the witness protection program. Hopefully that would come in phase two. Still, if media widely knew their story, the press would look everywhere for the two women. The authorities would fight that line of inquiry every step of the way, but there were enough unscrupulous, amoral media types out there who wouldn't give a damn if they exposed Susan's and Liz's new identities. Berger would have a small army of reporters unwittingly engaged in his cause. They'd be looking everywhere for the two protectees. What a coup it would be to find one of them and get an exclusive interview.

It may or may not happen, but if he could pull off what he had in mind, he would have enlisted some of the best investigative reporters in the country to start digging deep. They would rationalize that the women could always be whisked away to new locations and given other identities. Regardless, their obligation was to get the truth. The public had a right to know.

Susan and Liz would become the focus of the media's most ambitious and aggressive minds. Berger would have a crack team working on his behalf once he pulled the trigger, and what a trigger it would be. He could hardly contain his glee at the thought of it. At the very least, Susan and Liz would be spooked by becoming the center of national attention. Maybe they would make a forced error. Maybe they would show themselves.

The second concept would take time, but he could roll out the two operations simultaneously. It took a while for that one to crystalize. Berger had images of Susan in his mind. He recalled her doing research in the lab, innocent and driven—driven by the memory of her grandmother to find a cure for Alzheimer's. When those thoughts percolated to his conscious mind, he had a eureka moment. Obviously, Susan had been given a new name, identity, and location. Wherever she was, both she and her protectors knew she might be there for a long time, possibly years or even decades. The situation had been forced upon her, and she had little or no choice in the matter. Would she really have given up her central mission in life? Could she actually have put that on hold indefinitely, letting the years go by, sidelined with no purpose? Would she really have given up any opportunity to continue her research?

She would not have. That was Berger's insight, the breakthrough to his conscious brain. He was sure of it. Of course, there was no guarantee, but he knew Susan. He understood what made her tick. He could see her giving up everything else, agreeing to witness protection, and taking on a new life. She had to do those things as a matter of self-preservation, but the research? Berger would have bet his life—or, more accurately, Susan's life—that she could never have walked completely away from the research. If he accepted that fact as a given, then it provided a path to find her. They had provided Susan a new life, but Berger was sure that whatever her cover, they'd constructed a scenario that had allowed her to resume the research. If that was the case, it was a thread that needed to be pulled.

Berger put together a plan to implement the second part of his strategy. After all, he had all the time in the world. He would do some research himself and compile a comprehensive list of every medical institution in the country with a research arm. He would scour websites as well as every medical journal and publication that ever had produced an article on the topic of Alzheimer's. He would cross-check bibliographies and references, assembling a master list of articles and contributors.

He didn't really expect Susan, or her false identity, to turn up on any of the lists. His objective was to complete a directory of every name and institution even tangentially associated with Alzheimer's research. He would define the entire universe, and then he would look for clues to narrow the field. From there, he would go to the blogs and anonymous chat rooms. He planned to create his own false identity as a young graduate student interested in Alzheimer's research. He would place provocative posts, seeking to prompt a response—most likely not a response from Susan but maybe close enough to home to attract her attention if she was watching.

After all, who knew more about the subject than he did? He also knew the angles Susan had been working on back at MIT. He wouldn't be too obvious about it, but he could come up with some stuff that might lure her into a chat room. If he got a wide enough conversation going in enough different chat rooms and blogs and planted a couple of tidbits about how tau reduction in brain synapses was more impactful than amyloid beta reduction, he would reach her sooner or later, assuming she was still in the field.

Berger whitewashed an entire wall of his apartment to turn it into a huge writer board. He got himself a package of multicolored markers, and as he identified institutions, he created a giant map on the wall. Next to each institution, he wrote columns of names uncovered in his own research. He drew lines and circled names to indicate people from different institutions who had a connection, perhaps in collaborating or publishing together or exchanging views on a blog or in a chat room. He worked tirelessly to create a visual mural defining the entire universe of Alzheimer's research. Then, if need be, he would look for what wasn't there. Who didn't fit? Who was new? Who knew whom? What clues could he find?

He would be patient, but if Susan Pearce was in that universe, he would find her. Sooner or later, as always, the variables would better define themselves.

CHAPTER 21

Acadia National Park, Maine

The deed was done. He stood back and looked at the Liz doll. *Not bad*, he thought. Of course, it wasn't a perfect likeness, but no one would miss the connection. The custom T-shirts he'd picked up at a sidewalk shop a few weeks earlier in Rye Beach, New Hampshire, would help to ensure that. Written across the front in bold red lettering was "Book Club." On her head, he placed a maroon baseball-style cap emblazoned with black letters: MIT.

He had cut and dyed the cheap wig beneath the cap so it approximated his best memory of Liz's color and style. To make the scene even more surreal, he applied makeup and bright red lipstick to give the face a doll-like appearance, emphasizing her lips and enlarging her eyes with blue shadow and black liner. *Perfect*. His fans would get a charge when word got around about this one.

He turned his attention to the lifeless mannequin lying on

the ground behind him, which would soon become the Susan doll. He dragged her over to the low-lying folding camp chair next to Liz and flipped her around, maneuvering her into a sitting position in the chair. With a bit of a struggle, he raised her hands over her head, removed the soiled lightweight "Maine: Life in the Slow Lane" sweatshirt she was wearing, and gently cleaned blood away from the ugly gash on her throat. He pulled a matching "Book Club" T-shirt over her torso and arranged a blonde wig atop her head. Within minutes, the makeup was done, and another MIT baseball cap was in place.

He pushed the chairs a little closer side by side and put the dolls' hands together with their fingers interlaced, as if they were holding hands as a last gesture of their deep friendship. From his backpack, he removed a half dozen science textbooks. He put an open book in each doll's lap and stacked the others next to their chairs, a symbol of their deep commitment to academia and the pursuit of knowledge. He did love his imagery.

The last step was to leave the message and place the name tags. He smiled again as he thought about the media frenzy he was about to unleash. They all wondered if there were more book club members. He would spell it out for them and then sit back and see what reaction he got.

He used black magic marker to write out on one name tag, "Hi. I'm Liz McFarland." He removed the backing and stuck the sticky side on her T-shirt, above her right breast, just as if she were attending an academic conference. On a second name tag, he wrote, "Hi. I'm Susan Pearce," and he affixed it above the doll's left breast. Lastly, he removed from his knapsack a carefully crafted note handwritten in neat black script on double-bond paper. The message said, "The truth will win out." He folded the message and tucked it between two pages of the open book the Susan doll held in her lap.

Berger had been camping and hiking around Acadia National Park for five days, patiently seeking the closest match. There had been a couple of other possibilities, including a threesome, but in that case, he'd have had to dispose of the third body in order to stage the final scene the way he wished. Then good fortune had smiled upon him when he stumbled across those two candidates. They were just what he'd been looking for. They'd made the final cut.

Berger was in character; he'd dyed his long naturally blond hair and beard jet black. With sunglasses and a cap, he was just another hiker. Of course, everyone would know it was him after the fact. That was the whole idea, exactly what he wanted. Until that point, he wanted to blend in.

With his task complete, he hustled back to the trail, hiked back to the campground, retrieved his gear, and then moved on to the parking area.

He had one last curveball to throw at Dimase and his cohorts. This time around, they would not be able to withhold any details of the crime scene. More importantly, Liz McFarland and Susan Pearce were about to become national celebrities—household names. An army of media would be looking for them, willing to sacrifice anything for an exclusive, career-making story. He wondered how that would make Susan and Liz, hiding and waiting in the false security of their new identities, feel.

Safely back on the highway, he took a burner phone from the Volvo's glove compartment and called the regional desk of the *Boston Globe*. He waited for a live voice to come on the line.

"Good morning. I have an exclusive story for you if you hurry. On the downside slope of the Beehive Loop in Acadia National Park, approximately one thousand feet from the summit, use a compass, and leave the trail, walking due west for two hundred feet. You and everyone else have been looking for additional members of the so-called book club in the Phantom Professor case. In that area, you will find the last two remaining members."

"Who is this?" the reporter asked.

"Shut up, and look where I told you. Your choice. I'm just trying to help you out. You'd better get moving if you want to be the first one there."

Berger hung up the phone, ending the conversation.

◆ ◆ ◆

Acadia National Park, Maine

Dimase clasped his hands behind his back as he stood in front of the macabre scene. Obviously, the call to the *Globe* had come from Berger. Obviously, the brutal murder of the two women had been his work. Obviously, Berger had wanted the reporters to find the scene and report on it.

"The guy is back in true form," Larson said. "It seems clear he's trying to draw the ladies out of hiding."

Dimase nodded. "That's what I think too."

"Well, he sure as hell is gonna get lots of press on this one," Coyne said. "That'll feed his ego a bit, I'd say."

"Sadly, I think you're right," Dimase said. He knew the story was going to get out sooner rather than later.

◆ ◆ ◆

Twenty-four hours later, Dimase opened the *Boston Globe* and saw pictures of the two murder victims on the front page. His hands shook slightly as he read the headline: "Who Are Liz McFarland and Susan Pearce?" The accompanying story was filled with speculation and inaccuracies, but the gist was that authorities had not yet confirmed the identities of the two women. The story raised many questions but provided few answers. Were the two unfortunate women actually Liz McFarland and Susan Pearce? Were they members of the book club? What was the motive? Why the staged production? Was their killing related to the murders of Gussie Watkins, Angela Mancini, Ellen Klein, and Cicely Blackwood? Was it related to the similar killing of two hikers on the Appalachian Trail? Who were Liz McFarland and Susan Pearce?

The reporters had promised to keep the story under wraps for at least a day or two, and Dimase was furious that they hadn't. Frankly, he wasn't surprised, just angry and disappointed because the press coverage played right into Berger's hand. The cat was out of the bag. The Associated Press quickly picked up the story, and almost immediately, the two doll-like figures became macabre instant celebrities in death. Most cable TV channels tried at first to pretend they had standards that prohibited them from running pictures of the corpses, but the images were ubiquitous throughout the internet, and once the *Globe* broke protocol and set a new precedent by publishing the pictures, most media and news outlets quickly followed suit, citing that once the pictures were so widely distributed, they became part of the public domain.

It wasn't long before the real identities of the dead women were discovered. They were friends from New York City on a weeklong camping trip to the park. They had no known relationship to any of the previous victims and no connection to MIT. In fact, they had hardly spent any time at all in Boston. It appeared they had just been in the wrong place at the wrong time—random victims selected perhaps solely on the basis of age and gender. That begged the question of who the real Elizabeth McFarland and Susan Pearce were.

◆ ◆ ◆

Davis Square, Somerville, Massachusetts

Berger was giddy as he flipped through channels on the TV, monitoring the latest coverage. He thrilled at each news segment featuring a breathless reporter hyping the story for all it was worth. His goal was to shake things up for Susan and Liz. He still had no idea where they were, but he knew they must have been aware of the media maelstrom surrounding them and feeling pretty uncomfortable. It was time to ramp up the second phase of his operation.

He looked at the twelve-foot-long, six-foot-high white wall covered with writing, a schematic of Alzheimer's research institutions and scientific publications. Hundreds of names were written on the wall, sorted by different affiliations and cross-connections, with lines to indicate relationships. He would find Susan Pearce somewhere in that universe. He was sure of it.

◆ ◆ ◆

Davis Square, Somerville, Massachusetts

Dimase stood front and center at the podium in the media room at Cambridge PD. Flanking him to either side were Larson and Smith from the FBI. The room was filled to capacity with reporters of all stripes and was quiet for the moment. Dimase knew that as soon as he finished his prepared statement, all hell would break loose.

"Thank you for coming. The two women found murdered in Acadia National Park last week have been identified as twenty-six-year-old Roberta Clapper of Connersville, New York, and her lifelong friend twenty-seven-year-old Hannah Walsh, also of Connersville. The two women were childhood friends, apparently on vacation together in the park. The cause of death for Ms. Clapper was an acute knife wound to the throat. For Ms. Walsh, the cause of death was a broken neck. We don't believe either of the women has a connection to MIT or the so-called book club. They do not appear to have spent any time in Boston as adults and have no significant connections to the Greater Boston area that we know of at this time. Their deaths are being investigated as possibly being part of a series of serial killings. We have no motive as of yet. That's all I have for you at this time."

The room exploded in chaos with a cacophony of shouted questions.

"Why were they staged as Susan Pearce and Liz McFarland?"

"Is former MIT professor Hans Berger a suspect?"

"Where are the real Pearce and McFarland now?"

"Are Pearce and McFarland dead or alive?"

"Do you have any leads on the whereabouts of the Phantom Professor?"

"Can you confirm Pearce and McFarland were part of a book club with previous victims?"

The questions went on and on. Dimase waited for the furor to die down and then signaled for quiet with the palms of his hands. "Professor Berger is a person of interest in this case and several other murders. His current whereabouts are unknown. If anyone has any information on him, they should call the FBI. He is considered armed and extremely dangerous. I caution members of the public not to engage with him under any circumstances but to call authorities immediately should you have any information."

"What about Pearce and McFarland?" a reporter shouted. "Where are they?"

"We have no comment on the whereabouts of Susan Pearce or Elizabeth McFarland." With that, Dimase turned and left the room through a hail of shouted questions, followed closely by Larson and Smith.

Back in Dimase's office, the three of them sat and contemplated their next move. The site at Acadia National Park was clean of DNA and other direct evidence linking the crime to Berger. Of course, it wasn't a blind crime scene. They already knew with certainty who the perpetrator was. There was no doubt about that. This was no copycat killing. The use of Susan's and Liz's names was proof of Berger's involvement, and to erase any trace of doubt, the professor had reached out to them the previous day with a text to Susan's account, which was now on Dimase's phone: "How many more have to die? How about giving me a clue, Dimase? Where are they?"

They had not shared Berger's communication with the press. None of them wanted to get into a public war of words with Berger through the press. The media exposure would only have excited him and possibly even prompted further acts of violence to entertain his fans.

"What do we do about Susan and Liz?" Dimase asked. "Do we leave them in place or pull them out?"

"Pull them out?" Larson said. "What good would that do? We'd only have to establish new identities for them somewhere else. Just going through that process of relocation would be more exposure than having them shelter in place. The longer they stay where they are, the more established they'll become in the new identities and the harder they will be to locate."

"I don't disagree," Dimase said, "but if that's the case, we have to harden our defenses. Most times, when people go into the witness protection program, they disappear into anonymity. No one is looking for them. Susan and Liz have the entire national press corps trying to figure out where they are."

"That's probably exactly what Berger wants. That's why he

dressed up the two girls in Acadia to look like them. The son of a bitch has recruited thousands of reporters to help him find them. What do you have in mind?"

"We have to hold a secure conference call with each of them separately. I want each to have a panic-button device on her person at all times and perhaps some kind of tracking device as well. More importantly, at least for the time being, I want each of them to have a shadow. I want someone placed near them in an undercover position that even they do not know about. If there's a panic-button call, that shadow should be right nearby. We'll place the shadows in housing near the protectees. They'll have no direct contact. They'll observe and protect. Maybe their cover is as a janitor, a groundskeeper, or something like that. Susan works in an institutional environment. A janitor might have freedom of movement around her buildings. At night, they will be in a nearby apartment or house."

"What if the shadow spooks them?" Larson asked.

"Would you rather spook them or have them wind up dead? If we use the right people, they won't get spooked, and neither will anyone else. Their presence will be totally innocuous, part of the fabric of the community. Until this is over, I don't want Susan and Liz dangling out there on their own. I also want a rapid response team that is fully prepped on this case and ready to go at the drop of a hat to back up the shadow should there ever be a need."

Larson agreed. "It's not the normal procedure for witness protection, but then again, this is a totally different situation. I don't like the idea of them being out there all alone either, not as long as Berger is at large and actively looking for them, along with everyone else. He's not your everyday criminal, and he seems to have a knack for keeping one step ahead of us."

◆ ◆ ◆

Davis Square, Somerville, Massachusetts

Berger paced back and forth in front of his special wall. He eyed the names, stopped, and then started pacing again. His plan called for a two-pronged attack. He'd executed phase one to perfection. He'd enlisted an army of media to search everywhere for Susan Pearce and Liz McFarland. Thanks to the murders at Acadia National Park, as planned, the two women had become household names. Wherever they were, they must have been nervous, wondering every time someone looked at them if that person was suspicious of their true identity. They had been dropped into new communities out of the blue, and they were the right age to be the missing women. Surely someone would be curious about their background and look a little deeper. The heat was on.

At the same time, Berger had spent weeks constructing and adjusting the large schematic map and organizational chart on his wall. He could have done the same thing on his computer, but he liked the visual impact and cathartic feel of the wall. His apartment felt like a war room, and he was the general in charge, the master mind orchestrating each strategic move.

Phase two was to establish a series of false online identities and participate in every chat room out there related to Alzheimer's research. Berger knew his way around the internet as well as anyone. He searched for chat rooms, most of them anonymous, and created an identity to suit each one. He read every blog and every research publication on the topic. He cultivated a different persona and backstory for his presence in each chat room.

On some, he was identified as Grinder1, a grad student engaged in research. On others, he was Grampacure, a family member trying to keep up on the latest research, looking for hope for a loved one. He created chat room identities as teachers, students, family members, and journalists. On one site, he even represented himself as an early stage dementia patient. It was a full-time job to track all the activity every day and keep responses and information up to date. He was immersed in the Alzheimer's community online.

Phase two was a giant coordinated fishing operation. He was trolling for a tuna and had to be just as patient. If Susan Pearce was still in the world of Alzheimer's research, she was represented or connected somewhere on his wall, either listed with a pseudonym or as an unlisted person invisibly associated with one of the institutions or organizations represented on his operational map.

Weeks before the murders at Acadia, Berger had begun the early stages of the construction and implementation of phase two. As the wall filled with multicolored notes, lists, and diagrams, he systematically conducted deep research on any appropriate names. Many were easy to rule out. Having come from the same field, he already knew many of them. He quickly eliminated others on the basis of gender, age, or ethnicity. He was trying to narrow the pool, and at the same time, he was hoping to engage possible candidates in conversation in chat rooms, looking for any inadvertent clue that might point to the identity and location of the person he sought.

As the scope narrowed, he focused on young female researchers who were in new situations; had recently joined an organization; or were newly affiliated with a university, publication, or project. There were many. Berger also realized the person he sought might not publicly list herself, in an effort to shield her true identity. In that case, he reasoned, he would have to look for the footprint she created—in a sense, he'd have to work backward from specific research initiatives that had some similarity to the work at MIT and look for a false name in the credits, a name with no matching background on the deep net, a repeat commenter in a chat room, or a reference to unattributed work.

It was slow, painstaking forensic work, but Berger was up to the task. He was back to doing what he was good at: working a complex, multilayered research project. In the weeks after the Acadia murders, his days were consumed by the project. He was a recluse in the apartment, sorting through names, developing profiles, disregarding prospects, and adding new candidates, only to repeat the process again and again. Like a fisherman putting multiple lines in the water, patiently plying his task, patrolling from pole to pole, and jigging each line with an occasional tug, Berger checked his chat rooms each day.

The universe was getting smaller. Either the press would flush Susan out, or Berger would hunt her down. As always, the variables would eventually define themselves. The puzzle would be solved, and the picture would come into focus. Berger could be a very patient man.

CHAPTER 22

Feinberg School of Medicine, Chicago, Illinois

Susan was feeling the heat of the national media search for her and Liz. She didn't even know where Liz was—a precaution in shielding each other's identity and location—but she hoped she was okay. There was no longer any communication between the two women. That was strictly forbidden. Phones and computers had been confiscated and replaced with devices that wiped the slate clean.

Ever since the horrific murders of the two unfortunate stand-ins at Acadia National Park, Susan had been a basket case. The anguish she felt for the two innocent women was accompanied by a sense of deep foreboding for her own safety. The follow-up conference call with Dimase and the feds hadn't helped much. They were obviously nervous too.

Every time she interacted with a colleague, Susan felt naked, exposed, as if she had a sign around her neck that said, "I'm the one. I'm the one everyone's looking for. I'm Susan Pearce." She tried to shut out the media madness, but it was hard to avoid. Every time she turned on the TV or looked online, it seemed there was a reference to some aspect of the case. Everyone wanted to know: Where were Susan Pearce and Liz McFarland? Where was the Phantom Professor?

There were all kinds of speculation and false leads. What was the motive behind the murders? Was it a love triangle?

In her mind, she felt it must have been painfully obvious to others around her that she was a good candidate to be one of the missing women. After all, she was the right age. She had shown up at the right time and out of nowhere, from her colleagues' perspective. She flipped the argument around, debating it endlessly in her mind. It was a circular thought pattern from which there was no escape.

Don't be silly, she would tell herself. *There must be thousands of young women moving around the country every week, changing jobs, schools, and cities for a myriad of reasons. I'm just being paranoid.*

Her natural reaction was to retreat from contact with people. Her only escape was to lose herself in the research. The less visible she was, the less exposed she felt. Her depression began to return. A fog of hopelessness enshrouded her day as the emotional and physical isolation took a toll.

The research itself was going well, although progress was glacially slow, in part because she wasn't using any direct lab assistants or coresearchers. As a means of self-preservation, she filled her days and nights with work-related tasks: data analysis, technical reading, and related subjects. She avoided the news.

Typically, she gravitated to reading the blogs of other scientists, which eventually drew her into a half dozen chat rooms. The chat rooms provided an anonymous way for her to have some social interaction with like-minded people.

Over time, one particular chat room caught her interest. The participants seemed to be a bunch of research geeks, and the topic broadly revolved around the differing roles of tau and amyloid beta in the brain. Discussion ranged from how and why each type of protein was generated to where in the brain each tended to concentrate, any differentiation in symptoms, and the efficacy of possible chemical compounds to reduce the presence of one or the other. Much of the conversation was right up her alley, and the anonymous platform was the perfect forum for her to be able to participate.

Susan's tag was 1researchgeek. She had no idea who the other participants were or where they were located, nor would they have known about her. One evening, unexpectedly, Cureboy, which flashed in Susan's mind as a wordplay on *choirboy*, made a random reference to PKC Group in Boston, questioning whether they had made any progress since leaving MIT and going private. Another participant noted that they hadn't published or released any information since the crazy professor who'd founded the company had left. Another asked if that was the Phantom Professor, the one who'd committed all the murders. That sparked a vigorous exchange about whether PKC ever really had been onto anything or actually had nothing. Maybe that was why the guy had left.

Of course, none of that explained why he'd started killing everybody, but almost comically and in stereotypical character, the geeks in the group focused less on the sensational murders that had captivated the rest of the country and more on whether there was anything of value in the work at PKC.

Susan, who had been actively involved in the conversation up to the point it veered into the discussion about PKC Group, now sat back and didn't participate. Her emotions were screaming to set the record straight and blurt out that there was something real at PKC, but her rational brain forced her to stay quiet.

◆ ◆ ◆

Davis Square, Somerville, Massachusetts

Back at his apartment in Davis Square, Cureboy, a.k.a. the Phantom Professor, a.k.a. Hans Berger, made note of her lack of participation. Why the sudden radio silence from 1researchgeek? Was it a sensitive subject, one that struck too close to home? It seemed odd. He decided to prod.

Berger looked at the schematic on his wall and typed out a general comment: "I heard the government is funding some new programs in other parts of the country that are also focusing on tau compounds, similar to the work at MIT that led to PKC Group."

Susan responded, "I think there's something happening on the West Coast. Not sure. I heard somebody in administration talking about it. Stanford maybe?"

Berger's mind started churning as his eyes scanned back and forth over the wall chart. "Stanford? Why is it they always give all the money to both coasts? What's wrong with the rest of the country?"

One participant responded, "Sorry, Cureboy. Can't help you with that. I am on a coast and happy to take the money. LOL."

Three or four others made similar comments. One mentioned being located in the South, and another was in the Midwest. Cureboy noted that 1resarchgeek again remained silent during the exchange, other than her initial remark diverting attention to the West Coast. *Interesting*, he thought. *Could fit the profile. Knowledgeable on tau research, didn't speak at all during the discussion on PKC Group, seemed aware of government funding but directed everyone to the West Coast, and was the only one not to comment when people disclosed which regions of the country they were from.*

It wasn't much to go on, but when trolling big game fish, one had to expect long hours and long odds, which was okay because Berger had both the time and the patience.

He logged out of the chat room and walked over to the writing-covered wall. With a red marker, he drew a large circle around the entire middle of the country. With a blue marker, he drew a large circle around southern states from Texas to Florida. He took out a pad of paper and started writing down potential research centers within the circles. He remembered that 1researchgeek had referred to someone in the administration when mentioning government research funds being directed to the West Coast. Had that been an intentional misdirection? The word *administration* implied that 1researchgeek might be in an academic environment, possibly a medical school engaged in research.

On a whim, he googled "top medical research schools in the Midwest" and came up with a list. He did the same for the southern states. He had to start somewhere.

Berger came up with a plan. He'd been confined to the apartment for weeks. It was time to plan another field trip. He was proud of his detective work. Now it was time for an action step.

He looked at the list for the Midwest and resolved to begin there. He would develop an identity of his own and visit each school. Susan might not be at any of them. Then again, she might. He was winnowing the field, narrowing the scope, one step at a time. If he got lucky, it would be a spectacular win for him and his fans. If not, he could cross those institutions off his list. In the meantime, he would keep a close eye on 1researchgeek in the chat rooms. Maybe he could glean some further tidbit of information that narrowed down her location. That one definitely had potential. He knew the variables would better define themselves sooner or later.

◆ ◆ ◆

Davis Square, Somerville, Massachusetts

Dimase parked his car at a meter about a block from the newsstand he was looking for. The tip had been phoned in earlier that morning and forwarded to Dimase, who'd decided to handle it himself. Dimase strolled casually down the sidewalk and waited patiently until the vendor selling newspapers at the outdoor stand had a lull in the action.

"Mr. Salta," Dimase said, flashing his badge. He then identified himself. "I'm here to talk about the information you called in this morning. What can you tell me?"

"Well, I sell newspapers for a living, as you can see, so I read them all the time. When the *Globe* started running that picture of the Phantom Professor guy, he looked familiar. I knew I seen him somewhere. Just wasn't sure where. Then it came to me. I ain't seen him lately, probably at least a year, but he used to come in here a long time ago."

"How long ago?" Dimase asked.

"Not sure, like I said. At least a year. Maybe more. That's why I couldn't place him. It was back before all those murders started, back before they was all talking about this Phantom Professor, but it was him."

Dimase felt a surge of hope. If that were true, it might mean Berger still lived somewhere in the area. He pulled out a set of photos of Berger, and the man confirmed it was the same person he'd seen at his stand.

"How many times did you see him?"

"Oh, back then, lots of times off and on. Sometimes he'd come in and buy newspapers and magazines. He kind of stuck in my mind because he would always buy science journals and stuff like that if we got something new in." The clerk took a swig of his soda, put the can down on the counter, and leaned toward Dimase.

"Was he always on foot, or did he ever park a car? Which direction did he come from? Did he always come the same time of day? Did he always leave in the same direction?"

"I don't know," the vendor replied. "I didn't really pay attention, but one thing I did notice was I saw him jogging sometimes. It was always real early, just when the morning papers were coming in for the day—you know, hardly anyone out on the street yet. He'd come from down there"—the man pointed—"and about a half hour later, he'd pass by again, like on his way back."

Dimase thanked the man and handed him a card. He hoped the information could be the break he'd been waiting for. "Call me immediately if you see him again or you think of anything else that could be important."

Dimase pondered what his next move should be as he walked back to his car. He got in and took out his cell. He called headquarters and instructed Rodriguez and Coyne to meet him at Davis Square. As he waited for the detectives to arrive, he scoped out the area, looking for residential units and apartments above storefronts or in stand-alone buildings. It appeared that with the three of them, there might be a manageable number of doors to knock on if they split up and worked east from the newsstand.

When Rodriguez and Coyne arrived, he gave them the latest intel and assigned each a section of a few blocks. "Let's knock on doors and show Berger's picture to anyone who answers. Be careful. If he's still living in this area and we stumble into him, he's got nothing to lose. Don't try anything heroic. Let's try to see if anyone else has seen him, and maybe if we get lucky, we can start to narrow down a location."

The men separated, taking their assigned areas, with Dimase starting on the opposite side of the street. Progress was slow.

They often received no response, as many people apparently were at work or school. Occasionally, Dimase could see Rodriguez and Coyne working farther down the square and venturing down side streets. Dimase had pretty much exhausted all the possibilities on the main drag, and he decided to head back in the direction of the newsstand, this time checking out side streets as he worked his way.

Just off the square, Dimase approached a two-family house with a single set of steps to the foyer. He rang the bell for the unit on the left, and an elderly woman answered the door. "Excuse me, ma'am," he said, holding out his ID. "We're doing a routine inquiry. Ever see this man in the neighborhood before?"

The woman squinted as she examined the photo. "Can't say as I have," she said at length. "Why? Did he do something wrong?"

"No, ma'am, just a person of interest. Can you tell me who else lives in this building?"

"Don't know. Never seen 'em or talked to 'em," she said, pointing at the door of the other unit.

Dimase noted a plastic grocery basket filled with sundries by the door of the other unit. It contained an assortment of grocery supplies, a newspaper, and a couple of magazines. He bent over and picked up one of the magazines: *Scientific American*. Dimase felt a shot of adrenaline. He thanked the woman, handed her a card, and waited for her to close the door. He put his ear to the door of the other unit, straining to hear anything at all. He wasn't sure if he imagined it or if, for the briefest moment, he heard distant, rhythmic grunting, as if someone were engaged in heavy exercise.

Dimase continued to listen for several minutes, but there was only silence. Finally, he rapped on the door. There was no answer. He knocked again, but still, there was no response. He bent over to examine the contents of the grocery basket more closely. There was an unsealed envelope with no addressee. Inside the envelope was a bill for the groceries. The heading on the bill read, "Pemberton Farms Marketplace." Dimase took a picture of the bill with his cell phone and replaced the envelope in the basket.

◆ ◆ ◆

Berger's Apartment, Davis Square, Somerville Massachusetts

A signal went off on Hans Berger's laptop, indicating the button camera he'd secreted in the foyer was now active. He stopped doing push-ups and stared at the image on his computer screen. *Holy Shit*, he thought. *Dimase Augustin! What the fuck is he doing here, and how did he find me?*

Berger ran to the kitchen area and grabbed the eight-inch hunting knife he kept handy in the unlikely event he had to deal with intruders, a duplicate of the knife he had used on Gussie Watkins. He ran back to the front door, lugging the laptop with him, and took a position off to the side, ready to strike should the door swing open. He held his breath and placed the laptop on the floor, angling the screen so he could continue to watch.

The detective was talking to the old lady next door. *The old bitch.* He wondered what she was telling him. Berger pressed his ear hard to the door, straining to catch any tidbit of the conversation. The lady retreated back into her apartment, and Augustin examined his grocery basket. *Shit, shit, shit. This is not good. Not now.*

Berger contemplated bursting from his apartment to take the detective by surprise, ending the threat. Augustin stood up and knocked sharply on the door. *If I throw open the door, I could probably get a knife in him before he knows what happened*, Berger thought. His fingers coiled and recoiled, opening and closing around the handle of the knife. *But what if there are others waiting outside? What if the building is surrounded? It can't end like this, not when I'm so close to finding Susan. Go ahead. Open the door, Dimase. I have a surprise for you.*

All at once, Augustin turned to leave and was out the door in a hurry. Berger could barely breathe with the tension and excitement. He half expected a SWAT team to swarm into the foyer as soon as Augustin was clear. He switched the laptop to a series of outdoor camera perspectives. He saw nothing—no activity. Augustin was gone. One thing was certain: Dimase would be back soon, and he would not be alone the next time.

Berger crossed the room to his whitewashed wall and started writing the names of medical schools in the Midwest that had significant research programs. He returned to his laptop and pulled up a map of the midwestern states, ranging west to Minnesota, Iowa, and Missouri and east to Michigan and Ohio, with Wisconsin, Illinois, and Indiana sandwiched in between. The fact that Dimase was closing in excited him more than it scared him. Nonetheless, it was time to go.

Chicago stood out for two reasons. If one envisioned the region as a wagon wheel, Chicago, at the southernmost tip of Lake Michigan, was centrally located, the hub of the wheel. From there, he could branch out along the spokes to the other states. The second and more important reason was simple mathematical efficiency. Two of the research medical schools on his list of ten were located in Chicago. He could knock two schools off his list by starting in one city.

The University of Chicago's Pritzker School of Medicine and the Feinberg College of Medicine at Northwestern University were both venerated institutions. A few days or weeks in Chicago would be a good use of his time. He turned again to the wall and, with a red magic marker, began circling the two medical schools in Chicago over and over, working himself into a frenzy. Finally, he pumped his fist and howled in exultation.

Berger gave some thought to what identity he should assume when casing out the schools. He settled on posing as some sort of PhD candidate doing research on the breakdown of public versus private funding in the area of brain research. The purpose of his supposed study would be to evaluate the most efficient use and distribution of funds.

The cover was believable, and he could easily fake some student credentials from MIT. He would call ahead to each school's director of funding and development to schedule an interview. If he approached them properly, he was sure the directors would be more than willing to accommodate a fellow academic working on his postgraduate thesis.

He certainly couldn't walk right into a lab and come face-to-face with Susan Pearce. Even if he was in character, that might alert her. An indirect approach made much more sense. Scheduling an interview with someone in senior administration would give him a free pass about campus. In addition to gathering information from the interview itself, he could wander about campus without raising suspicion. He could eat at the cafeteria, conduct random student interviews, and even hook up on a formal tour to tag along with prospective students and their parents. He could identify any appropriate buildings and keep an eye on people coming and going. If he was lucky, he might even be able to walk around inside various facilities in the relative obscurity of a group tour. That would be a perfect way to conduct surveillance.

He would promise the directors a copy of his final paper, a useful tool as a barometer to relate their relative standing to other research universities. Berger wrote and rewrote the questions many times. The finished product was like a psychological test, asking similar questions in slightly different ways, systematically sorting to the desired information.

Now that the game plan was in his head, Berger was powerless to resist the urge overwhelming him. This time, he would not have to settle for a surrogate. This time would be the real thing. This time, it would be Susan. He was sure of it.

◆ ◆ ◆

Somerville, Massachusetts

Dimase sat in the manager's office at Pemberton Farms Marketplace. The delivery boy stood in the doorway, fidgeting nervously, having been summoned by his boss. Dimase introduced himself and motioned for the boy to sit. He pulled up the photo of the grocery bill from his cell phone and showed it to the boy.

"Did you deliver these groceries today to this address off Davis Square?"

"Yes," the boy replied.

"How long have you been making deliveries there?"

"Off and on maybe a year or two."

"Off and on," Dimase repeated. "How so?"

"Well, sometimes the guy would be gone for a long time, and I'd stop deliveries. Then he'd come back, and I'd start up again."

"Did you ever see him or speak to him?" Dimase asked.

"No, he'd call the order in or leave a note for next time in the grocery basket by the door."

"When was the last time he stopped delivery? For how long?"

"I'd say he started up again a few weeks ago. Before that, he was gone for a few months. I don't know exactly. I don't keep track."

Dimase's sixth sense was now on high alert. He had a possible ID from the newspaper vendor, a mystery tenant whom neighbors never saw, and absences that coincided with the timing of the various murders around the country. The mystery tenant definitely needed further investigation.

◆ ◆ ◆

Feinberg School of Medicine, Chicago, Illinois

Berger sat on a bench in Lake Shore Park, facing Lake Michigan, looking out across Outer Lake Shore Drive. It was a beautiful, sunlit, cloudless day with a brisk breeze blowing in from the lake. Berger's first interview, with the director of development, was in an hour. He unfolded the campus map he'd picked up at the bookstore and made note of how to find the administration building. He also put his finger on the Robert H. Lurie Medical Research Center, a likely location for Susan if she was at the school.

On the off chance they happened to bump into each other, Berger's current character was quite different from anything Susan would have remembered. His blond hair was now dark brown and trimmed short, just long enough to part on one side. His thin mustache, which was cut almost too short, and thick glasses gave him a somewhat geeky appearance. His healed broken nose didn't give off the vibe of a prizefighter. Instead, one might have interpreted it as a sign that the poor guy couldn't see straight or had been so preoccupied that he probably had walked into a wall.

At the appointed hour, he made his way to the administration building and, after a short wait, was ushered into the office of the director of development. The man was receptive. He asked a few questions about MIT, more out of professional curiosity than anything else. Of course, Berger, with his background, handled those with ease, adding detail and anecdotes that only an insider at MIT would have known.

The two men quickly built rapport, and Berger learned that the medical school had a long history of research in the area of heart disease, having been mainly funded several decades earlier by a benefactor named Feinberg after he suffered a heart attack. Of greater interest to Berger was the fact that the university had recently expanded work in the area of brain research, particularly a two-year government grant to fund a start-up program specializing in Alzheimer's. That was a first for the university, and if successful, it could greatly expand their standing in the community of research hospitals and medical schools. The government had seeded the capital and brought in their own scientist to oversee the program with the idea of handing it off to private funding after the initial two-year period. The program had something to do with an Obama-era initiative designed to stimulate medical entrepreneurship. So far, the program was in its infancy, flying under the radar, pending any kind of results that could be publicized and published in the future.

Berger could hardly contain himself. He may or may not have found Susan, but the timing and profile of the project was a perfect match. "I don't want to violate any privacy or confidentiality, but as part of my background work, do you think I could tag along on a student tour of the research building sometime while I'm here? I'll be here about a week."

"Of course," the director replied. "We do those all the time. I'll arrange it."

"That would be great," Berger said. "It would help me get

a feel for the scope and scale of the overall operations here and to put that in perspective with the statistical information you've provided. I can't thank you enough. Your help will be invaluable to my thesis paper. I promise to give you a final copy. Hopefully, if I can achieve my objective, it might provide you a better feel for the national landscape of research funding, how it varies from institution to institution, and the direction of trend lines in the future."

The director smiled appreciatively, and the two men shook hands after making arrangements for Berger to join a campus tour the next morning. Berger headed back to his temporary quarters at the Raffaello Hotel at the corner of Mies van der Rohe Way and Delaware Street. As he walked down Fairbanks Court toward Superior Street, he saw a single woman exit a side door of the Lurie Medical Research Center. Berger felt a shot of adrenaline course through his system and quickened his pace. He only caught a brief side profile before the woman turned and walked away with her back toward him. His antennae were up. His first reaction was that it was her. The woman was the right age and the right build. The hair was different. That was to be expected. What sealed it for him was her gait, even from a distance and watching her from behind. It was hard to define specifically, but he recognized the way she walked. Like an individual fingerprint, there was something about her stride, posture, and body language. The old Beatles lyric "something in the way she moves" flashed in his head. It had to be her.

She was walking about a hundred feet in front of him. There were quite a few other pedestrians out and about. He didn't want to pass her and take even the remotest chance of being recognized, but he needed to get a closer look. There was a bus stop in front of the Museum of Contemporary Art, and the woman turned and sat on a bench in the partially sheltered stop.

She was facing directly toward him, seated thirty feet away. It was her.

Berger maintained a sideways orientation toward Susan as he blended with other foot traffic and walked past, taking a quick right on Mies van der Rohe Way. There was no need to maintain contact. He knew all he needed to know. She was the government scientist running the new brain research program. He didn't yet know her new name. That was irrelevant. He knew what her new identity was and where she worked. She had been a needle in a haystack, and he had found her. There was plenty of time to plan the next step. Berger practically walked on air as he glided the two blocks back to his hotel.

◆ ◆ ◆

Davis Square, Somerville, Massachusetts

Dimase stood behind the assembled SWAT team, across the street from Berger's apartment. He felt sure the mystery tenant was Berger. Two things cinched it for him and for the judge who'd issued the search warrant. First, the newspaper vendor had reconfirmed that the man he'd sold to was the same man in the photos Dimase had shown him of Berger. More importantly, Dimase had tracked down the landlord, gotten the name of the mystery tenant, run the name, and discovered that the person had died ten years earlier. Now it was the moment of truth, a time for justice.

On his command, the team formed into two separate columns and jogged across the street, approaching the front corners of Berger's building from two different angles. Dimase clicked his throat mic and received a double click in return, which indicated that additional men were in position behind the building.

Fully armored, the men were mere silhouettes in the predawn light. Dimase gave three clicks on the mic, and two men from each of the groups at the corners of the house broke off and ran up the front steps, forming a four-man entry team, as their colleagues remained outside. Two officers with a battering ram took the lead, followed by the short man carrying a full-body shield and the tall man angling his military-style assault rifle over the top of his partner.

The team flew up the stairs and crashed the heavy battering ram into the door of Berger's unit. The door flew off the hinges, and the team exploded into the room, identifying themselves and shouting commands to freeze. Dimase hustled up the steps behind them with his sidearm drawn and ready for action.

It took mere seconds to clear the small space. Berger was gone. It looked as if he'd left in a hurry. Debris was strewn about, as if someone had quickly rifled through cabinets and drawers in search of essential items to take with him. Curiously, there was a mattress on the floor, neatly made up with blankets tucked at the corners. It was strangely at odds with the mess throughout the rest of the apartment. Apparently, no one had slept in the bed.

One of the SWAT officers called Dimase over to a drawer in the kitchen. It was filled with cutout newspaper articles and computer printouts relating to the murders attributed to the Phantom Professor, along with the latest media speculation regarding Liz McFarland and Susan Pearce.

Dimase's attention was drawn to a large wall taking up one entire side of the apartment. The wall was densely covered with writing and diagrams in multicolored magic marker. There were crudely drawn maps of geographic regions; names of government institutions, charitable organizations, colleges, and universities;

and hundreds of individual names, some crossed out and some not. The writing and schematics virtually blotted out the white space of the backing.

Dimase studied the wall carefully, scanning the lists of names and institutions, when suddenly, he saw it. There in the middle of the almost indecipherable hieroglyphics were the names of two medical schools in Chicago. They were circled multiple times in bright red magic marker. To the other personnel in the room, that would have been as meaningless as the rest of the chaos on the wall. To Dimase, it was a cause for panic. One of the schools was the Feinberg School of Medicine at Northwestern University in Chicago, the school where Susan Pearce now worked as a research professor under a false name as a temporary protectee in the witness protection program.

Dimase had to get to Chicago—and fast.

◆ ◆ ◆

Feinberg School of Medicine, Chicago, Illinois

Berger took the campus tour as offered the next morning. Planning was his forte, and getting the lay of the land was crucial. The tour helped to cement his understanding of which buildings housed which departments. Between that and the campus map he'd picked up the previous day, he quickly assimilated the overall layout and various functions of the campus.

He continued his charade as a postgraduate student working on a thesis, and once the tour was over, he wandered about, occasionally asking questions of students or faculty passing by. Between the original interview with the director of development and his own meanderings and impromptu exchanges, it became clear by the second day on which floor of which building and in which department Susan Pearce worked.

He was careful not to run directly into her but did catch a glimpse or two from a distance. He'd completed the most difficult aspect of the operation. Against all odds, he had found a proctectee in the witness protection program. What happened next would be critical.

He was in no hurry. He doubted she would be going anywhere. The detail and anticipation of the planning process were perhaps the most enjoyable parts. The subliminal thrill of some primitive stalking instinct kicked in. He felt like a prehistoric man, only equipped with a superbrain, circling his prey until the moment was right to strike. It was exhilarating.

Susan proved to be somewhat a creature of habit. He observed her over the next two days, and she always exited the same building via the same side exit at approximately the same time each day. He also learned she had an office and lab in that building, on the back side of the third floor. She worked alone and kept to herself. Her project on brain research was somewhat segregated from other work happening in the research center, as the school's focus traditionally had been on heart disease research, something for which the Feinberg College of Medicine was well known. Susan was the scientist brought in for the special project, the one the director of development had spoken of.

Berger was confident in the efficacy of his disguise, but it was prudent not to get too close or have any direct communication with his quarry until it was time. He wanted to fill in the other half of the equation: the variables of where she lived and her habits and patterns during her off time away from the school.

Berger obtained a bus schedule and noted that Susan's stop in front of the Museum of Contemporary Art was the third on a route that looped through campus and then past the outskirts of the city and ended in the center of Chicago itself.

He got on at the first stop and positioned himself near the back of the bus, where he could observe passengers coming and going. His first run was a bust, as Susan did not get on the bus. When he realized she wasn't coming, he exited the bus at the next stop and speed-walked across campus back to the first stop by Fairfield Inn on Ontario Street, where he repeated the process.

His second attempt was rewarded. Susan entered the bus and settled into a seat about halfway down the aisle, several rows in front of Berger. He kept a newspaper folded in half to shield his face, and although he appeared to be engrossed in his reading, he was keenly observing Susan and their fellow passengers.

He repeated that process, getting a feel for who else was on the bus, how many were regulars, and who might stick out. Susan always got off at the same stop in front of a midrise apartment building on East Erie Street. He assumed she lived there. He confirmed it by following her into the building at a safe distance and noting the floor the elevator stopped on. He was almost ready to strike.

He took the elevator to the seventh floor, Susan's floor; got out; and scanned the hallway. Nobody was there. The units had no names posted on the doors, only numbers. There were eight units on the floor, four on each side. Susan had to have been in one of them. Berger had gathered a lot of intelligence. Now a more concrete plan was starting to take shape in his head.

He reentered the elevator, and on the way out of the building, he made note of a sign in the entryway: "A proud property of the Prentice Group, 761-999-8888."

He committed the number to memory. Berger knew from his widespread reading that most apartment buildings carried at least a 5 to 10 percent vacancy rate, even in the best of times. The normal turnover of a mobile society pretty much guaranteed that some units would be available to rent. He quickly did the math: ninety-six units at 10 percent vacancy rounded to ten empty units. Five would have been half that. If he was lucky, the building would have an average of just under one vacant unit per floor. It wasn't essential that he procure a unit on the same floor as Susan Pearce, but it would certainly reduce his exposure if he didn't have to maneuver her to another level of the building.

While still in the entryway, he looked at the mailboxes. Most had names next to the unit number. The unit numbers were hyphenated, indicating floor and unit. Berger smiled. There was only one unit on the seventh floor without a name attached to it: unit 7-703. It was obvious. At Northwestern and at Feinberg School of Medicine, there was no directory listing of a guest scientist working on brain research. The director of development had referenced the program, but he hadn't supplied any names. In fact, he'd said the program was flying under the radar for the time being. The tour hadn't taken him by Susan's office, so he didn't know if there was a nameplate on the door or not. He imagined colleagues in her department must have called her by name—some name—but if a person was in the witness protection program and was trying to keep a low profile, maybe one didn't put his or her name on a mailbox or list it in a faculty directory, even if it was a new name.

Well, Berger thought, *things are about to change, and you won't be safe*. It didn't matter what her new name was. It only mattered that Susan Pearce was working on the third floor of the Lurie Medical Center at Feinberg College of Medicine at Northwestern University and living in unit 7-703 on the seventh floor of a nearby apartment building on East Erie Street. Berger pulled out his cell and dialed the number for the real estate management company. He was surprised when a real person answered the phone.

"Prentice Real Estate Group. How may I help you?"

"I'm moving to Chicago to work on my postgraduate thesis. A friend told me you had some vacancies in your building at 330 East Erie Street. Is that true?"

"Please hold for a minute while I check," the pleasant female voice responded. In a moment, she returned to the phone. "We currently have four vacancies in that building."

"That's quite low for a ninety-six-unit building. You must do a good job for your tenants. May I ask what floor they are on?"

"Of course. All the available units are two bedrooms. They range in rent from three thousand to thirty-five hundred per month, depending on how high up they are. We have openings on the third, seventh, eighth, and eleventh floors."

"Excellent," Berger replied. "How soon can I make arrangements to look at them? I'm anxious to get settled."

◆ ◆ ◆

Feinberg School of Medicine, Chicago, Illinois

Dimase had a dilemma. He was one of the few people aside from the witness protection program administrators who knew the new identity and placement of Susan Pearce as a research professor in Chicago. For the protectee's security, that type of knowledge was strictly on a need-to-know basis. Dimase had been kept in the loop because of his intimate involvement in the case and as a means to aid his continuing pursuit of Hans Berger. Plus, Susan had declined the formal protection route, choosing instead to accept the FBI's help in going underground without a commitment to disappear forever. She'd told him she hoped to reemerge from the shadows one day to reclaim her life after Berger was caught.

Dimase was forbidden to break protocol and contact Susan directly unless there was a clear and immediate threat to her safety that overrode the ongoing need to maintain her secret identity. That was the rule, not only to limit communication and avoid any inadvertent leak or compromise but also so the protectee would not subconsciously change her natural behavior or do anything to inadvertently give away her identity.

Dimase could not just show up out of the blue and notify campus police of the possible threat, nor could he bring in local police or the FBI. Unless there was an actual attack or a preponderance of evidence that one was about to occur, Dimase's options were limited. Ironically, the procedure had been designed for the protectee's benefit, and mandate required that all adhere to it.

The only person Dimase could work with at that stage of the game was the US Marshal charged with being Susan's shadow. Upon his direction or if Susan hit the panic button, an FBI rapid response team could be deployed, and local police could also respond to any unfolding emergency. Absent that, Dimase and the shadow would be on their own to assess the threat, and Susan would be kept in the dark.

When Dimase met with the marshal, he brought the man up to date on his suspicion about Berger possibly being in the vicinity. They agreed that beginning the next morning, they would split up in an effort to provide more comprehensive coverage of Susan. The marshal would pick up surveillance on campus when Susan got off the bus in the morning, surveying the area in advance to scope out any possible threat. Dimase would cover her apartment from the street below and then reconnect with the marshal to double-team her office building during the day.

Still, as Dimase watched Susan leave the Lurie Research building that afternoon and walk briskly toward the bus stop, he wondered if he should somehow break protocol and warn her of Berger's possible presence. From a distance, he saw her get on the bus, knowing that her shadow, the marshal, had already boarded at an earlier stop. Dimase scanned the students around him as they strolled across campus, innocently heading for whatever was next for them. He fixed his gaze briefly on anyone within range, trying to determine in that instant if any bore even a remote resemblance to Hans Berger. Dimase moved about, trying to take in as many faces as he could, but none were a fit. The little voice was going off in his head. He could feel Berger's presence. If only he would show himself. It was a perfect day and an innocent setting, but Dimase could not ignore what every nerve in his body was telling him. He was in the presence of evil. Berger was near.

◆ ◆ ◆

Hans Berger lurked behind a tree, surreptitiously observing Susan exit her building for the day and start toward the bus stop. He smiled with pleasure as he fantasized about how events would play out in the morning. All his months of planning, searching, and dreaming were about to become real. He clenched his jaw and silently stented in excitement.

That was when he noticed Dimase Augustin trailing behind Susan, hiding among a group of students, watching, looking everywhere—but not at him.

"Well, well, well," Berger said out loud to himself. "Welcome to the party. This should be fun. Game on, my friend. Game on."

CHAPTER 23

East Erie Street, Chicago, Illinois

Berger stood just inside the threshold of his new unit at 330 East Erie Street. Unit 7-702 had proven most suitable for his needs. As he'd explained to the rental agent, he wanted to be high enough to feel secure from intruders and low enough that he could still afford the rent. Of course, the most important reason, the only reason, was that the apartment was situated diagonally across from the unit of Susan Pearce, between her unit and the elevator.

Berger knew that with certainty because it was his second morning surreptitiously observing through the slightly cracked door. He wanted to get a good sense of whether or not she left at the same time each day and if any other tenants were likely to be out at the same time. Both issues were favorable to Berger. She left her apartment at precisely seven o'clock, presumably because she had a bus to catch. The other six tenants on the floor were apparently on a different schedule. Thus far, none had exited their units within fifteen minutes of Susan's normal departure time.

It had been five days since Berger arrived in Chicago. That morning was a Friday. He hadn't had time to observe her weekend comings and goings but imagined they were more random. He didn't want to wait three more days until Monday. Even more compelling, now that Dimase was in town, he had to act sooner rather than later. That morning was zero hour. It was time to strike. Every nerve in his body tingled. His senses were heightened to an almost superhuman level, and his focus was absolute.

He'd spent the latter part of the week planning, visualizing, and rehearsing in his mind. It occurred to him that he was as deranged as ever, but that was of little consequence at that point. He was what he was, and he had a purpose—a purpose he was about to fulfill. All the physical training, mental preparation, and emotional trauma of his metamorphosis were about to be actualized in the next few minutes. He had dreamed of that moment for almost two years.

It would be a stunning victory. His fans would go nuts. He would vanquish his tormentors and defeat and demoralize his would-be captors yet again. The door was cracked less than an eighth of an inch. The crack was invisible to the naked eye, just enough of a gap to provide a sliver view of Susan's door. He heard the click of the dead bolt before he saw the doorknob turn. A quick glance up and down the hallway confirmed there was no one else in sight.

Berger watched as Susan stepped out into the corridor. The door to her unit locked automatically behind her. She carried an oversized bag that looked to be a cross between a purse and carry-on luggage. Before she took three steps, Berger burst from his unit and hit her square in the face with a long, continuous stream of pepper spray. Susan's hands flew to her face. She coughed and choked as her bag dropped to the floor, and she doubled over. Berger grabbed her around the head and midsection and dragged her across the hall.

As he forced Susan through the door, he kicked her bag toward his unit, knocking it across the threshold just before pulling Susan in and closing the door. He was careful to make sure none of the contents of the bag spilled. There was no evidence to indicate what had just happened. The entire operation had taken less than twelve seconds.

Susan was too incapacitated to resist. Berger quickly zip-tied her hands behind her back and bound her feet with duct tape. There was no furniture in the apartment, so Berger knelt over her as she lay on the floor. He'd picked up whatever supplies he needed during the previous three days. He went to the bathroom and retrieved a warm, wet cloth, which he used to carefully and gently wash her face and eyes. Now that she was secure, he wanted to have a conversation, and for that, he needed Susan to be calm and lucid. He was patient as he waited for her to recover.

◆ ◆ ◆

Minutes passed, and Susan's breathing and vision began to normalize. She looked at the figure standing above her and knew it could only be one person. He looked different from how she remembered him, but given the circumstances, she had no doubt. Some of his facial features were vaguely recognizable now that she knew what she was looking for. There was a long silence as Berger smiled down at her, waiting for her to come around.

Susan broke the silence. "What happened to you, Hans?"

His smile vanished, replaced by a twisted sneer. "What happened to me, Susan? You would know that better than anyone. You and your friends destroyed my life. You took everything from me. I never had a chance, and it was all based on lies, wasn't it, Susan? You were never raped. You know that, and I know that, but everyone else in the world doesn't think so. They don't care about the truth."

"I'm sorry, Hans. Truly, I'm sorry!" Susan cried. "If I could take it all back, I would."

"Yes, I'm sure you would, but you can't. It's a little late for that now, isn't it, Susan?"

"All those people, Hans. How could you kill all those people? They had nothing to do with this."

"I guess you could say a seismic shift in moral standards. The moral construct with society didn't do me much good, did it? I was discarded like a piece of garbage. All those years of academic pursuit, excellence, discipline, and respect gone in a week—gone on a lie. There was no presumption of innocence. You, Susan Pearce, said I was guilty, so I was. You were the angel of my destruction, Susan, but our sick and warped culture permitted it to happen. All are complicit. None are exempt."

Berger squatted down on his haunches, moving closer to her face. His eyes were cold and dead.

"Hans, you've gone insane. This can be stopped. I'll give a full confession. I'll retract my accusations. I'll tell the world I was never raped. I'll take the shame away from you. I'll wear it, Hans. I'll wear the mantle of shame. Let me do it. Please."

"Oh, I have other plans for you. I'm afraid I've done some things, as you know, that won't allow me to go back. I'll never be a part of our corrupt, shallow, immoral society. I'm better than that. You left me few options, but you know what they say: 'One door closes, and another one opens.' I'm good at this. Don't you think?"

Susan said nothing.

Hans shouted, "I said I'm good at this! Don't you agree?"

"Yes," Susan responded almost inaudibly.

"I found out something else. I enjoy it. There's no fairness to it. If all are complicit, then all are guilty. There's no exempt card. People turn a blind eye to truth as long as it serves their own purpose. There is no moral code. Not anymore. Not for me. I'm a shark in open water. I seek, I kill, and I disappear. It is my purpose in life. You left me no choice, but now I thank you. We all have to die sometime. It's not that big of a deal. I'm not afraid of death. You shouldn't be either. You opened up a new door for me, Susan, and I ran through it. I enjoy the game we've created—more than I can tell you."

"How did you find me?" Susan whimpered.

Berger stood up, walked to the window, and kept his back to her. "It wasn't hard. Do you really think that second-rate minds who settle for a government job would be any match for me? It's entertaining to toy with them. Their thinking is so transparent. You can't hide from me, Susan. Ever! If I decide to let you go, you must realize I can get to you anytime I want, however and whenever I please."

"Let me go?" Susan whispered hoarsely with a flicker of hope in her voice. "Are you going to let me go?"

"I'm toying with the idea," Berger replied. "If I kill you, then a lot of the fun is over. Oh sure, I can stalk and plan and kill other people, and I'm sure it will be fun, but you are special, Susan. It might be more fun to try something a little different, a little more creative. After all, I can always come back and kill you in the future if that's what I decide is best. It would give me something to look forward to in life."

Susan couldn't imagine what he was driving at. She was terrified. What could possibly have been worse for her and more satisfying for Berger than to kill her right there at that moment? After all the murders of her friends and all the time and effort he'd put into staging their elaborate deaths one by one, now he had her. What was he talking about? Her heart pounded in time with the massive throbbing in her head. Her eyes still burned, and her body was shaking. Berger was enjoying her discomfort.

"I can disappear for as long as I want and come and go as I please. They will never catch me if I don't want to be caught. Still, you took my old life away, and you're going to pay dearly for it."

"You forced me out at PKC Group," Susan said, her voice raspy. "You were cooking the books. It was the only way I could get you out without blowing up the whole company."

Berger turned to face her. He crossed the room and stood over her with his arms folded across his chest as if he were giving himself a hug. "Was it worth it? All you had to do was play along. All I wanted was for us to succeed, to buy more time. We had something. We may even have been onto a cure. I took it on my shoulders to keep it going. It could have all come out in the end, but you decided to be judge, jury, and executioner. You lied. You are no different from me. You lied to get what was important to you."

"Hans, you've killed nine people. That's a whole lot worse than lying. You've gone insane. You realize that, don't you?"

"No, Susan!" he shouted. "You killed those people. You are directly responsible. You killed each and every one of your friends. Only Liz remains, and when I'm through with you, maybe I'll visit her as well. Your lies and corruption were what killed them. They would be alive today if you had been truthful. All who have died would be alive if you were not such a deceitful bitch. It's on you." Hans seethed as he spit out the words. "Would you make a deal with the devil to save your life?"

"Are you the devil, Hans?"

"I guess you could say for you, I am. What if I slice you up just enough to let you live? You could have some physical scars to match your emotional scars. An eye for an eye. A life for a life. Only in this case, we are both still living. You and me, connected forever—a bond that can never be broken. You must return to the research. You will find a cure, even if it takes the rest of your life, and I will share in the credit. It would be a cure made possible only because I chose to let you live. I would be responsible for the cure the same way you are responsible for your friends' deaths. We are at a crossroads. If I kill you now, maybe someone else someday will find a cure, but it would have nothing to do with us. If I let you live, we are linked together forever. In a way, we'd be a team again—both responsible for the events that follow. Do you understand?"

Susan nodded.

"Good." Berger squatted in a catcher's position and leaned forward so his face was next to hers. "These are my conditions. I'll be watching. First, you must dedicate your life to the research. That part should be okay with you. You will have no other purpose in life."

Susan nodded.

"Second, I will allow Liz to live. If you resist me or break any of the conditions of our agreement, she will die. If I could find you, I can find her. Nod if you agree to follow my orders."

Susan nodded.

"Third, you will live a solitary life, just like me. You will live with the weight of responsibility for your friends' murders for the rest of your life. You will have no lovers, no friends, and no family. If I find you are dating someone, I will kill them. If you involve anyone in your life, I will kill them. Nod your head if you understand."

Susan nodded.

"Agreed." Berger smiled. "But you still must pay a physical price for your transgressions."

◆ ◆ ◆

Dimase Augustin sat alone in a parked car, watching the entrance to the apartment building at 330 East Erie Street. He felt uneasy. The marshal had told him that most weekdays, Susan was out the front door of the building by 7:05 a.m. in order to catch the 7:12 bus. Dimase glanced at his watch for the tenth time in ten minutes. The 7:12 had come and gone. It was 7:25. Something was wrong.

Dimase reached over to the floor on the passenger side of the front seat and retrieved a small case, from which he removed an electronic device. The device was larger than an iPad and smaller than a laptop. He flipped a switch, and a white grid with green lines appeared on the screen. GPS coordinates were labeled along the horizontal and vertical axes. Three-quarters of the way up the screen, a red dot pulsated. The pill-sized tracking beacon Dimase had insisted upon was now active and indicated Susan was still up on the seventh floor of her building. He watched for several minutes. She did not seem to be moving about. That was odd. Not only had she missed the bus, but she now seemed to be fixed in one position. He wondered if she had somehow fallen and maybe hit her head. Perhaps she was sick and still lying in bed. It was impossible to tell the configuration of the apartment on the tracking device. GPS coordinates were generally only good to within fifty to one hundred feet. Speculation was useless. He had to check it out.

Dimase exited his car and produced a master key card that had been supplied to Susan's shadow for emergencies. He took the elevator to the seventh floor and cautiously entered the corridor. Training and discipline dictated that he be on high alert. He stepped softly down the hall with his gun still holstered, his eyes scanning right and left. At Susan's unit, he paused to put his ear to the door. There was no sound. He didn't want to scare her, nor did he want to give away his presence.

He placed the card key against the code reader, and the door clicked open. He crept silently across the threshold, prepared to make a quick, clandestine exit if he heard any evidence of her moving about the apartment. There was only silence. Working quickly and quietly, he cleared the apartment, which was puzzling since the tracking device clearly showed Susan as being present somewhere on the seventh floor.

Cursing himself for not bringing the device with him, he raced back down the hallway, took the elevator back to the lobby, and retraced his steps to the vehicle. The tracking device was on the seat, where he'd left it. He tapped a key, and the screen sprang to life, showing the same red dot pulsating on the seventh floor. There were only two explanations: either the tracker was malfunctioning, or the beacon itself was stationary somewhere on the seventh floor. He doubted the malfunction theory but was at a loss on how to proceed without going from apartment to apartment. He supposed she could have been visiting a neighbor, but that would have been out of character. To his knowledge, she didn't have any friends in the building, and there was no explanation as to why she would miss her bus while the beacon was motionless in a neighboring apartment.

Dimase began to panic. Was it possible the beacon had become separated from her body? It was possible but highly unlikely, given that he personally had insisted on having the pill-sized capsule implanted by injection into the soft tissue of her buttocks. Removing it would have required a minor surgical procedure.

The most likely explanation was the simplest: the beacon was still in place, and Susan was stationary somewhere on the seventh floor. She was not in her own apartment, and she was not moving. She wouldn't have been sleeping. Even if she'd been sitting in a chair, having a conversation, she would have moved a bit by then. The only explanation left made an alarm go off in Dimase's head: Susan had been kidnapped.

CHAPTER 24

Dimase grabbed the tracking device, sprinted back across the street, flashed his badge to throw people off the elevator, and returned to the seventh floor. He stepped off the elevator into the seventh-floor hallway with the tracking device in hand. He wasn't looking at a detailed schematic of the floor layout. On the screen, he could see only if the flashing red dot was in front of or behind him and to his left or right. He angled the device back and forth, walking slowly down the corridor.

Suddenly, the last door on the right opened, and two people dressed for work appeared about forty feet in front of him. Their startled looks were quickly replaced by fear when Dimase waved his firearm in their direction and, in a loud whisper, instructed them to get back inside.

As best as he could tell, when he had his back to the elevator, Susan was in one of the units to the right. If he assumed she wasn't in the apartment from which the two tenants had just tried to leave for work, the process of elimination left three possibilities. He decided to start with the second-to-last unit from the far end and work his way back toward the elevator.

The tracking device was no longer of any use to him now that he'd narrowed the scope of Susan's location to one of three units. He gently folded the device and leaned it against a wall. Gun in hand, he held the key card against the code reader and quickly opened the door. There was no sign of activity within his range of vision.

Dimase entered the unit with his .45-caliber pistol pointed out in front. He moved catlike through the unit, clearing the kitchen, the living room, and a bedroom. In the second bedroom, he encountered a sleeping woman who sat bolt upright in the bed, gathering the sheets about her, as he made his entrance. She looked as if she were about to scream but thought better of it when Dimase waved his gun and put a finger to his lips in the universal gesture for silence. He held out his palm in a calming motion and then fished out his badge and held it forward for the woman to see. He whispered instructions, and the woman climbed under the bed, where she remained. *One down, three to go*, he thought as he readied to repeat the process on the next unit in line.

◆ ◆ ◆

Berger toyed with a terrified Susan Pearce. Blood was everywhere as he tenderly, almost lovingly administered a series of cuts to her thighs and stomach. He held a hunting knife with a serrated eight-inch blade designed to terrorize as much as inflict serious damage. The cuts were deep enough to scar permanently but intended not to be fatal. Berger leaned over his victim as the tip of the blade pricked into her face, just above her right cheekbone and under her eye. A drop of blood trickled down her cheek and gathered speed before splattering onto the floor next to her. Susan tried to turn her head away as Hans promised she would never see the same face in the mirror again.

Hans was in a euphoric, trancelike state. This was the culmination of all his fantasies. How creatively brilliant and satisfying it was to construct a living hell for her rather than just kill her and have it be done. That was fine for the others. Their deaths were necessary to punish Susan and make her ultimate fate all the more unbearable. There would be plenty of time to kill others. Susan would not die that day. Not unless she broke the rules he had just laid out for her. Susan was special. Her place in his story was unique, and now he had done to her in spades what she had done to him.

Berger pushed the blade a little deeper into the soft flesh of her face. Somewhere in the animal part of his brain, he heard a sound that didn't fit with his fantasy. He wasn't sure what it was as he peered into Susan's eyes, reveling in her terror. It didn't quite register in his present state of preoccupation.

◆ ◆ ◆

Dimase cracked the door to 7-702. The living room was clear. He listened carefully for any sound. There was none. He moved through the kitchen and started down the hall to the bedrooms, when he first heard it: the slightest of whimpers, followed by a male voice. His senses heightened to another level, if that were even possible. The sound had come from the last bedroom on the left. He could see the door was open. He crept up to the threshold. Half expecting to get his head blown off, he extended far enough to allow one eye an angle on most of the room.

His reaction was instantaneous. His only thought was to stop the knife. Without hesitation, he fired off a double tap, one to the shoulder of the arm holding the knife and the other four inches lower and to the left—center-mass torso. The knife toppled to the floor as the man's shoulder exploded, and then the body shot spun him around and landed him on his back.

◆ ◆ ◆

Northwestern Memorial Hospital, Chicago, Illinois

Dimase Augustin and Bill Larson stood next to Susan's hospital bed at Northwestern Memorial Hospital. She was lucky to be alive. Dimase's decision to utilize the tracking beacon and deploy the undercover shadow had saved her from a horrible fate.

Berger had done a pretty good job of carving up her thighs and stomach. There would always be some faint scarring in those areas. Fortunately, he'd just started on her face when Dimase took him out. The doctors were confident that with a little plastic surgery, no one would ever know the difference.

Berger was in the same hospital, several floors down, fighting for his life in intensive care. Dimase had not been worried about preserving Berger's life when he'd taken his shots. He'd passed on a head shot only because of his years of professional training. The head had a lot more movement than center torso and presented a smaller target. There had been no time to think. The first priority had been to take the knife out of play, and the second had been to take the most certain shot to take Berger out of play. In the event of a glancing wound to the head or a miss, anything could have happened. Dimase had taken the correct action: center mass and no miss.

Dimase smiled and patted Susan's shoulder. "You are free again, Susan—you and Liz. You can have your own lives back now. Berger is no longer a threat to you."

Susan smiled weakly. Bandages covered half her face. "Thank

you, Dimase. Thanks to all of you. I can't believe any of this happened, but I'm so grateful to all of you. I'm so relieved it's over."

"You can go back to your research now," Dimase said. "Maybe you can fulfill your original purpose. I believe there is a reason things go as they do. You were not meant to die, Susan. You have a mission to fulfill, a reason for being here. You will recover. Find your purpose, and live your life. All this is behind you now."

"What about Berger?" Susan asked.

"They say he's touch-and-go," Larson said. "It's fifty-fifty he'll make it. Either way, we have enough evidence to put him away for three lifetimes. He'll never be a threat to you or anyone else again."

Dimase smiled once more. "I look forward to seeing your research published in your own name someday. I doubt I'll understand any of it." He chuckled. "But I promise to read it."

EPILOGUE

The passage of time changed life considerably for Susan and Liz. Liz found her calling, happy to have a second chance at life as a small-town teacher in rural Alaska. The two women kept in touch, but they rarely, if ever, brought up the past. Communication was sporadic and centered mainly on birthdays, holidays, and significant family events. They kept conversation light, more than willing to move on from the intimacy of the nightmare they once had shared.

Berger eventually recovered from his wounds. Both Liz and Susan testified at his trial. Dimase proved to be surprisingly clairvoyant with his bedside prediction. Berger was given three consecutive life sentences in a maximum-security federal prison.

Susan's research went well. She immediately resumed using her own name.

There was an extraordinary level of publicity surrounding the sensational arrest and subsequent conviction of Hans Berger, the Phantom Professor. Over the course of the trial and public proceedings, the truth about Berger's motivation came to light.

Berger was steadfast in maintaining that he never had raped Susan Pearce, but no one believed him. It became clear that his motive in the so-called Book Club Murders had been to punish Susan and her friends for their role in his humiliating dismissal from PKC Group.

The prosecution did a superb job of painting a vivid picture of Berger's transformation into a cold-blooded serial killer who murdered innocents purely for the thrill and for bloodlust. The trial also brought to light the issue of Berger falsifying data at both MIT and PKC Group, tainting what had been considered promising research.

Due to the unusual circumstances and keen public interest, government negotiators helped broker a deal among the Feinberg College of Medicine, PKC Group, and Susan. All parties were willing; it was just a matter of making it happen and having a viable outcome. The Department of Health and Human Services was persuaded to make an additional grant to bridge any differences and facilitate a fair outcome.

Susan returned to PKC Group as chief scientist in charge. She was able to integrate her work from Feinberg Medical College, which itself became an affiliated partner in the venture. The angel investors were happy. The director of development at Feinberg was thrilled. Most importantly, Susan was back where she belonged.

The new collaboration proved to be fruitful. Susan completely overhauled the research protocols, and the group identified a variation of one particular compound that consistently produced improved results. Five years after Susan's dramatic rescue, PKC was on the verge of going to human trials, a result made possible in part by the additional funding and sympathetic viewpoint of government regulators.

Susan's personal life changed as well. For the first time in her life, she found the joy of love, companionship, and compatibility. It was a foreign experience for her, and she treasured it. Far from being a hindrance to her work, the balance allowed her to bring more energy and focus to her research. Brad was a fellow scientist hired after Susan's reunification with PKC Group. Within a year, they found each other, and three years later, their shared passion was the foundation for a relationship firing on all cylinders.

Together they shared a roomy apartment in one half of an old two-family home a short bus ride from Kendall Square. Perhaps the only interest they didn't have in common was Brad's fixation on all of Boston's professional sports teams. Susan found it laughable that he could get so animated about rooting for laundry, as she called it.

To her, it seemed as if players were always changing teams, and whichever owner had the most money simply bought the best players. Hence, fans ended up cheering for whoever happened to be wearing the uniform for their team. It seemed pointless in Susan's view, but if that was her future husband's only vice, she could have done a lot worse.

They both had their morning rituals before catching the bus to work. They sat together, always touching but temporarily immersed in separate worlds, each with coffee in hand. Susan would surf the internet, catching up on world events, while Brad lost himself in the sports section of the *Boston Globe.* Brad was old school when it came to his newspaper. Something in the way he was brought up—some nostalgic, engrained, pleasurable, comfortable routine from his youth—compelled him to forgo the internet when it came to sports news. For Brad, the only proper way to get his daily fix of sports was to digest each column of the sports section word for word. The only way to start the day was with coffee, newsprint, and nestling up with Susan.

Susan suspected it was a coping mechanism, a way to maintain a bond with his long-deceased dad. Brad had little use for the day-old news in the rest of the paper. He enjoyed the opinion pieces by the sports columnists the most. Who was playing well? Who was not? Who was on the trading block? Whom should they sign? Whom would they draft? What did they need to do to change up the chemistry?

Susan noted the time on the screen of her laptop. "Come on, lover boy," she said, tugging at his hand. "We've got a bus to catch."

"Okay, okay." Brad smiled, halfway through an article. Reluctantly, he folded the newspaper and placed it on the side table. He gave Susan a quick kiss on the lips, and they both got up to put their cups in the sink. Brad gave her a hug from behind and kissed the side of her neck. Susan reacted playfully and kissed him back. They pulled on their coats. Susan grabbed her bag, and Brad gathered his baseball cap and soft leather briefcase as they tumbled out the door. Neither one of them noticed the small article halfway down the open page of the folded-over newspaper. It was only a quarter column, tucked between a piece about a local robbery and an article on rising crime rates in Boston.

Inmate Escape Foiled Again

Associated Press

Bruceton Mills, West Virginia

A high-level federal inmate was captured yesterday after two hours of freedom. It was the third time former MIT professor Hans Berger has made it past prison walls in an attempt to escape. Berger is serving three consecutive life sentences for murder, conspiracy, and kidnapping. Berger, also known as the Phantom Professor, has boasted that no prison can hold him for a lifetime. He was picked up in nearby Bruceton Mills, West Virginia, at a bus station. Authorities were at a loss to explain how he managed to escape his maximum-security cell and find his way to the town.

CPSIA information can be obtained
at www.ICGtesting.com
Printed in the USA
BVHW030507111219
566264BV00001BA/18/P